THE PATCHWORK MARRIAGE

Also by Mary de Laszlo

Breaking the Rules

THE PATCHWORK MARRIAGE

Mary de Laszlo

HEADLINE

First published in 1996
by HEADLINE BOOK PUBLISHING

10 9 8 7 6 5 4 3 2 1

British Library Cataloguing in Publication Data

Laszlo, Mary de
    The patchwork marriage
    1.English fiction - 20th century
    I.Title
    823.9'14 [F]

ISBN 0 7472 1591 X

Typeset by
Letterpart Limited, Reigate, Surrey

Printed and bound in Great Britain by
Mackays of Chatham PLC, Chatham, Kent

HEADLINE BOOK PUBLISHING
A division of Hodder Headline PLC
338 Euston Road
London NW1 3BH

To Martin, Rupert, Oliver and Lydia with love

Chapter One

'A close family is a precious thing,' Leonie had once heard her mother, Zinnia, remark to a friend, 'but that means one has to live with their mistakes too.'

Leonie remembered this now as her mother drove with her back from the airport towards home. She glanced at Zinnia with affection. She was still wearing her gardening shoes. She had obviously been working in her beloved garden right up to the last minute, thrown on her expensive suit – bought in a hurry from some well-bred shop – and rushed to meet her. She also saw with a little shock that Zinnia's hair, golden brown like her own, had become greyer in the three months she'd been away. She did not want her mother to grow old. She sat quietly, waiting for Zinnia's reaction to her news that she had returned from Florence engaged to be married.

'So, who is this new young man in your life?' Zinnia said at last, with a good attempt at nonchalance.

Leonie couldn't help herself glowing as she thought of Julian, then winced as Zinnia flashed close past a car, almost catching its wing mirror.

'Do be careful, Ma,' she said. 'Shall I drive?'

'No, darling . . . I just hope *Daddy* will like him. I liked Dominic. I know he was selfish, but what man isn't? But Daddy made such a fuss, snobbish reasons I'd say, wrong public school.'

'Oh Ma, Dad's not that bad,' Leonie laughed; almost said, besides, it's you that minds about those sorts of things. 'These days you can't be like that.'

'Well, tell me everything, darling. I suppose I ought to ask you about your art course first, but I'd rather hear about Julian.'

'You'll like him. He's studying History of Art, wants to write about it – or work with it, anyway. I told you we wanted to live in Florence after we're married, didn't I, Ma?' She said this quickly as if hoping her mother wouldn't take it in and start raising objections.

'Lovely place to live. Maybe we can come and visit you and I can paint out there,' Zinnia said in what Leonie recognised as her 'I'm not going to get rattled, she's only doing it for attention' voice.

Zinnia had quite a name in the village for her flower painting, but although every year she swore she was going to branch out and try something more ambitious, so far she hadn't done so.

'But do you really love him, darling?' Zinnia couldn't help herself asking. 'I mean, after a broken love affair one is awfully vulnerable, and marriage without love would be pretty bleak.'

'I do love him, and he loves me so much,' Leonie said, remembering with a pang of desire the warmth of their lovemaking a few hours before. The wrench of leaving him had been terrible, even though in a couple of weeks he too was coming back. Her last picture of Julian was him lifting one hand in a brave farewell, his beautiful large eyes gazing at her with grave intensity, as if they could hold on to her and keep her with him.

Zinnia said nothing, but glancing at her profile as she spoke, Leonie saw a slight tightening of her mouth, a wariness in her eyes.

'We have so much in common, we just fitted together . . . you know, like you and Dad,' she said, willing her mother to understand and approve, not trot out endless obstacles to diminish their love.

Zinnia smiled, 'Your father and I have come a long way together – like two old trees growing into each other. We annoy each other like hell sometimes, as you know, but there's always been a spark of love there. It may almost go out sometimes, but then it flares up again, and on we go. Have you and Julian got that, do you think?' She took her eyes off the road and regarded her daughter intently. A car overtook them, swerved, hooting madly.

'Oh Ma, do watch it!' Leonie almost snatched the steering wheel from her hand, her stomach lurching in panic.

'Don't fuss so, dear, you're so nervy. It's just some impatient man trying to bully me,' Zinnia said cheerfully. 'Thinks he owns the road.

2

You said Julian's parents were divorced, and that he is a very sensitive person.'

'Yes, but so many people divorce these days. That's hardly his fault.' Leonie felt the familiar nudge of irritation Zinnia often provoked in her.

'Of course it's not, darling.' Zinnia recognised her annoyance. 'It's just from what you've said on the phone and in your letters, I wondered if he needed you too much?'

Irritation really took a hold of Leonie now. 'That's a ridiculous remark,' she said. 'Love, need . . . you need Daddy. You know you're hopeless with coping with money and modern machines, and he needs you to come home to at the end of the day. What's wrong with that? That's marriage, isn't it? Being needed, being loved?'

'In a way, but love should be stronger.'

'It is, in our case,' Leonie protested, recalling the feeling of awe that had suddenly come over them the first time they had made love. A wonder, a delight in each other's body and the passion and intensity of love they had engendered between them.

'Don't worry so, Ma. I've seen the dangers of wanting to be needed. Look at all those middle-aged women that fall to pieces when their children have gone and they're no longer relied upon. I mean, you're not too bad.'

'Thanks.'

'Not like some of my friends' mothers, who moon about "looking for themselves", gulping down gin and Prozac, making everyone around them feel guilty. You have your painting and your garden. As we got older and left home you painted, or gardened more. But you still like to be needed by Dad . . . or us. You've just got it in perspective. Look at you, coming to meet me off the plane – not every mother would.'

Zinnia gave a pleased smile at this back-handed compliment. 'I expect they would,' she said without conviction.

'So what's wrong with need as long as you don't become a slave to it?'

'Nothing, dear,' Zinnia said hurriedly. 'I'm . . . we're longing to meet Julian. When did you say he gets back?'

'On the fifteenth,' Leonie said, then added longingly, 'I do wish I'd

3

stayed out there with him, but he had so much work to finish, and anyway I had nowhere to live. Signora Lelli needs her month's rest before the next lot of students crowd in.' Leonie did not mention that she had spent much of her time in Julian's room instead of the house run by Signora Lelli, where she was staying to do her art course.

'You could live in this vast cupboard, no one would ever know,' Julian had said once when they were in his bedroom in the decaying palace where he was lodging.

'It's almost big enough for both of us,' she'd agreed. They'd made jokes about the huge pieces of ornate furniture that towered over them as they lay together in his four-poster bed.

Zinnia and Leonie arrived home without mishap. The large, rambling house, where Leonie had lived all her life, was Georgian and stood on the outskirts of a village near Chichester. An elderly wisteria, its grey trunk thick and twisted, meandered over the walls. Inside, the furniture was good, but didn't quite blend together, as it had been passed down from both sides of the family. Each piece held a memory from George or Zinnia's own childhood, and would never be changed for something smaller or more useful. The colours of the once-expensive curtains and the chair covers were faded by the sun, which had also bleached the edges of the wood floors unprotected by rugs, to a pale honey. The house resembled an old person of good breeding, unmistakably elegant and beautiful, but touched by the passing of time.

As Leonie opened the front door, three warm, frantic bundles threw themselves on her and Zinnia, jumping, barking and squeaking their delight.

'Hi, dogs,' Leonie said, letting herself be licked and scratched by tongues and claws. 'Oh don't get too wild, Mitzi.' She playfully pushed the white terrier away. Mitzi was the youngest of this trio, all related to each other, and the most excitable.

'I suppose it must be dreadful being a dog,' Leonie'd said when she was a child, 'being left and never knowing if someone will come back to you. Feeling abandoned every time we go out shopping, or to a party.' She'd never quite got over this feeling, so she let the dogs show their relief with their frantic slavering at being reunited again.

'My darlings,' Zinnia greeted them, then with a voice like the crack of a whip ordered: 'Marcus, here, no rabbiting.' Marcus crept back miserably, looking at her with anguished eyes. 'No, my darling,' she bent down and stroked him. Gratefully he jumped up and covered her face with licks. 'You scared me witless by disappearing last week. No more rabbiting.' She emphasised the last words as if to get through his language problem.

'Did he run off?' Leonie said, dumping her cases in the corner of the hall and going over to the table to leaf through some letters that were piled there. There was none for her; her mother had sent her post on. Was she hoping, she wondered fleetingly, for a letter from Dominic? She hadn't heard a word from him since they'd broken up, and though she knew she loved Julian, was far happier with him, her pride wanted her last affair to be rounded off neatly and tucked away to rest in peace.

'Yes, for two days we lost him. I thought he'd been run over. Then Giles Harding found him down a rabbit hole when he was out shooting. Poor, naughty boy,' Zinnia hugged Marcus to her.

'Was he all right?'

'Yes, hungry, muddy but ready to go off and do the same thing again. Weren't you, my naughty boy?' She kissed him again. 'Hungry, darling? Want some tea?' This remark she addressed to Leonie.

'I'm starving . . . plane food was filthy as usual. Why they can't provide really nice sandwiches and fresh fruit, I'll never know.' She went into the kitchen, her fingertips running over familiar surfaces as she went. She loved it here, felt warm and secure whenever she returned. Of course, it would drive her mad to live at home all the time. She loved her freedom and the tiny flat in London that she shared with her sister, Melanie, but it was reassuring to return to touch base every so often. She found herself wondering if she and Julian would be able to create such a haven for their children.

'I must ring Julian, Ma,' she said. 'I promised him I would.'

'Have some tea first.' Zinnia followed her into the kitchen and put on the kettle. 'I don't know if there's anything left in those tins – I'm trying not to eat tea – but there's plenty of bread if you want toast.'

'I'll look.' Leonie went into the larder and began to open the row of battered tins on the shelf. 'Mmm, Christmas cake, but it will be off, won't it?'

'No, it keeps for ages. You should make it three months before you eat it anyway, and I only got round to it two weeks before this time.'

'I'll try a piece.' Leonie took some and a cup of tea and sat down at the kitchen table. Zinnia leant against the Rayburn, sipping at her tea. The dogs lay quiet now in a heap at her feet, exhausted by their greeting. It was a familiar sight. Italy and Julian seemed a long way away. Home was always the same, and yet of course it wasn't. Once this table had been crowded with three children and often their friends, all squabbling and snatching food, all competing for air space with the things they wanted to say. They'd gone to boarding school, they'd come back, Melanie and Harry had gone to university. Leonie, having failed to get into Exeter, where she wanted to go, rebelled and refused to go to university at all. Now Melanie had a good job in the City, and Harry was in his last year, but she could earn money as a top cook, as indeed she had, cooking lunches for some firms in the City before she went to Florence.

'Melanie said she'd be down tonight, Harry tomorrow after a party,' Zinnia said.

'I suppose Melanie's still with Jason?' Leonie said. She envisaged her whole family here: her father tall and square, still young-looking though his hair was white, sitting awkwardly at the table, the kitchen chair being too small for him; Melanie always reading a balance sheet or a report, which she would look up from and remark about, usually in a derogatory way. Harry would lounge, his long legs half across the kitchen so everyone always tripped over them, his hair flopping over his eyes, a brooding melancholy on his face while he contemplated, often out loud, life or love, or some injustice connected with either.

For an instant Leonie saw Dominic as he'd been the last time he'd come here, early in October. Flung on a chair or pacing restlessly round the kitchen, his shoulder-length, blond hair glinting under the light. Leonie had called him her lion, as he reminded her of the magnificent beasts caged in the zoo, forever pacing up and down, round and round. Only when he painted was he still, absorbed in his own world of creation.

Zinnia said, 'I think they are still together, but as always her job comes first.' She sighed; it was a problem she'd long worried over. 'I

6

must go and shut up the chickens.' She rinsed out her cup. She didn't allow mugs in the house – being without saucers, people might put them down on her beloved furniture and leave ring marks. 'I'll be back in a minute, darling.' She went outside, the dogs scrabbling after her.

Leonie watched her go. The chickens were an ornate collection Zinnia had acquired over the years. They laid so spasmodically that they were useless for their eggs. Zinnia was the only person who liked them.

Leonie suddenly felt rather bereft, as if with Zinnia's departure the others had gone too. A big house needs people, she thought, remembering the clamour there used to be here. When it was dark outside, like now, the house seemed emptier. She wondered how her mother felt when she was alone here. She got up briskly and went through to the drawing room to ring Julian. She dialled his number, knowing she'd have to get through to one of the impoverished noble family who'd rented him a room in their crumbling palace, before she could speak to him.

'*Pronto.*'

'*Potrei parlare con Julian, per favore?*' Leonie said, recognising the voice of the young nanny who looked after the children. She tried to picture Julian in his room, working at his cluttered desk, one fine-boned hand propping up his beautiful head with its glossy dark hair, and those wonderful, huge eyes, with thick eyelashes to die for.

'*Un momento, per favore.*' The receiver was put down and she heard receding footsteps, then the cry of a child followed by the quick words of the nanny. Then steps coming back, slower.

'Hello?'

'Julian, it's me.'

'Darling, are you safe?'

'Of course I am,' she laughed. 'Back home. How are you?'

'Lonely without you. It's not the same now you've gone.'

'You've got all those lovely pictures and statues to keep you company, and soon we'll be there together again.' She felt pleased and sad that he was missing her.

'I can hardly wait. If I've time, I'm going to try and look for somewhere for us to live. It may be simple to start with, but we can

7

get something better when I get a job.'

'Of course we can. Anywhere will be wonderful. I can hardly wait to come back, be just us again.'

'Let's get married straight away, darling, the minute I get to London. I mean, there's no point in hanging about is there?' He sounded anxious.

'No . . . but you'd better meet my parents first, and I'd better meet yours. And it does take a bit of time, you know, ordering the dress, writing the invitations.'

'It can't take longer than a month?'

'Couldn't we get married in June, or July? That's only three months at the most.'

There was a silence. She could sense him all that way away, standing there by the antiquated telephone in the passage, tense and anxious. 'I want to get back out here, start looking for a job and a place for us to live, and I'd like us to come out together.'

'I'll come with you whether we're married or not,' she laughed. 'I love England and being home again, but already I miss Italy.'

'So why this sudden rush to get married?' Melanie asked the following day from the depth of an armchair by the fire. 'I mean, four months ago you were madly in love with Dominic.'

'I thought I was *then* but it's been over since Christmas. You know that, Mel,' Leonie said impatiently.

'Of course I know it's finished. Why you stayed so long with him, I'll never understand. A useless painter, though I'd admit he was attractive. He slept with all his models—'

'He wasn't useless, his pictures were . . .' Leonie jumped to his defence, then remembering his large canvases dotted with cogs, nails, bits of this and that, compared to the wonders she'd just seen in Florence, found herself floundering for a complimentary adjective to describe them.

'Forget him, but why *marry* this one, Leo? You hardly know him. And when you're somewhere lovely like Italy, one always falls in love with someone. I'm just surprised he's not an Italian. They are so amazing, really know how to get on with women.' She rolled her eyes as if the room were full of them.

8

'Why don't you find one then?' said Harry, who was lying on the floor with a dog asleep on his chest. 'That pointy-faced Jason is hardly the world's most attractive specimen.'

'Get lost,' Melanie said mildly. 'But serious, Leo,' she lowered her voice, 'surely you're not . . .'

'No, big sister, I am not pregnant. I've enough sense, although I didn't go to university, to take care of that side of things.' Leonie hated it when Melanie put on her bossy voice. Just because *she* had never put a foot wrong in her life; had sailed through school, sickeningly being top of the form, captain of the netball team, and, if that were not enough, head girl too, not to mention getting distinctions at Cambridge. Now she had a top job in a prestigious financial firm in the City she felt she knew everything.

'That's a mercy, but why marry him quite so quickly? He hasn't even got a job, has he?' Melanie said. 'Love will soon pall in a squalid bedsit on the dole – if they give it to you out there.'

'He'll get a job. He's fluent in Italian, has endless degrees in History of Art, Fine Art, whatever. Florence, of all places, should be stuffed with opportunities for him,' Leonie said impatiently.

'It is also bound to be stuffed with art experts already,' Melanie went on.

'Maybe Leo wants him with her,' Harry came to Leonie's defence. 'Maybe she doesn't want someone who has to find a "window" between board meetings and takeover bids to have sex with her.'

Zinnia came in, catching the end of his remark. She threw him a despairing look. 'Oh Harry, do get up off the floor and stop talking about sex all the time. Surely at university they teach you more than that?'

Harry grinned, pushed Mitzi off his chest and sat up. 'We were talking about finding windows for sex,' he said mischievously, knowing she would misunderstand and be shocked.

'Silly boy,' Melanie said. 'Don't try and be clever—'

'Wouldn't dream of it. After all, you had an overdose of "clever" genes. There was none left over for Leo and me.'

'Oh children, do stop squabbling,' Zinnia said wearily. 'We are so rarely all home together, and then you spend the time fighting.'

'We love it really,' Harry said, getting up and hugging her. 'Melanie has been interrogating Leonie on her love life, and why she has to marry this man so quickly. We've established she's not pregnant so—'

'That is enough, Harry,' Zinnia said firmly.

'I'm touched by your concern,' Leonie said sarcastically. 'But may I remind you that Julian and I are both in our twenties, we are very much in love, and he wants to marry me at once. I think it's rather wonderful, especially these days when people shy away from commitment.' She looked pointedly at Melanie, knowing that she and Jason thought commitment meant imprisonment.

'Of course, it's up to you,' Melanie broke in, 'but you know how upset you got over breaking up with Dominic. Poor old Dad having to send you to Florence on an art course to get your mind off it. Well, it's done that, I suppose, though perhaps a degree in History of Art would be more lasting than a marriage certificate.'

'Dad didn't have to . . .' Leonie said, feeling now rather ashamed of her hysterics when she'd split up with Dominic. 'You know he didn't like Dominic much. I think he sent me there partly in relief and partly in the hope that we would not start it up again.'

Melanie shrugged. 'Anyway, you went, and now you're back saying you're going to marry someone else immediately. I just think you should be careful. Marriage is meant to be for life.'

'Let's all go out for a walk,' Zinnia said hurriedly. 'I think it's silly to talk about it until we meet Julian. After all,' she smiled bravely, 'you haven't seen him at home yet, darling. Things may have been wonderful in Florence, which is *such* a romantic place, but back home . . .'

Leonie let out a leaden sigh. 'Ma, he is not an Italian waiter who is going to appear here in a shiny suit, greased down hair and no social graces. He is British, went to public school and university and is doing a further course on History of Art. He is well bred and house-trained.'

'So you can breathe again, Mum,' Harry said, putting on a plummy voice, 'and hold your head up in the village after all. He's one of us.'

'I hate you all.' Leonie felt like crying. 'You're impossible. Julian's right, we should have got married on our own, out there in Florence, kept away from bloody families.'

Chapter Two

'My mother wants to meet you, darling. Naturally my father does too, but he's not in London at the moment,' Julian said, when, a fortnight later, he was holding Leonie close to him in her bed, in her flat in London. 'I think we'd better get the meeting over, don't you? So we can set the date for our wedding as soon as possible.'

'Of course,' she said, wondering why she could feel his body tauten with sudden tension about such a normal thing as meeting his mother. Though remembering how intrusive and suffocating with their concern her family was sometimes, Leonie thought perhaps it wasn't surprising. 'Do we have to meet everyone at once? There's your sister too, isn't there, but we can keep today just for us, can't we?' She smiled, kissing his mouth, wriggling her body against his.

He didn't respond to her kiss, but let her go, turned over and lay on his back, staring at the ceiling. She noticed a slight tic at the corner of his mouth. He said gravely, 'The sooner everyone meets us, the sooner we can get married and go back to Florence.'

'OK, so what's the plan?' She tried to sound jokey, to push away a small feeling of unease that was creeping through her.

'I said we'd go round for lunch today. She's going out this evening.'

'Lunch . . . today! But, darling, that's going to massacre our day. Why can't we go tomorrow?' she retorted, looking at her watch. Then she said more gently, 'Let's go tomorrow. It's your first day back – she must understand that we want to be together today.'

He did not look at her, but got up from the bed and went over to the window. Watching him, Leonie thought again how beautiful he was. His long, lean body so perfectly proportioned, his profile with

11

the straight nose, the downcast eyes with their long eyelashes. She felt a surge of love, of desire for him.

'You remind me of Donatello's *David*,' she said. 'I shall never be able to look at that statue again without thinking of you.'

He turned, gave her an awkward, but pleased smile. 'Don't be silly.'

'It's true.'

'You remind me of Botticelli's *Venus* then,' he grinned.

She laughed. 'When we are really old and saggy we can hobble off on our walking frames and look at what we once were to each other,' she said, sadness inexplicably hitting her as she realised that only in pictures did people never change.

Her melancholy was coupled to his change of mood, this new tension running deep in him. She wanted to ask him outright why he was feeling this way, but she was a little insecure about their love and feared he might say he had a change of heart about their plans now he was back. Instead she said, 'How will life treat us, do you think?' willing him to say something reassuring.

She expected him to laugh, make a joke. He hated it when she was sad. But he stared out of the window as if the answer were in the London street.

'I don't know,' he said gravely, turning back to the room, his shoulders slightly slumped as if his previous buoyancy was slowly being deflated. 'I don't know.'

'Whatever do you mean, Julian?' she said, annoyed and fearful that he hadn't found her a word of comfort. She felt suddenly afraid of the precariousness of love, terrified that their warm passion and hopes for their future together would turn to ice and shatter before them.

'Oh nothing,' he said impatiently, weary of her questions. He went out of the room and she heard him go into the bathroom and shut the door.

She forced herself to stay in bed and not go running after him, to take him in her arms and hold him, beg him to reassure her of his love. But after that wonderful lovemaking – and her body warmed again thinking of it – it was surely obvious that he loved her. She was just overwrought at seeing him again; they both were.

She lay on her pillows and tried to calm herself. They needed time to settle back together again without the heady feeling of freedom and romance in Florence. *Without* their families. How much better it would have been to have today just for themselves.

Melanie, thankfully, was away on a business trip, so they could stay here undisturbed for a week if they wanted to, then go through the dreaded family meetings. Leonie began to feel buoyant again. She giggled. She'd seduce him, then when she had power over him, she'd suggest that, make him want to say here in bed with her for the rest of the day.

'Darling,' she held out her arms to him when he came into the room, 'come back to bed.'

'Not now, we must get dressed . . . go to lunch.' He didn't look at her but began to pick up his clothes from the floor.

'Couldn't we stay here today? It's so long since we've been together – two whole weeks – and I've missed you so much.' She tried not to whine.

He found his boxer shorts and pulled them on, then sat down on the end of the bed with his back to her to put on his socks.

'Come on, darling. The sooner we meet everyone, the sooner we can get married,' he said levelly. 'Please, Leonie. Please, darling,' he threw her an anxious smile, 'let's get it over with.'

'God, what sort of woman is your mother?' she grumbled as she got out of bed. But seeing his stricken expression she felt mean. After all, *her* parents were making enough fuss at wanting to meet him.

'I'm sorry,' she said, putting her hand on his bare shoulder as she passed. 'I just wanted us to be alone today, your first day back. I find families, well, mine anyway, make such negative remarks about one's plans. They think they are being kind, I suppose, but somehow they end up just being depressing. I . . . I just don't feel like putting up with it today. I want to spend it alone with you.'

He put his arm round her, laid his head on her bare stomach and kissed her. 'I know, darling,' he said, his voice slightly desperate. 'You know what families are like. But once we're married and in Italy . . . we'll just be us, as we were before.'

'I wish we had got married quietly in Florence, then told everyone,' she said, remembering her family bickering over their plans.

'I do too,' he said, 'but your mother wants you in a beautiful dress and all the trimmings,' he released her, giving her a little pat on her bottom, 'and so do I. A beautiful start to a beautiful life.' He got up and put on his shirt. 'Now cover that sexy body of yours or I will never get dressed in time either.'

'Good,' she said, turning to him again.

But he smiled, kissed her chastely on her forehead and said, 'Don't tempt me, darling. We mustn't be late, we'll make up for it tonight.'

Reluctantly Leonie obeyed him. She fussed with her hair, finally tying it back with a black silk band, so it lay like a glistening rope down her back. She wondered what to wear to impress his mother. Should she be simple in a jersey and skirt, or more formal in a suit, or even a dress? She kept asking Julian and throwing garments on the bed for his approval, but as time went on he seemed to be getting increasingly agitated.

Eventually he said, 'All these things are pretty and you always look good. Wear what you want.'

'You're no help. Don't blame me if I make the wrong impression,' she wailed, finding a smudge of makeup on the collar of her cream silk shirt. She settled at last for a lavender linen shirt and beige skirt, putting a thin gold chain round her neck.

'Do I pass?' She pirouetted before him.

'Yes, oh darling, you'll always pass for me.' He grabbed her to him and held her tightly in his arms.

'Let's hope your mother's as easy,' she said, returning his hug with such fervour that they both had to restrain themselves before their clothes were torn off again and crumpled under them on the floor.

They left her flat and got into Julian's car. He had flown home last night, and despite her pleas to meet him at the airport and take him home to her bed, he had told her, firmly but gently, that his mother was sending someone to pick him up.

'I'll ring you when I'm home and I'll be with you for breakfast,' he'd said.

'Early breakfast,' she'd replied, trying to hide her disappointment.

'Very early breakfast.'

She had spent the evening in restless anticipation of his call, and when he had rung soon after ten to say he was back, she had found it almost impossible to sleep, so determined was she to be up and beautiful when he arrived. He had come at seven and they had loved each other with such joy and abandon, she couldn't now help feeling rather resentful that they had to stop, get dressed up and go out into the real world to meet his mother.

Glancing at Julian as he drove, she saw how taut his face and body had become. He exuded tension. Leonie felt the atmosphere was so thick, she could cut it in slices like a fruitcake. It made her feel sick with trepidation.

'Where does your mother live?' she asked, to try to lighten the mood in the car as they drove down Kensington High Street. The pavements were crowded with lunchtime shoppers dressed in warm clothes against the chill spring air, in contrast to the skimpily clothed plastic mannequins in the shop windows, optimistically predicting a summer heat wave. He hadn't told her much about his family, but she knew he was living with his mother at the moment. 'You know, darling, I don't even know your London address.'

'It's just off here,' he said, turning off the High Street, up a tree-lined residential road. In a moment they arrived outside a large house.

'Is this it?' Leonie said, thinking how smart and expensive it looked. She began to worry about her clothes – were they elegant enough for such surroundings? It would be too gauche and too late to ask him now.

He parked the car in the garage beside the house, the door opening automatically. She could feel the tension running through him. For a terrible moment she wondered if he were ashamed of her, if his mother were a duchess or something and wanted at least a duke's daughter for her son.

'What shall I call your mother?' she said, hoping that he would tell her if she had a title.

'Oh, I . . . well . . .' A flash of desperation crossed his face. It was gone so fast she thought she'd imagined it.

'Has she got a title or anything?' She did not say that her mother had looked him up in Debrett's, which she called 'the good book', but as Leonie didn't know Julian's father's first name, she hadn't got very far. 'There are so many Hunters,' Zinnia had said, 'have you no idea which one his father could be?'

15

'Oh no, sorry, darling.' Julian briefly touched her hand. 'I haven't filled you in. She's Mrs Maitland, Anita. After she divorced my father she married someone called Piers Maitland. It didn't last long. We'll go in this way.' He led her through a small door in the back of the garage and she followed him up some steps into a square hall. He put their coats on a chair, and dropped the car keys on to a silver dish on the table.

Everything was spotless and gleaming, not a single thing superfluous to the room. Their dumped coats on the straight-backed chair felt like an insult to the room's perfection. Leonie followed Julian into a large, long drawing room with a grand piano at one end. The sofas and chairs were done up in dark red with an army of small chintz or tapestry cushions lined up in precision along their backs. Again, nothing extra was there to spoil the effect – no newspapers hurriedly folded, or letters, or sewing or books discarded on a chair or table. It was as if no one lived here.

French windows opened on to a large patio decorated with stone tubs and pristine plants, a white wrought-iron table and matching chairs. There were steps leading down to a garden.

'Do sit,' Julian said, curiously stiff and formal now. 'Can I get you a drink?'

Leonie, fearful of the change in him, wondering why he was so tense, and afraid to ask, longed for something strong to give her strength, but she didn't dare seek courage in alcohol. She had never felt so on edge meeting someone before. Shy, often, but never before this crippling nervousness. She knew it was because Julian was so tense and she was picking it up from him.

She remembered her first meeting with Dominic's mother, a round, wispy-haired woman who kept glancing in amazement at her son as if she couldn't believe that her baby had grown into this huge man. She'd been sweet and vague and very welcoming. She'd made a cake for Leonie, and brought out the best china, made her feel special. Leonie felt that 'the best china' was the only china used here, and it was used to show off the superiority of the hostess, not as a treat for a guest.

'Will your sister be here for lunch?' Leonie asked, curious to meet her, wondering if she was as beautiful as Julian.

16

'No,' Julian replied shortly, adding more gently, 'Diana's out all day. She's doing a course in china-mending. You'll meet her another time.'

'China-mending . . . how interesting. Where is she . . .?' Leonie began, wanting to fill this empty, dead-feeling house with the vitality of her babbling words. But her remark was broken by the sound of the front door opening . . .

She tensed, heard the door close, then a few staccato steps in the hall and a voice calling, 'Julian, are you there?'

Julian hurried towards the door, his face anxious. 'We're here, Mother.'

Leonie's first impression was of a bird. Anita Maitland was wearing a brown felt hat with a pointed brim; her nose and to some extent her chin were pointed, her eyes, large and dark, seemed to take in everything at once. She was elegant, very slim, and quite formidably beautiful. Leonie felt hysterically that she was like a blackbird, but a tall, superior kind of blackbird. She wished for one crazy moment that she could say that to Julian, make him laugh, agree with her. She got up from the sofa and walked towards her, smiling shyly.

'Darling, what a time I've had. I mean, shop assistants these days, I don't know where they find them.' Anita addressed this remark to Julian as if Leonie weren't in the room. She took off her coat and hat and handed them to him, giving him a dazzling smile.

'Mother, this is Leonie Eldridge,' Julian said loudly, awkwardly, as if he feared her opinion.

'Oh, yes . . . how do you do?' Anita nodded vaguely towards her and did not offer Leonie her hand. It was as if she were automatically following some social custom, not meeting the girl her son wanted to marry.

'How do . . . you . . .?' Leonie said, agonised. She shot Julian a quick glance. Had he not told his mother he wanted to marry her? Did she think she was just a passing acquaintance, someone here in her drawing room by chance?

Anita was dressed in brown cashmere with a brilliant orange and blue silk scarf tucked into her neck. She carried on her conversation with Julian as if they were alone in the room. 'I want you to drive

Janet down to Liberty's this afternoon and pick up some material they've got in especially for me. I want the house in Ladbroke Terrace finished this week if possible.'

'But, Mother, I—' This time he did shoot a glance towards Leonie.

'Taxis are so expensive, and she may have to wait while they find it. They can't deliver it for a couple of days, and my curtain maker said she'd start on it today. I knew you'd go, darling. It is important to me.' She flashed him another smile and touched his cheek with her hand. Leonie thought her long, maroon nails might just as easily scratch him if he declined to help her.

'I've had to spend so much doing up that house, the sooner I can get it on the market the better,' she continued.

Leonie standing there in the middle of the carpet didn't know what to do with herself. Her feet and hands felt huge, she longed to sit down, but didn't like to until Anita did – not that Anita seemed to know, or care that she was there at all. She longed to say something to Julian, anything, just to make contact with him. Unconsciously she moved a step towards him.

This seemed to wake him up. He said briskly, 'I'll get us a drink. Mother, you must ask Leonie about her art course in Florence. She had a strict old bag trying to lock her in every night, rather like the one you told us about when you were there.' He darted off to pursue the drinks.

'Really?' Anita looked at her now, but as if she were too insignificant to waste breath on.

Leonie longed to leave. To be alone with Julian back in her flat. She yearned for his reassurance that all that mattered was each other, being together. She wanted to say to him, 'I want to go home. She doesn't like me. She won't give me a chance. I just don't feel comfortable here.' But before she could follow him into the hall, he was back. He opened some double doors revealing another, smaller room, its windows looking on to the road. He poured a gin and tonic from the drinks tray on the side and said to Leonie, 'What will you have, darling?' The 'darling' must have slipped out involuntarily, Leonie thought, seeing him clench his lips as his mother glanced at him sharply. It gave her a little surge of hope and courage. He loved her after all, but he didn't want to show it in front of his mother. She

18

felt a pang of sympathy for him. If anyone showed too much passion for their boy- or girlfriend in her family, the others were maddening with their teasing.

'I'll just have tonic . . . or a bitter lemon, thank you, darling,' she said as warmly as she could, determined suddenly to show Anita that she was important to him.

When he handed her her glass she stroked his hand and smiled up at him. She was rewarded with a smile back. 'Thank you, darling,' she said, covetously watching Anita's exaggerated indifference.

Then, telling herself that first meetings were often sticky and she must try for Julian's sake to make it go smoothly, she said into the icy silence: 'Julian and I are going to live in Florence, or near by, when we're married. I love it out there, don't you, Mrs Maitland?' As she said the words she saw Julian stiffen, send her a warning with his eyes.

Anita said coldly, 'There comes a time when one's student days have to end. Julian has to get down to a job.'

'Of course he'll work out there. I'm sure he'll find something without much trouble,' Leonie said, feeling as if she'd put her foot in it, but annoyed at the same time that Julian hadn't paved the way, told his mother where they wanted to live after they were married.

'It all depends where the best job for him is,' Anita said smoothly, smiling at Julian. Then she lifted her eyes to the doorway where a thin, blonde-haired woman in a pale blue overall was standing.

'Thank you, Janet, we'll come at once. Julian will take you to Liberty's this afternoon, about two thirty. Will that be all right?'

'Thank you. I'll be ready,' Janet said and left them.

Anita tucked her arm through Julian's and walked with him to the door. Leonie, left behind and feeling she could hardly bear any more, felt tears of misery, of frustration rise in her.

She suddenly realised why he had insisted that they live in Italy. He had to get away from Anita. She'd never let them lead their own lives if they stayed here. She forced herself to remember those wonderful three months they'd spent together in Florence. They had loved each other, they *did* love each other. Anita was just a possessive mother,

19

and once they were away from her, everything would be wonderful again.

At the door Julian turned back, his eyes searching for hers. He saw what she was feeling in her expression and the way she stood. He pulled himself from his mother's arm, came back to her and held out his hand.

'Coming?' he said gently.

'Julian . . . I . . .' She was about to say she wanted to leave. She would slip away quietly. She wasn't hungry, could never eat a mouthful in this house, with his mother criticising her in her silent way with those dark, sharp eyes. Looking up into Julian's eyes, she thought, they are the image of his mother's, yet they are soft and kind. What happens to a person, to change them so?

'Come on, darling,' he urged gently. Under that gentleness she felt a steely determination in him. He knew how she was feeling but he was not going to let her go. She went with him reluctantly, down the stairs into the dining room.

Anita was already seated at an expensive glass table, carefully laid with silver and three glasses at each place, a bowl of white gardenias in the centre. Their heavy smell seemed oversweet and sick-making to Leonie, who mechanically took her place next to Julian, who sat at the head of the table. Anita was opposite her.

A plate of melon and Parma ham was in front of her, which she picked at. It was followed by chicken breasts and green beans.

'Leonie is a marvellous cook, she trained at Leith's,' Julian said in one of the silences in between Anita's telling him about the houses she was buying, doing up and reselling or letting.

Anita barely lifted her eyes to her.

Julian went on: 'She cooks directors' lunches.' He smiled encouragingly at Leonie. 'Are you going to go back to working for your friend . . . Caroline, isn't it? You thought you might.'

'I don't know.' Leonie kept her eyes on him. 'It depends . . .' her voice tailed away. She was going to suggest there would not be enough time before they went back to Florence, but now she didn't know what to say.

Sitting here with Anita so icy, so unapproachable, everything so different from what she'd imagined, she felt a surge of panic. She thought she would choke on her food. Her throat closed up and she couldn't swallow.

Anita finished her chicken, then rang the bell for Janet, who came in with cheese and fruit. She told her of a few other things she could get her that afternoon, then gave Julian instructions as to where to wait for Janet while she fetched the material.

'It's so sweet of you, darling, to give up your time for me,' she said softly, looking into his eyes, smiling at him.

He flushed, looking . . . almost grateful, Leonie thought bitterly. Every word, every gesture between them made her feel more isolated, more excluded. It would have been easier to bear if Anita had been rude to her, ridiculed her remarks. Instead she carried on as if Leonie were too insignificant to bother about, not worth including in the conversation, however domestic and trivial.

Leonie kept her eyes on her plate, willing the meal to end, trying to persuade herself that she was overreacting. Just because her own mother made such an effort to welcome her children's friends, it didn't mean that other people's mothers did. Anita was a tough businesswoman by the sound of all her talk of deals in the property market; she was probably someone who hadn't time for the trivia of social chatter, Leonie told herself firmly, but still she felt utterly wretched.

She loved Julian, she could not live without him, but how could she marry someone with a mother like this? A mother who seemed to dominate him, fill him with tension followed by gratitude when she chose to bestow her charm on him. She would, surely, destroy them both.

Chapter Three

Julian felt sick. He had so hoped his mother would take to Leonie. She'd always been a little difficult with the few girlfriends he'd brought home in the past.

'I'm afraid she's got her eye on the money, darling,' she'd said of one. 'I hope you've told her not to be taken in by this house. You will have to earn your own living.'

Another time she'd said, 'You'll have to keep your eyes on that one. Goodness knows whose bed she'll be in if you turn your back.'

Later, he had to admit, her remarks, though cutting at the time, had turned out to be true.

But Leonie wasn't like that and he'd done his best to persuade his mother that she was different, she meant more to him than anyone had before, but Anita had said airily, with an impatient toss of her hand, 'Oh darling, love at your age is so prevalent, like chicken pox. Have lots of girlfriends, you don't want to be drearily settled with one for at least another ten years.' And she'd let out a peal of laughter as if he were being frightfully amusing.

'But I love her, and I want you to make her feel welcome, love her too,' he ventured, trying to swallow his anguish that his news of his engagement to Leonie had displeased her.

Ever since he'd been a small boy he'd craved her love. She was such a beautiful, feminine woman and his first memories were of her floating upstairs to the nursery to say good night. She was always wonderfully dressed in clothes of rich fabrics and colours, trailing a scent that seemed to surround him like a soft mist, drawing him in. She would drop kisses in the air above his head, and when, overcome with love and longing to touch her, to feel the soft silky fabrics of her clothes, to be enclosed in the voluptuousness of her skin, he would put out his arms to her and try and hold her, she would shake him off, saying laughingly, 'No, my darling, I've just done my makeup . . . my hair . . . you'll crush my dress.' Then she would be gone, calling out good night as she whisked down the stairs and away somewhere into the dark night and he would be left lonely, despite the companionship of his sister and the warm kisses and hugs of his plump, plain nanny.

Later, when he was at public school, she always caused a sensation. Other people's mothers had, it seemed, let themselves go. Their clothes were dowdy and if they wore makeup it was only a token, a snatch of lipstick, a dab of powder. His mother was so glamorous with her beautiful, glossy hair, impeccable makeup, trim figure in sensational clothes from Paris. He remembered the older boys saying with a mixture of envy and probably sexual admiration, 'Have you seen Hunter's mother?' and the warm feeling and pride this had evoked in him. She was his . . . *his* mother.

But as he grew older he saw how elusive she was. You had to earn her love. She turned it on and off, making him, making anyone who wanted her, yearn for more.

After lunch with Anita, Leonie said she had shopping to do and made Julian put her out at the tube station. With Janet in the car neither could say much, but when he came later to her flat she let him have it.

'I have never felt so unwelcome in all my life,' she burst out, near tears. 'She hates me – no, she doesn't even hate me, I'm not even worth that amount of emotion. We can't possibly get married.'

'Darling, we can, we can.' He caught her hands, tried to pull her to him. 'I know she can be difficult—'

'Difficult! She's impossible.'

'It's us that's important, when we get to Florence . . . when we're together.' His voice was imploring now. 'Darling, I love you, we love each other, want to spend the rest of our lives together. That is all that matters.'

'Don't you see that it's not? She doesn't want me to marry you, perhaps anyone to marry you – or has she her eye on someone else for you?' she asked bitterly, despair throwing in more doubts.

'No, of course not. She just . . . well, she doesn't like change. She's shy—'

'Oh Julian, who are you kidding?' she exclaimed, so hurt by Anita's disdain, she wanted to hurt someone in return, hurt him if she couldn't get at his mother.

He let go of her and paced the room, his hands thrust in his pockets, his face desolate. 'I know she's impossible . . . but she can be so charming. She does this sometimes. I expect it's because I've been away and obviously wanted to be with you more than I wanted to be with her . . .' He rattled on, desperate to find some reason she'd understand.

'*My* mother loves us and wants us to herself, but she knows life's not like that. She'll be welcoming to you, talk to you, show interest in you,' she retorted.

'I know, but . . .'

'We are adults, Julian, we can do what we want. She has no right to be so bad-mannered, so selfish.'

The row raged on, tight circles of anger and hurt whirring round and round. In the end, in sheer exhaustion, Leonie burst into tears and collapsed on the floor. Julian ran to her, crying too, and held her, soothed her, finally made love to her. Although she let him, and allowed him to stay with her the next day, she refused to discuss marriage with him.

'I don't want to mention your mother or marriage again,' she said firmly whenever he tried to bring the subjects up. 'Let's be just us and not make any plans for the moment.'

But even while she pretended to be strong and practical, Leonie felt bewildered, bereft of her joyful plans, and she could see no way out of her misery.

A couple of evenings later Julian said, 'Put on something special, darling. I want to take you out somewhere nice.'

'Where are we going?' she asked him.

'I told you, somewhere nice. Wear that pretty green silk dress – I love you in that,' he smiled. 'It makes your hair look so gold and your skin so creamy.'

'You make me sound like an ice cream,' she laughed, but she felt pleased.

He drove her to the Connaught, then left the car with the doorman. But just as they were going in he said, 'My father is here, he's longing to meet you.'

'Oh no, Julian, no way,' she said in despair, turning round and struggling to back out, though he had his hand firmly under her arm. 'I don't want to meet anyone else from your family. It's quite pointless anyway.' Her stomach plummeted at the thought of another unpleasant scene.

'I promise you, darling, he's different from Mother. You'll like him,' Julian said encouragingly, giving her a kiss.

'No, Julian, I don't want to.' But before she could escape another couple had come up behind them and she was forced to go in.

A tall, grey-haired, well-built man, with rather heavy features but none the less striking good looks, came forward as they entered.

'My dear, I'm so very glad to meet you. In fact I'm going to kiss you.' Tony Hunter put his hands on Leonie's shoulders and kissed her smartly on both cheeks. 'My, you're lovely,' he smiled. 'I always hoped I'd have a pretty daughter-in-law.'

Leonie smiled shyly, feeling warm in spite of her inner turmoil. Julian was right, his father was completely different from his mother.

They sat down and Tony ordered drinks. When they came he lifted his glass to her. 'To you, my dear. Welcome.'

'Thank you,' she smiled at him, liking him even more.

'So,' Tony said a little later, as she sat with him while Julian was in the gents, 'you met the dreaded Anita and I hear she barely spoke to you.'

'Y-yes.' Leonie was momentarily taken aback by his forthright remark.

He patted her hand. 'You're not to take any notice of her, my dear. She's a selfish woman, used to having life her own way. Julian is the only man in her life at the moment; she's just broken up with some poor bugger. She'll soon find another, then she'll behave better towards you.'

'Mr Hun—'

'Tony, please, my dear.'

'Tony, I can't marry Julian,' she burst out suddenly, feeling she must tell him before things got much further.

He looked at her quizzically and said soothingly, as if he were a doctor trying to massage a secret from her, 'Don't you love him?'

'Oh yes, of course I do, but—'

'Then you must marry him. He loves you. You must go for it, both of you. Don't let Anita win, ruin his life.' His full mouth clenched, his eyes blazed. 'I don't mind telling you, my dear, she's the most selfish woman I've ever met.' He took a long drink of his whisky and soda, and settled back as if to tell a story.

'She was the only child of an older father and an invalid mother – anyway she thought she was an invalid, but if you ask me I think she did it for attention,' he winked. 'They lived in that wonderful house, I don't know if you know it, Hopewell House, in Kent.'

Leonie shook her head.

'It belongs to the National Trust now. Her father overindulged her, made her impossible for any other man to live with. After her father's death her mother remarried.' He laughed. 'So much for the invalid. Then the money went. Oh, I was fool.' He leant forward confidingly. 'She was – is still, for all I know – a beautiful, desirable woman. She was determined to have me. I had money, you see,' he said in a deprecating voice, as if that were all he had to make him attractive.

'At first I was flattered. I loved her,' he smiled sadly, 'she can be so charming. We had the children and she began to manipulate them, manipulate us all. I hung on for the children until they went to boarding school, which saved them a bit from her. Then she began to have lovers and I couldn't take any more.' He took another drink.

Leonie felt a wave of sympathy for him. For an instant he looked so dejected, diminished. She could imagine Anita reeling him in when she needed him, discarding him when she'd taken whatever she wanted from him.

'I was lucky, I fell in love with someone else. A sweeter woman you couldn't find.' His face lit up for a moment, then went serious again, as if he had remembered a less happy fact. 'We live in Scotland, which is rather far for the children to come often. Also by then they had their own lives. But still Anita managed to do a lot of damage to them. That's why I'm so happy Julian has found you.' He took her

27

hand just as Julian came back. He gave a tiny, tight smile when he saw his father holding Leonie's hand.

'Flirting already, Dad?' he said a little sharply.

Tony smiled at him. 'I was just telling Leonie not to mind about your mother. I could have guessed she'd try to muck things up. Pity you two can't go off and get married in secret, but I suppose your mother wants to give you a do.' He addressed Leonie.

'Yes . . . but . . .' she glanced quickly at Julian, slightly surprised at his displeasure over something as innocent as his father holding her hand. She didn't want to hurt him, or his father, but she really felt she couldn't take on Anita.

'If you love each other, get married, none of this living together instead, that's short-changing yourselves,' Tony said seriously. 'Believe an old man. Life is short enough, don't throw it away because of a selfish, scheming woman. Just carry on with your plans,' he winked at Leonie, 'and if Anita sees they're going ahead and she's being left out of them, she'll behave. You see if she won't.'

Leonie was about to protest when Tony looked up, then got to his feet. 'There you are, darling,' he greeted a rather plain, slender girl in her early twenties, with dark brown hair sweeping back from her forehead like his, and his intense blue eyes.

'Daddy!' She flung herself into his arms, and the two held each other a moment before he released her, looking intently into her face.

Leonie thought how contrary nature was, giving Julian the beauty of his mother and Diana the sturdier looks of her father. And Diana hadn't helped herself by wearing a rather dowdy, red wool dress, which surprised Leonie knowing how elegant Anita was. But then again, she thought, with a trace of spite, Anita may not want to encourage her daughter to look attractive in case she drew some attention away from her.

'You look a little pale, my darling,' Tony said, 'and too thin, but come on, we'll have a good dinner. Now meet Leonie Eldridge, the lovely girl your lucky brother has found. Though,' he said, picking up Leonie's hand, 'she hasn't got a ring on her finger yet, Julian, so it can hardly be official.'

'He bought me one in Florence—' Leonie began.

'Only a joke one. I was just waiting to get home,' Julian said.

28

'We have some lovely rings, family ones, especially for this occasion,' Tony said, then seeing her expression laughed. 'Don't worry they're not cast-off engagement rings of failed marriages, like mine to their mother.'

'I didn't mean—'

'Of course you didn't, and if you don't like one of those, don't be afraid to say so. We'll try to go to the bank vault tomorrow,' he said to Julian, then turning back to his daughter said, 'So, Diana, this is your new sister-in-law-to-be.'

'How do you do?' Diana said formally and held out her hand to her. Leonie took it and smiled. 'I suppose I ought to say congratulations,' Diana said shyly. 'It is so exciting.' She kissed Julian and then sat down beside him.

'So tell me what you've been up to,' Tony asked her. 'Hope your mother's not been bothering you more than usual.'

'Oh, no . . . not much,' Diana said a little guiltily.

Tony gave his daughter an intense look, which Leonie felt was almost a warning. She began to feel uncomfortable again. She longed to get up before Tony spent a fortune on her dinner, and say, 'It's lovely meeting you, but I can't marry Julian. We'll just have to "short-change" ourselves and live together.' But before she could, Tony had whisked her up into the conversation again, then the menus arrived and it became too difficult to leave.

Diana was quiet throughout dinner, letting the others talk. Leonie often caught her looking at her in a shy, almost disbelieving way, as if trying to assess her as the wife of her brother. But she was friendly enough, and got quite animated when they talked about living in Florence.

'I'd love to live there,' she said wistfully.

'You must come and stay with us, though God knows where we'll be living – probably some dank cellar under a bridge,' Julian said, half smiling at Leonie as if fearful she would start on again about not marrying him.

'Oh, I'd love to,' Diana said eagerly. 'I really would. Are you sure?' She turned to Leonie, an expression of anxious hope on her face.

'But of course you must come,' Leonie burst out, quite forgetting that she wasn't going to marry Julian. She felt a sudden compassion for Diana, that she couldn't bear to disappoint her hesitant wish to come to Italy. She found herself watching her interact with Julian. At first they had seemed ordinary together, perfectly friendly, Julian doing most of the talking. He asked her about the china mending course she was doing, how various friends were. They never touched each other, or showed undue affection, but Leonie came to the conclusion that there was a deep closeness there, a dependence on each other that she didn't have with her brother and sister. She felt that Julian and Diana were tied together by the bond made by their parents' troubles. She wondered what Tony's wife, their stepmother, was like. He had said she was the sweetest woman, yet Julian had hardly mentioned her.

'What is your wife's name? I've forgotten,' she said with an awkward laugh, aware that she'd never known it. She felt rather than saw a despairing look flash between Julian and Diana.

'Clemmy,' Tony said, smiling, 'short for Clemency.'

'And she's in Scotland?'

'Yes. We live near Inverness, as no doubt Julian's told you. She's just opened a book shop there so she couldn't get away.' He told Leonie all this in a serious way, as if he was explaining something difficult to her. He didn't once look at his children.

'How nice.' She wondered why Julian and Diana stayed so silent.

'I don't know how she's going to manage running the shop and coping with the children,' Tony said with an affectionate smile.

'Children?'

'Surely Julian's told you?' Tony was still not looking at his son. 'I have two small sons, four and three.'

'Oh yes . . . I . . .' Leonie fought to hide her surprise. Julian had told her his parents were divorced and that his father lived in Scotland with another wife. He'd never mentioned small brothers. She looked surreptitiously at Tony. He looked sixty and she'd imagined his wife to be near his age, or anyway forty-something, and past having babies. She longed now to know how old his wife was but didn't know how to ask, as Tony obviously assumed that Julian had told her all about his stepmother.

'It must be fun having a young family,' she said lamely.

'Exhausting, my dear,' he smiled, 'but if you two have some soon they can all mix in. Fancy, they'll be uncles to your children.' He laughed uproariously. 'I can't imagine Ben and Tom being uncles.'

Leonie laughed too, but Julian drank rather desperately from his glass while Diana played with her bread, crumbling it and making little piles with the crumbs.

'I think it's time to go home,' Julian said suddenly. 'Lovely dinner, Dad. Thanks so much.'

'A pleasure, my dear boy, and such an occasion. I couldn't be more delighted.' He put his hand over Leonie's and squeezed it. 'I really want to welcome you into the family, my dear. Any time you want to come to Scotland, Clemmy and I will greet you with open arms.'

'Thank you. I'd love to come. I don't know Scotland very well, but I'd like to get to know it better,' she said with real enthusiasm. She glanced at Julian, but he didn't look at her or take up his father's invitation. Instead, while Tony called for the bill, he began an earnest conversation with Diana about Florence and what avenues he was exploring for a job.

'Remember what I said, Leonie,' Tony, who was staying at the hotel, said after he'd signed the bill and they were hovering in the foyer. 'This is your life, yours and Julian's. Don't throw away your happiness together because of a selfish woman.'

'I won't.' She kissed him back, feeling strong, defiant now. She was marrying Julian, not Anita. They would escape to Italy and leave her behind.

In the car, going home with Julian and Diana, Leonie said as nonchalantly as she could, 'You never told me you had little brothers. Your stepmother must be quite young then?' She glanced at him from the corner of her eyes and saw his mouth tighten.

He said, 'They are just babies; we never see them.'

'And your stepmother?' She turned round now and addressed this question to Diana. From the light of passing streetlamps that crisscrossed Diana's face, Leonie saw a troubled expression, saw her throw a nervous glance at Julian's back view.

'We don't go to Scotland and she's too busy to come South,' she said lamely. Then, seeing Leonie's puzzled expression, she added quickly, 'But she's nice, you'd like her. I mean . . .'

Diana was grinding her hands desperately in her lap and Leonie was certain she was blushing. Leonie was sure she meant to say, 'She's not like my mother, she'll be pleased for you and Julian.' She smiled kindly at Diana, sympathising at her discomfiture.

'I'm glad,' Leonie said. 'I do so want us all to get on.'

Diana's face lit up eagerly, like a child being offered a place in a coveted gang. 'I do too. I'm sure we will . . . in time,' she added hastily, again looking desperately at the back of Julian's head.

When they'd dropped Diana back at the large house in Kensington, Leonie said, 'I wish you'd told me about Clemmy and the little boys. It was rather embarrassing for me not to know.'

'I'm sure I told you, darling,' Julian said a little impatiently. 'Anyway, as Diana said, we don't see much of them, living all that way away. Only my father comes South sometimes for his business.'

'I wonder how much more I'm going to find out about your family,' Leonie said dubiously. She did not feel quite convinced by his laughter that followed her remark.

Chapter Four

'I've never heard such nonsense,' Zinnia said when Leonie took Julian down to Sussex for the weekend to meet her parents, and told her mother about her meeting with Anita. 'I hope she's not one of those tiresome women who think no one is good enough for her son.' She basted the meat with such fury that she splashed the gravy over the hotplate, which hissed and splattered.

'No . . . I don't think it's as simple as that, Ma, but—'

'I expect our blood is bluer than hers.' Zinnia was firmly in the 'good book'. 'She sounds thoroughly rude to me, not even possessing common courtesy to a guest in her house. But I like Julian, poor young man,' she added as if she had never questioned Julian's background. 'And at least you say his father is very nice.'

'He's charming, I liked him very much – and his sister, though she seems very immature, perhaps because she's bossed to bits by Anita, still living with her, no doubt as her slave,' she said with feeling. 'But I didn't tell you,' Leonie smiled, 'Tony has a young wife and two little boys.'

'Good gracious! Well, you know what men are.' She banged the door of the oven shut, and prodded the cauliflower boiling on the top. 'Shall we have a white sauce?' and before Leonie could answer she went on: 'I think it's nicer. Fetch me some milk, dear. But if that woman thinks she can mess up your marriage for some selfish reason of her own, she's another think coming.'

'Tony says she'll come round when she knows the marriage will go ahead whatever she thinks, and now I have the ring.' She looked at it shining on her finger, a beautiful deep sapphire with diamonds round it. She still hadn't got used to it. Julian had given it to her the day after she'd met his father.

'If you'd rather I bought you a new one do say,' he'd said, slipping it on to her finger. 'This is a family ring, from my great-grandmother.'

'It's so beautiful.' She hadn't been able to take her eyes off it. The setting was unusual – the main stone raised, the diamonds falling away around it.

He'd smiled and kissed her, pleased with her obvious delight. 'Everything will work out, darling, I promise you it will.'

'It is the most lovely ring. Nothing can beat those old settings,' Zinnia said now, pausing in her cooking for a moment to look at it again. 'I think he is perfect for you too. You must not let his tiresome mother come between you.'

'I think . . . hope she may be easier now she's found another man,' Leonie said, putting down a bottle of milk near Zinnia and fetching the flour.

'*Another* man?' Zinnia said sharply. 'What on earth has that to do with her son's marriage?'

'Well . . .' Leonie thought it was nonsense too, but remembering what Tony had told her, tried to explain, 'she needs a man in her life and if Julian marries—'

'How very selfish of her.' Zinnia splashed the milk on to the roux in the pan and stirred it briskly. 'I can't be doing with these women who won't function without a man. What would have happened if she'd been widowed suddenly, or had lived through the last war?'

'I don't know.'

'You say she had lots of lovers while she was married, and I suppose after handing herself round like that, no decent man wants her so she's determined to take it out on her son. She's probably jealous of his happiness with you.' Zinnia crashed the saucepans about some more.

Leonie smiled. Her mother had very distinct ideas about people and jumped to outrageous conclusions, which often did turn out to hold some truth.

Harry flopped into the kitchen in his old school dressing gown, which was far too short for him, his hair tousled, his feet bare. He was immediately followed by Julian and George, both looking windswept. George had taken Julian to see his boat moored at Chichester

Harbour. He rarely sailed now, but anyone new that came to stay, especially someone he thought one of his children fancied, was always taken to see it.

'What a sight you look, Harry,' Zinnia said affectionately. 'Go and get dressed, darling. It's almost lunchtime.'

Harry grinned at Julian. 'Old man been doing the boat test on you then?'

Julian looked puzzled. 'Boat test?'

'Stop making inane remarks and go and tidy yourself up,' George said firmly.

Leonie looked quickly at Julian, knowing Harry's supposition was true, though George would never admit to it. He smiled at her. 'Great boat,' he said. 'I'd love to go out in it one day.'

'We will,' George said beaming, 'next time you're down. Time for a drink before lunch, darling?' he asked Zinnia.

'If you're quick,' Zinnia said, 'and when you've had it, I want to discuss the date of the wedding. I don't think there's a minute to lose.'

'Don't you, darling?' George shot Leonie a rather red and flustered look.

Leonie laughed. 'I'm not pregnant, Dad. There'll be no concealing a huge tummy under my bouquet. But you know what Ma is like once she's got the bit between her teeth.'

'Oh, I didn't mean to imply, darling . . .' blustered George who obviously had thought Zinnia meant it was to be a shotgun wedding.

'I shall never tell any of you if ever I want to get married,' Harry said, switching on the electric kettle and spooning a mound of instant coffee into a cup. 'Subject some poor girl to pregnancy tests, Aids tests, means tests, not to mention questioning where she's been bred as if she were a prize bitch and our offspring will be entered for Crufts—'

'That's enough, Harry. Go and get dressed,' George interrupted.

Leonie and Julian giggled.

'Don't worry, Julian, they won't let you get away. Mum is longing for one of us to get married so she can outdo some of those toffee-nosed cronies in the village,' Harry grinned as he left the room.

'I really appreciate your getting the wedding organised so soon,'

Julian said when Harry had gone. 'I've been telling . . . George,' he shot him a half-embarrassed smile at using his first name, even though he'd been told to, 'I am sure I will get a job in the art world in Florence, but the sooner I go out there to look for one the better.'

'I'm sure you'll get a job. They'll be lucky to have you. An Englishman that's obviously so well educated and speaking their language too,' Zinnia said airily. 'Besides, one of the so-called good things about the Common Market is opening up a wider field for jobs, isn't it?'

'Yes, so let's hope it comes off for him,' George said briskly.

Leonie caught Julian's eye and guessed that her father had been interrogating him on his 'prospects'. Harry was right, she thought ruefully, feeling sorry for Julian being so bombarded. At least it would have been done with better tact and manners than Anita had shown to her.

'Dad,' she slipped her arm through his, 'you haven't been giving Julian the third degree on keeping your daughter how you hope she should become accustomed, have you?'

'Well . . . I . . .'

'Well don't.' She playfully flicked her finger against his cheek. 'I'm working, doing a bit of cooking with Caroline and I've saved some of my allowance, and both of us are prepared to turn our hands to anything until the right job comes along for Julian. OK?'

'I have a bit of money of my own too,' Julian said, in case Zinnia were about to say something about husbands being supposed to support their wives. 'And with my qualifications—'

'Everything will be fine, I know it will. After all, at your age life is just beginning,' Zinnia said quickly, shooting George a sideways glance. 'I'm really looking forward to having this wedding,' she beamed at both of them.

George coughed, thinking about the cost, and said to Julian, 'Let's go and have that drink before lunch.' He took his arm and led him out of the kitchen.

'If we get it all settled, then his mother can't do anything to stop it,' Zinnia said firmly.

'But surely we have to fix the date with her, and Tony?' Leonie said.

'I'll write to her tomorrow, say how much we love Julian, and how pleased we are, and that we thought we'd have it mid-June. Daddy can go and see her . . .' She paused, draining the cauliflower. 'On second thoughts he'd better not in case she tries any tricks on him. You know how susceptible men are.'

Leonie laughed. 'Ma, you can't be serious. She's not Dad's type at all.'

'You never know what wiles these women come up with. Of course, *we'd* see through them at once, but men are much simpler creatures. I'll meet her first. I don't want her persuading him that the marriage is a bad thing.'

'But Dad wouldn't fall for that. After all, he likes Julian, and,' she sighed, 'Julian seems to have passed the immensely high standards the Eldridge parents have set for their children's spouses.'

'Oh darling, don't be silly. You know we love you and want you to be happy. Marriage, even when you are both so madly in love, as no doubt you are, is a big step.' She put her hand on Leonie's shoulder.

'I know, Ma, but give us a chance to take it without putting too many obstacles in our way.'

'We don't mean to.'

'I know, not like *his* mother, who I'm sure was determined not to like me whoever or whatever I was.'

'We'll get round her, darling,' Zinnia said a little gleefully, as if she looked forward to the fray. 'I'll come up to London next week to see her, and Daddy and I will invite her to dinner – just on her own.' She smiled, deftly stepping over a sleeping dog on her way to the stove. 'Better to know the enemy first.'

Chapter Five

The following week, Leonie and Zinnia met for lunch at the General Trading Company, where they had planned to look at possible wedding presents and open a wedding list there.

'So, Ma, tell all! How did your meeting with Anita go?' Leonie asked eagerly as they settled at their table.

'Quite well, really. As you know, she invited me to tea, then we took her out to dinner. Really, that mausoleum of a house!' Zinnia exclaimed incredulously. 'It has no character or warmth whatsoever, just like a magazine spread. I felt uncomfortable denting the cushions when I sat down, and my yellow jacket clashed with everything.' She laughed.

'But how was she?' Leonie insisted.

'Charming, distant but charming. All "how delighted I am that my . . ." well, she didn't actually say "little boy", but she implied it.'

'Oh Ma, you do exaggerate,' Leonie giggled.

They ordered their lunch and when the waitress had gone Zinnia said, 'She kept on about this new man in her life. Let's just hope he'll last until after the wedding. She's off to the South of France with him . . . whoever he is . . . for three weeks soon. That should keep her out of your way for a while,' she smiled, 'and give me carte blanche for the arrangements.'

'So she didn't bring him to dinner?'

'No, we didn't actually ask him, but I gather he's away on business.'

'I wonder what he's like, probably some ageing cosmopolitan gigolo,' Leonie said. She had not discussed with Julian the parents' meeting, finding it easier on her nerves not to mention his mother.

He was usually loving and fun, but the minute she mentioned Anita, that closed, tight look came over his face and he became distant and uncommunicative.

'Anyway, if she is going away, we should be left alone – that is, until she gets back – and I hope to have it all arranged by then.' Zinnia sprinkled dressing on her salad. 'I said you'd drop in the invitations, which should be ready in a few days. She gave me a detailed account of how to organise a reception, as if I'd never done it before.'

Leonie laughed. 'But you haven't, Ma.'

'Darling, stop being aggravating. I know I haven't actually done a wedding reception, but we've done enough entertaining over the years to know how to cope. Anyway, I told her we were having it at home, hiring a marquee for the garden as the weather is so unpredict-able. She made a bit of a do about the caterers, suggested some frightfully expensive French ones in London.'

Leonie jumped in, 'I'd like Caroline Smythe to do the catering, I told you. I could help, and she is a marvellous cook. She wants to break into weddings.'

'Of course.' Zinnia looked relieved. 'I'd forgotten about Caroline. But you can't do it, darling, you're going to have so much else to do.'

'I suppose so.' Then, looking at her mother, she felt a sudden surge of love.

'Thank goodness I've got you to help me, Ma,' she said gratefully, and before Zinnia could say anything she added with a laugh, 'and how clever you are to have brought Anita to heel.'

On Friday of the following week, Leonie went round to hand over the wedding invitations to Anita. They lay wrapped in white tissue paper on her knee, as Leonie waited for the appropriate moment. She and Julian had called in to the house in Kensington on their way down to her family for the weekend.

Anita kissed her on this second meeting, an icy social kiss into the air beside her cheek.

'I so enjoyed meeting your parents. Your mother came to tea, as you know, and then they took me out to dinner, to such a *dear* little place in Pimlico. I'd never heard of it before.' She smiled as if she were surprised and relieved that Leonie's parents were able to behave properly in public.

'They liked meeting you,' Leonie said politely, remembering her father praising Anita's good looks, and her mother's caustic remark: 'They've been her undoing, all those foolish men hovering like moths around her, being burnt to pieces when she's bored of them.'

'I know you'll forgive me a moment, Leonie dear, while I take Julian upstairs. I've a bill I want to show him. He's so clever over things like that.' She threw him a warm look that made him flush with pleasure. 'I'm sure I've been overcharged,' she continued, her voice confidential. She smiled at Leonie, making her smile back in pleasurable relief. Tony had been right. Now that the wedding was going ahead and she had met her parents, and not forgetting she had a man, Anita was perfectly reasonable.

'Of course, I'll wait down here.'

'We won't be long. Can Janet bring you a coffee or anything?'

'No thank you.' Leonie smiled again, feeling almost relaxed. She settled back on the sofa, looking round in vain for something to read. Julian blew her a kiss.

'Only be a minute, darling.' He too, she thought, seemed more relaxed, catching the lighter mood from his mother. Perhaps everything was going to be all right after all.

She realised when they had gone upstairs that she hadn't handed over the invitations. In her confused emotional state – sick dread at meeting Anita again followed by amazed relief at her acceptance of her – she had completely forgotten them.

Half an hour later Julian came down alone. 'Ready to go, darling?' He came over and kissed her, taking one of her hands in his to pull her to her feet.

'Yes . . . but I forgot to give your mother the invitations. Shall I take them up to her?'

'I'll take them. She's working at her desk. She sends her apologies, and says goodbye. She's got a lot of paperwork to catch up on.'

He took the packet of invitations from her hand and she followed him out into the hall, watching as he went up the stairs and into a room on the first floor. She heard his voice softly talking to Anita, a silence, then Anita screamed out, making her jump.

'Don't tell me she's a Papist!'

Her remark hit Leonie like a blow. She took one step up the stairs as if to go up and confess at once that she was.

She heard Julian say anxiously: 'Yes, but it doesn't matter. It's never mattered to us.'

'The Church of Our Lady of Sorrows!' Anita screeched again. 'Surely they, you, should have said something to me about her religion. I suppose your father knows?'

'I don't know. But, Mother, I don't see why you care so much. I'm sorry I never told you; it just slipped my mind. It's not something that bothers me. In Italy we just went to any church—'

'In Italy! How I wish you'd never gone there. It's quite addled your mind, coming back with all these . . . these ridiculous ideas.'

Another door opened upstairs and Diana came out. Leonie was surprised – no one had told her Diana was at home, but she had obviously heard everything. Catching sight of Leonie she blushed and looked acutely ashamed as if it were she who had been over-heard. She closed the door so they could no longer hear exactly what Julian and Anita were saying, and came on down the stairs.

'Oh dear,' she said, her face quite pink, 'Mummy gets like this sometimes when she's upset. She hates not to know everything, you see. I'm sure she'd be horrified if she knew you'd heard,' she added not looking at her.

Leonie was convinced Diana had only added this last remark to make her feel better, but she forced a smile. 'We quite forgot to tell her I am a Catholic – not that I'm a very staunch one, rather a lazy one in fact. I wasn't trying to conceal it.'

Diana went on past her and into the long drawing room, motion-ing Leonie to follow her. She said awkwardly, her eyes still swivelling away from Leonie's, 'It's Clemmy, you see. She's a Catholic and . . . well, I know it sounds rather silly, but Mummy thinks she tricked Daddy into marrying her by getting pregnant and then saying she couldn't have an abortion because of her faith.'

'I see.' Leonie thought this made Anita sound even worse. 'But your father said that your mother was having affairs before he met Clemmy. Then he fell in love with her. He didn't have to marry her just because she was pregnant – people don't these days – and they went on to have another child, and he seems to be devoted to her,' she finished lamely, thinking what a mess some people made of their lives.

'Mummy didn't want him to marry again, or anyway not to someone so young who could still have children. She said it was hypocritical when everyone knows Catholics shouldn't commit adultery, and Daddy was still married,' Diana burst out as if she had been bottling up these words for ages, but that she felt they were obscene and it hurt her to say them.

Leonie smiled, touched her arm. 'How dreadful for you, for you and Julian, to have to put up with these muddles made by your parents. Does your mother think I've tricked Julian into marriage?'

'Oh no,' Diana protested too violently, making Leonie realise that Anita was not pleased about the marriage after all.

Leonie sighed heavily. Anita seemed to her to be a dog in the manger. She may be bored of her husband, use her son when it suited her, but she didn't want them to find happiness with any other woman. Well, tough, she thought, smiling grimly to herself. Tony and Clemmy are blissfully happy together, and so will Julian and I be.

Julian came in, his face white. He exchanged a despairing glance with Diana, who then wandered out on to the patio, saying as she went: 'I do so hope it works out.'

'Of course it will,' Julian said, taking Leonie in his arms. 'Darling, take no notice of Mother's outburst. It's my fault. I should have told her about your being a Catholic, but I never saw it as an issue.'

'Diana says she hates them because Clemmy used her religion to grab your father.'

He frowned. 'I don't think she did. She loved him, got pregnant, wanted his child. Mother just overreacted because she didn't know. She likes to know everything.' He smiled, not too convincingly.

Leonie said, 'I bet she's using it as an excuse to try to stop the wedding.'

'Nonsense, darling. Look,' he kissed her, 'forget it. It will blow over. She's a lot of worries at the moment and they're making her edgy. Come on, it's time to go to your family. Let's hit the road.'

Leonie said goodbye to Diana, who was deadheading the plants in the huge urns on the patio, and followed Julian out to his car.

'I rather wish we weren't going home,' she said as they drove away, past the solid white houses that wore their bright window boxes like jewellery, down into the bustle of Kensington High Street. 'I didn't think just getting married could cause such a commotion. I quite see why people would rather live together. Just move in and hang the relations.'

Julian smiled, curled his hand over hers as it lay on her lap. 'I know, darling, but I expect they mean well.'

'Do they?' Leonie said under her breath, knowing that Anita certainly didn't.

'Is your mother a deeply religious person?' Zinnia asked when they'd told her about Anita's reaction to Leonie's religion.

Leonie groaned inwardly. It annoyed her when her mother tried to be 'understanding'.

'I mean,' Zinnia went on, 'does she perhaps belong to a religion that does not want an alliance with a Christian family?'

'No, not at all,' Julian said. 'It's nothing. Really, it isn't. I just should have told her. I can't think why I didn't.'

'Well, my dear,' Zinnia said in amused tolerance, 'tell her not to worry, we won't be blowing up Parliament or plotting against the monarchy or anything like that.'

'Oh Ma, honestly!' Leonie said in disbelief at her trivial remark. 'Are we to call it off then, or get married in a registry office?' She addressed Julian rather sharply, impatient with her mother.

'Of course not, darling. Everything will be fine,' Julian said desperately.

'I'll telephone her,' Zinnia said cheerfully. 'I'm really sorry, Julian, if I've caused any offence.'

'Please don't worry about it,' Julian looked dubious at Zinnia's cheerfulness at dealing with his mother.

But it was George who sorted it out. He said, 'I'm so sorry, Julian, about our arrogance at assuming she'd know or not mind. I know religion's a touchy subject.'

Leonie went into the garden, not able to bear any more. Zinnia came and found her a few minutes later.

'That's settled, your father's smoothed it over. He's right, it was better coming from him. Now I wonder if you both ought to see Father Bennet . . . I mean, I know he's going to see you before the wedding, but to discuss things like . . .' she coughed, then blurted, 'the Church's views on birth control.'

'Ma, do leave it alone. Oh, how I wish we had got married in Florence and come back to a party after the event,' she said impatiently.

'Darling, don't say that. You'll forget all this and look back to a wonderful wedding day. I still think of mine sometimes. It's lovely to start off one's life together with an extravagant fanfare.' Zinnia linked her arm through her daughter's.

'Maybe, but without all this talk of religion and birth control. We are adults, quite able to decide what we want to do in our lives together. And if Julian doesn't mind my religion, then his mother must lump it,' Leonie said fervently. 'Where is Julian, by the way?'

'With your father. Let them be a while. Now tell me about the honeymoon. You're going to the South of Italy, aren't you? Then back up to Florence?'

'Yup, hopefully to find a little place to live while Julian looks for a job.' Leonie, recognising that her mother did not want to provoke an argument, allowed her to lead her on to safer subjects.

Among all the wedding preparations, Leonie found time to take on occasional cooking jobs with her old school friend Caroline Smythe.

'It's great that you can help me, Leonie,' Caroline said. 'It was wonderful of you to ask me to do your wedding. That should bring me in some new clients. But I'm sad you'll be going back to Italy. We'd make a great team cooking lunches together.'

'You should come out, then we could start up out there,' Leonie joked. She began to unpack the basket of fresh meat and vegetables she had just bought in Leadenhall market.

She loved this job, loved the old-fashioned market with its arched roof, silver dragons on each pillar, the stone urns and carved entrances. If she had time she enjoyed wandering round the tiny shops painted in dark red, cream and holly green, choosing vegetables that spilt out from the greengrocers on to the cobbles, or fish which lay glistening in lines on beds of crushed ice, their eyes staring balefully at her. But she was nearly always in a hurry, picking up meat here, cheese there, the smells of coffee and fresh baking tempting her to dart into the shop to grab something to eat herself.

They were cooking for a small firm of solicitors today. Leonie pulled out the leg of lamb, some glossy, purple aubergines and red onions from her large wicker basket. Then she took out a triangle of just ripe Brie wrapped in waxed paper, some smoked farmhouse Cheddar, and some soft Italian cheeses.

'Those look perfect,' Caroline said, unwrapping them to arrange on a cheeseboard.

'I've got some oatcakes as well as the Bath Olivers,' Leonie said, plonking them on the table, then storing her basket out of their way.

'It's so exciting about your wedding. Where did you meet Julian?' Caroline began as they settled down to cook the lunch. A large, plain and cheerful young woman with many friends, she was fast building herself a good reputation with her cooking but despite all this, what she really longed for was a husband and babies. Romance had seemingly passed her by and so far the nearest she'd got to babies was being their godmother.

'In the Uffizi. I was supposed to be writing an essay on Botticelli's Madonnas when a voice interrupted me saying, "It's hardly surprising that some American art students need therapy after seeing such pictures, knowing they can't hope to match them." ' She giggled, remembering her first sight of Julian, tall in a dark coat, a red scarf flung round his neck.

'How thrilling,' Caroline, who lived on romantic fiction, breathed. 'He is . . . so attractive, so fabulously good-looking.' Her eyes shone, but Leonie saw there was no envy there.

She smiled. 'I know. I remind myself of that first meeting – the sudden rush of attraction, of recognition, the love that followed – every time his mother plays up.'

'But you'll soon be back together in Florence.'

'I can't wait,' Leonie grinned. 'Now come on. I'll prepare the aubergines if you get the meat ready. I see you've nearly finished the starter.' She glanced over at the bowl of seafood and fresh pineapple waiting to be put on a bed of shredded lettuce at the last minute.

There were not many days now that she could help Caroline. There was so much else to be done: dress fittings, sending out invitations, doing wedding present lists, writing thank you letters. Leonie felt she had no time for herself, and not much for Julian.

It was strange, she thought, to have other people taking over their lives, arranging events for them as each day rolled them nearer to 16th of June, the great occasion.

Anita was the only cloud on Leonie's horizon. She hadn't seen her for some time, as she was in France, and in her absence Leonie felt confident that she would, if not exactly get on with her, at least manage to have a polite relationship. She was very relieved Anita was out of the way, especially as she was sure she would have objected to Julian's brothers being pages. She had chosen them because she wanted to please Tony and include them in a special way. By the time Anita got back, it would be too late to go back on the arrangement.

Salting the aubergines and helping Caroline stuff the boned lamb, Leonie thought back to a lunch she'd had recently with a couple of her married girl friends. She'd laughed when they'd exclaimed in horror at her description of her first meeting with Anita.

'I thought *my* mother-in-law was bad enough,' Becky had shrieked, 'but yours sounds really horrendous.'

'Wait until you have a baby!' Jessica, who had recently had a little boy, exclaimed with fervour. '*She* thinks it's her baby come back again.'

Leonie laughed loudly to cover the unease that nudged at her.

'I'll cope,' she said with more bravado than she felt. 'It will be fine once we're married and back in Florence, out of her clutches.' She pretended to herself she hadn't seen the knowing looks exchanged by her more experienced girl friends.

'Make sure you never have a spare bed, or she'll be staying all the time,' Jessica warned her. 'Mine almost lives with me.'

We'd better find somewhere minute to live in case Anita develops a passion for visiting Florence, Leonie thought now, tying up the leg of lamb and remembering Jessica's warning. She smiled as she imagined a tiny room in an ancient, dilapidated palace with only enough room for the two of them, safely out of Anita's reach.

A week before the wedding Leonie and Julian were crashed out at her flat, exhausted by the preparations, longing for it all to be over. Since Anita had got back a week ago, Julian had been quieter, more withdrawn.

He said suddenly, 'Mother wants us both to go round on Sunday afternoon, to give us our wedding present.'

'Can't she give it to us later?' Leonie had hoped to go home, even though she knew her mother's last-minute panics would exhaust her.

'No.' Julian had that tight, determined look on his face again. 'We must go, she's very excited about giving it to us.'

'What is it?'

'I've no idea,' he laughed. 'Probably a wonderful piece of furniture or even a car; mine is on its last legs, or should I say wheels.'

They could not go round to lunch as Janet had the day off. Anita apparently could not cook, nor could Diana, and Leonie didn't feel up to offering her services, fearing criticism. They arrived just after three as they'd been instructed.

Leonie felt the familiar tightening of her stomach as they entered the house, and wondered what face Anita would put on for her today. They'd barely crossed the hall when Anita and a tall, attractive man with blond straight hair swept back from his forehead came out of the drawing room to greet them.

'Darlings!' Anita opened her arms in an uncharacteristic show of welcome. Leonie, fighting down a feeling of resentment at this false show, surely put on in aid of the boyfriend, allowed herself to be embraced.

'I have *such* a surprise. I just know you'll both just love it,' she gushed, linking arms with the man and smiling up adoringly at him.

'We're longing to see it, Mother. Is it here?' Julian asked.

'Oh no, we've got to go on a little mystery tour. Have you the car outside?'

'Yes.'

'Come on then, everyone aboard,' she said skittishly, dancing on ahead.

Leonie and the man nodded awkwardly at each other. Anita had not introduced them. She was now linking arms with Julian, chatting animatedly about her '*wonderful* surprise'.

Leonie caught the man's eye and said, 'I'm Leonie Eldridge,

Julian's fiancée, as you've probably gathered.'

He gave her a little bow and smiled. 'I guessed,' he said. 'I'm Philip Fraser.'

Anita turned round. 'Come on, darling,' she said, holding out her hand to Philip, making Leonie feel excluded.

'I forgot to introduce you,' Julian said suddenly, looking contrite.

'We've done it,' Philip smiled, giving Leonie a tiny wink, which made her warm to him.

'Isn't Diana here? She might like to come too,' Leonie said, looking round for her.

'She's busy,' Anita said offhandedly, hustling them all out of the house.

'Which direction am I going in?' Julian said as he started the car.

'Go to Putney Bridge,' Anita said, tapping him on the knee. 'Then I'll direct you.'

They reached Putney Bridge, passed the two churches, one at one side of the bridge, one at the other, and went down the road beside the river. Anita directed them through some sideroads, leaving the river behind them. Leonie, looking idly out of the window, wondered what on earth Anita could be giving them. When she'd mentioned Putney Bridge she wondered if perhaps she was going to give them a boat, but now she thought Julian's suggestion that it was a car seemed more likely.

'Right, stop here,' Anita said at last as they drove into a small street of pale grey stone terraced houses with white painted windows.

They all got out of the car, Julian saying, 'Well, where is it? Give me a clue.'

'Patience, patience,' Anita beamed at him, and taking a bunch of keys from her bag she went over to one of the houses, bright with its new paint and filled window boxes, and opened its shiny deep blue door.

'Come in, don't be shy,' she said, standing back to let them all in. 'Look, come and see.' She led them into a square, light room beautifully decorated in blue and cream, then rushed out again and went into a pale green painted kitchen running into a pretty dining room papered in the same green with a white pattern. She opened the double doors into a garden which was so neat with its dark, clean

49

earth and small plants all standing to attention, that it had obviously just been made.

'Very Chelsea Flower Show,' Philip said with a laugh, 'not a slug or snail in sight.'

Julian smiled stiffly. He and Leonie were numb, following Anita into each room in a sort of daze.

'It is pretty,' Leonie said at last, knowing Anita's profession was doing up houses, now praying she was merely going to offer to do up whatever they lived in in Italy for them, and was showing them her taste.

'Very nice, could live in it myself,' Philip said.

They all went upstairs.

'Four bedrooms, two bathrooms,' Anita said, pushing open doors to reveal the rooms luxuriant in chintz and cream fitted carpets. 'So,' she smiled to encompass them all, 'this is my present to you. Don't you just love it?' Her eyes gave Leonie a defiant look.

'What a present, what a wonderful love nest for you both,' Philip said warmly, making Anita glow at him.

'It's lovely, Mother . . .' Julian began, his eyes keeping firmly away from Leonie's.

'Leonie, what do you think of it?' Anita's voice held a barb under its honey tone.

Leonie looked fully at her. 'It is really beautiful, thank you. We'll be so happy here on our holidays from Italy.'

'Oh, Italy,' Anita laughed. 'My dear, Italy will always be there, but for the moment you're to live here.'

'But, Mother, I must find a job. I've written to a few people in Florence that we're going to see when we get there,' Julian said patiently.

'That is my other present,' Anita smiled proudly, cuddling up to Philip. 'Philip's brother is a director of Christie's. He says he'll give you a job.'

'But Florence . . . we are going to live in Florence,' Leonie said, the exhaustion of the last few weeks threatening to make her cry and stamp her foot like a child.

'But without a job, my dear. You can't live on love, you know. Julian, thanks to Philip,' she bowed towards him as if expecting

50

Leonie to prostrate herself on the floor at his feet in gratitude for his generosity, 'has a job in arguably the best fine arts auction house in the world. If he makes a name for himself there, then the world is your oyster.'

'I'll say that's the best start a young couple could have,' Philip broke in, making Leonie feel that he thought her crass and ungrateful over this more than generous wedding present.

She turned away and went downstairs and out of the house, tears of frustration and despair choking her.

A wedding was like a great theatrical production, Leonie thought bitterly as she stomped up the road – all those people caught up in the momentum of it, like Caroline with the catering, the dressmaker, the florist, the marquee firm. It wasn't just her and Julian any more, there were so many working hard for it, wanting to make it a day to remember. Not to mention the money her father had spent. She couldn't stop it now with less than a week to go. Anita knew this and had waited until the last possible moment to play her trump card.

Leonie loved Julian, she wanted to marry him. Most people, including her own family, would applaud Anita for her generous present. They would think Leonie unkind and malicious to suggest she'd only done it to keep her son near her.

She shoved her hands angrily in her pockets and stormed up the road and into the next street, lined too with little houses. She wanted Julian to herself. She couldn't bear to have Anita so near them, poking into every part of their lives. She felt sick with anger and frustration. How could she get out of this house, and worse still, would it be fair of her to force Julian to forgo the job at Christie's? If only he had stood up to his mother, refused the house and the job.

But maybe he didn't want to, she thought sadly. Maybe he was relieved that a job in such a prestigious company had been found for him, handed to him on a plate.

She knew she'd been trapped. Anita had scored the winning goal. She would have to learn to outmanoeuvre her if she and Julian were to stand a chance together.

Chapter Six

Leonie saw a black hearse glide out from the back drive of the churchyard when they arrived at Our Lady of Sorrows. She looked away, remembering that Father Bennet had said he had a funeral the afternoon of their rehearsal. She did not want to know anything about it, ask who the dead person was, in case they were young. If she must be reminded of death today, she only wanted to think of it in the context of old age, coming at the end of a long life, not at the beginning of a new one.

She followed her parents into the church with its simple stone arches, the late sun making the stained-glass windows glow like precious jewels. Father Bennet, or Father Jim to the more trendy members of the congregation, was standing at the altar steps, being confronted by Anita.

'As the mother of the groom I insist that I sit in the first pew,' she was saying loudly, 'next to his father.' She glared at Tony and the back view of a young, blonde woman who was desperately trying to control two small boys. Julian stood anxiously by Father Bennet, looking as if his mother's strident request might bring down the wrath of God upon them any second.

When he saw Leonie, Julian's expression lifted and he ran over to kiss her, but then his eyes slid away to his mother as if afraid of what she would say or do next.

Father Bennet, having just dispatched one parishioner to his heavenly home and shortly to be welcoming another into the holy state of matrimony, seemed unperturbed. Leonie wondered what he thought of the trivia of a woman fussing about the etiquette of where she should sit in church when he'd just sent some poor soul to his final resting place.

He came forward, hands outstretched to welcome Leonie, and Zinnia and George whom he knew well. He always seemed a little cowed by Zinnia, Leonie thought with amusement. She often scolded him for something she didn't approve of in what she considered the too trendy way the Church was going. Last time it had been over serving coffee and biscuits after Mass.

'I know we are meant to be so friendly these days, Father, but couldn't you tell Mrs Briggs not to turn the kettle on until after the last blessing? It is so distracting.'

Leonie was now waiting for her to find fault with the wedding service.

Harry lagged behind them with a sullen expression on his face. He was looking into Buddhism at the moment and thought the Catholic Church far too over the top. Father Bennet welcomed him extra warmly.

Zinnia, who always treated opinions she couldn't cope with with extreme vagueness and trivia, had put him into this bad mood, by saying to him on the way: 'What a lovely shade of orange the Buddhist monks' robes are, darling. So bright.'

Infuriated, he shouted, 'You're hopeless, Mum. You have no idea what goes on in the world at all. Most of it is starving, and you don't see many underweight Catholic bishops, do you?'

'Don't speak to your mother like that,' George said, as if Harry were six years old.

Leonie could hardly wait to leave them all behind and be alone with Julian. Tomorrow night, she thought longingly, it will all be over and we'll be on our own.

'Here we are, Father,' Zinnia said easily, with none of the stiff awkwardness apparent in the Hunter contingent. 'Funny how frightened church makes so many people,' she said loudly to George. 'No doubt it brings out primeval fears, especially in people who profess to be atheists,' she added with relish.

Anita obviously didn't have that feeling.

'Hello ... er ... Zinnia and ... George,' she said, saying their names as if she'd suddenly remembered the answer to a question on *Mastermind*. 'And, of course, Leonie.' She kissed the air vaguely in her direction. 'Now,' she said, with all the force of a major-general, 'I was telling . . .' she gestured towards Father Bennet, 'the padre, that as the *mother* of the groom—'

'Of course, my dear,' Zinnia said. 'The parents of the couple, regardless of whether they are married or not,' she somehow made it sound like a social gaff, not to be still married to each other, 'sit next to each other in the top pew. That's all arranged.'

'Tony,' Zinnia kissed him warmly as he came forward to greet her, 'that's correct, isn't it? And your wife . . .' She smiled archly towards the slim, blonde woman, who had now straightened up, and though looking rather dishevelled with her hair everywhere and her clothes crumpled, was very pretty. She was also, Leonie thought with a little shock, hardly older than she was.

'That's right,' Tony said, 'and this is Clemmy.'

'Hi,' breathed Clemmy, looking eager to be liked by them all.

'Delighted,' George said, going rather pink as he took her hand. Zinnia firmly sent him off to find the organist.

'I'm so pleased to meet you at last,' Clemmy said to Leonie, with a genuine look of pleasure in her expression. 'Tony is mad about you, and I'm so happy for Julian to have found you.'

'Oh . . . thank you.' Leonie felt touched at her warmth.

'I know we live miles away, but I do hope you'll come and stay when you get back from your honeymoon. You'll always be welcome.' Clemmy's eyes shifted very slightly towards Anita, who was now bossing Harry and two other young men into their role as ushers.

Leonie suddenly felt she'd found a kindred spirit in Clemmy, imagining fun, relaxed weekends with her and Tony, a bolt hole far away from Anita. 'I'd love to,' she said with enthusiasm, relieved that at least one side of Julian's family liked her.

A pair of small fat legs, with feet encased in white socks and red, button shoes, appeared over the edge of the pew, wavered, then disappeared. There was a thump and a wail.

'Oh Lord!' Clemmy left Leonie and rushed over. Another small body hurtled out from behind a statue of the Sacred Heart and in his excitement trod on the accident victim's hand, producing more screams.

'I hope it's not serious.' Father Bennet hastened closer to the scene.

'Sorry about the row,' Tony said wearily and marched forward, thundering, 'That is enough, boys. Remember we are in church, so you will please behave.'

The church door opened and the two small bridesmaids, daughters of Leonie's cousin, arrived with their parents. Leonie went to greet them and to introduce them to Julian. She saw with horror that Charlotte, the youngest one, was staring in terror at the screams of the boys, out of sight behind the front pew, and Father Bennet's dark form bending over them. Her mouth trembled and tears rolled down her cheeks.

'M-M-Mum,' she choked on her sobs, 'I don't want to do it. I want to go home.'

You're not the only one, Leonie thought wearily.

Chapter Seven

Leonie and Julian fell into bed at the country house hotel near the airport.

'My feet hurt up to my armpits,' Leonie complained.

Julian laughed. 'I never thought it would be so tiring, all that smiling.'

'So, married at last – I can't believe it.' Leonie cuddled up to him. 'Will it be as fun, do you think,' she asked playfully, 'and as passionate?'

'I jolly well hope so. Why do you ask?'

'Well, one of my girl friends – you know Nicola Braithwaite?'

Julian didn't know Nicola, or couldn't remember her among all the other guests who had peered at and poked him as if he were a prize stud in the market.

'She's married to Christopher, and she said that once they were married, Christopher had great trouble in making love to her because he kept thinking of his mother.'

'His mother?'

Leonie was shell-shocked with exhaustion and emotion or she would have instantly stopped the conversation, or not even started it, but she went on, 'For some extraordinary reason, once he had married Nicola, he sort of confused her with his mother. Anyway, that's what the psychiatrist told him.'

'What very odd friends you have,' Julian said, grumpy with tiredness.

Leonie, suddenly realising that mothers were the last people she should be talking about, changed the subject hurriedly.

'I loved your little brothers – so naughty, especially Ben,' she giggled, remembering four-year-old Ben holding up her aged

Great-aunt Prudence with a stick masquerading as a gun. She had rewarded him with a whack with her handbag, and he, respecting her for her show of courage, had become great friends with her.

'They're far too much of a handful,' Julian said sighing. 'I don't know what Father was doing having more children at his age.'

'I expect Clemmy wanted them,' she said quickly, remembering she was meant to have trapped Tony with a pregnancy. 'I must say, I do like her. She's much younger than I thought, and so pretty. Probably the prettiest person there.'

Her remark was greeted with a deathly silence. Julian's face went tight, as it did when she mentioned Anita.

'Whatever's the matter?' she said with irritation. 'What's wrong with saying she's so pretty?' She wondered for a moment if he was hurt that she obviously thought his stepmother prettier, not to mention nicer, than his mother. But they were two quite different types. Anita was more beautiful, more elegant, and older.

'Nothing . . . I just don't want to talk about it. I'm tired and we have an early plane. Let's get some sleep.' He lay down with his back to her, and she suddenly felt terribly hurt and rejected. It wasn't as if she particularly wanted sex, it was just she would like to have slept in his arms on their wedding night.

'Whatever's upset you?' she said angrily. 'Whenever I mention your family you clam up or get cross. I'm not like that about mine. You can ask all the questions you want about them. Why Harry thinks Buddhism is a better religion than Catholicism, why Melanie thinks marriage makes women slaves, even why my mother treats my father like one of the dogs.'

Julian turned away even more forcibly, pulling the bedcovers tighter round him as if his actions would deafen her words.

'I'm well aware that my family has peculiar traits and I don't mind talking about them,' she went on, rather frantically now, 'so why shouldn't I discuss your family's peculiarities too? You must admit Clemmy is young enough to be your father's daughter, so I quite understand how difficult it must be for you and Diana to have a stepmother virtually your age.'

Julian burrowed deeper into the bed.

Furious now, almost out of control with exhaustion, Leonie

prodded him sharply in the back. 'I noticed Diana hardly spoke to her, and it must be difficult for your mother, having someone so young and pretty as her ex-husband's wife. No wonder she made such a fuss about Catholics and hypocrisy. I also saw how Philip looked at her, in that sort of "lucky old chap" way. No wonder she's jealous.'

Julian spun round, his face working with emotion. 'All right I'll tell you,' he shouted, his face flushed, his mouth clenched. 'She was my girlfriend and my father took her. Now are you satisfied?' He glared at her and saw her face open in surprise, then cloud over as the full realisation of his words hit her.

'Girlfriend?' she said weakly, feeling all of a sudden close to tears.

'Yes,' he said quietly.

'And you didn't tell me?' Her mouth felt stiff, her words like stones against her tongue.

'I love you,' he said. 'What does it matter what went before? You had a boyfriend, you told me.'

'I know, but that—'

'It's not different. What's wrong with having lovers before you marry, before we knew each other? What matters is loving each other now, staying together.'

'But your stepmother?' she said, jealousy writhing like a tornado in her.

'She wasn't my stepmother *then*,' he said impatiently. 'She was a girlfriend.'

'A close one?' She would not look at him, she didn't want to see any vestige of love for Clemmy in his eyes. She'd die if she knew the details, yet she longed to know them.

'Yes, as it happens.' He sat up and hugged his knees, leaning his chin on them. 'I was nineteen, she was twenty-four. She was the first girl I went to bed with . . . well, properly. I took her home a few times. My parents had almost broken up, then they did. I went off to university and saw less of her but we met when we could.'

'And your father?'

'He left my mother. I can't blame him. She was unfaithful all the time. I was busy, threw myself into my studies, met a few other girls – oh, nothing special.'

'But Clemmy was?' She hated asking.

There was a pause. 'Yes, Clemmy was.'

'So . . .?' She sneaked a look at him, but he kept his eyes straight ahead.

'She began to make excuses not to see me. I soon guessed there was someone else. Of course I didn't realise it was my own father.' His mouth curled with anger.

'Do you still love her?' Leonie asked in a small voice.

'Of course not.' He turned to her now, then took her in his arms, kissing her roughly, pulling at her nightdress. 'It's you I love, you must know that.'

'I thought you did, but now . . .' She burst into tears. Anita, Clemmy, two mothers-in-law and both in some way her enemies. She pushed him away, feeling that it was Clemmy he thought of now, Clemmy he wanted to make love to, not her.

'What's wrong, don't you believe me?' He looked sulky. 'Look, I'm not angry about . . . Dominic, wasn't it?'

'Don't you see the difference?' she sobbed.

'Darling, don't . . . please don't.' His voice was frantic now. 'It will be all right, I promise you it will. I stopped loving her ages ago, long before I met you, and now I have you, that's all I want. You must understand that. I never loved her like I love you.' He went on begging her to understand, swearing he never had loved or would love anyone as he loved her.

Leonie was so tired she finally let go, let his words soothe her. They made love carefully, with great consideration for each other, but deep in her heart she felt a hairline crack shift the depth of her love for him.

'Don't you see, I have *two* mothers-in-law? One is bad enough, but *two* at the same time . . .' She howled silently into her pillow, feeling betrayed by the one woman in her husband's family she'd thought would be her ally against Anita.

Chapter Eight

'Here we are, our own little home,' Julian said with exaggerated sentimentality, laughing as he opened the front door to their house in Putney. 'Wait, I must do this right.' He put down the suitcases, picked Leonie up and carried her in, putting her down in the narrow hall, kissing her on her mouth before he released her.

'We'll be so happy here, darling, you'll see,' he said, as if she had said again that she wished they were starting their lives together in Italy, alone, away from both their families.

Leonie forced a smile to match his mood, and followed him into the drawing room. She felt apprehensive, a loss creeping through her. Yesterday they had been so happy, so invincible against the world.

They'd spent the last afternoon of their honeymoon at Paestum, a ruined city dating from the fourth century BC, near Naples. As they'd wandered hand in hand round the ancient temple of Neptune, its stone coloured a warm apricot with the glowing embers of the dying sun, she had felt certain that she'd made the right decision in marrying Julian, and that they would be happy together. They fitted together so well, getting pleasure and amusement from the same things.

Strolling here where countless dramas had taken place over the centuries, she felt that the petty problems of two such different mothers-in-law could be lived with. She would be firm, visit them occasionally, as she would her own parents – who, much though she loved them, could in their own way also be damaging. She would refuse to let them rule her and Julian's life, though how much easier that would have been had they lived in Florence.

'Darling, don't, whatever you do, live your life hankering over what might have been,' her father advised her when she'd flown to him in her anger at Anita's scheming to keep Julian in London. 'There was no guarantee of a job for him in Florence, and you might have been forced to come home with nothing. Christie's is a very good start for him and, believe me, in these difficult days that is something.'

She'd taken his advice, and apart from the occasional regretful remark about it, kept off the subject.

'But imagine having *two* mothers-in-law at the same time,' she joked with Julian while they were on honeymoon, determined with this newfound strength to make light of it.

'Better than two husbands,' he'd said.

'My next husband will be an orphan,' she'd answered too quickly, and then seeing his stricken face had laughed loudly and kissed him to show she was only teasing him.

Now, back in the house – Anita's house, as she thought of it, felt it to be – she didn't feel so confident.

'Lots of letters,' Julian said, skimming through a neat pile of mail that had been put on the sofa. There was not much furniture, and what there was had been scrounged from their parents. Julian had bought a new bed, which had been delivered the day before the wedding. The drawing room had an old sofa and two chairs, which Leonie wanted to re-cover. There was one small table in the dining room with four assorted chairs. One of Leonie's first tasks was to go to the auction rooms and buy some more furniture.

'I'll come with you,' Anita said imperiously, when they'd discussed it before the wedding.

'I'm sure you haven't the time, so please don't worry. Anyway, I take ages to find what I want,' Leonie had said in as friendly a way as she could manage, not looking at her in case Anita's icy look would intimidate her into giving in. She could imagine Anita's disdain at her choice of furniture, insisting that she buy things that went with her furnishings, instead of those she liked, or which had character.

She went through to the kitchen and there was a huge box of groceries from Harrods and a card propped up beside it: 'Welcome home, love Anita.' There was also a large vase of flowers with another note: 'Left these in here as it was cooler. I thought they would look nice in the drawing room.'

Leonie felt as if she were being drawn into a poisonous web. This act, which would have been thought of as kindness on anyone else's part, she felt was just another way of Anita reminding them that she had a hold over them, which she would not easily give up.

Julian came in. 'Lovely flowers, oh and Harrods,' he laughed. 'Bet that's Mother. She's never heard of Sainsburys. I expect she just ordered a box of groceries.' He went to it and began to pull out the packets. 'My favourite muesli, and Chocolate Olivers, Marmite, and that French coffee,' he said, falling on each thing delightedly.

Leonie, watching him, felt like crying. She wanted to buy him his favourite things, but, she realised suddenly with a pang, she didn't really know them all yet. She would never know him as his mother did.

'We can't afford to buy everything from Harrods,' she said sharply. 'You'll have to make do with what the local shops have.'

'But of course I will, darling,' he said, but he didn't follow her when she left the room. She heard him open the fridge and exclaim about his favourite cheese and favourite flavour of yoghurt.

Upstairs their bed had been made up with their new sheets and blankets. As she thought about it, Leonie became convinced that Anita would not bother with such menial tasks. She had surely instructed Janet to do it all, down to ordering the food from Harrods and bringing it here in a taxi, leaving herself to take the credit for it. Leonie chided herself for her mean thoughts, then felt angry all over again when she realised she would have to thank Anita nicely and pretend to be grateful.

One advantage to Leonie of returning to London for the foreseeable future was that she could resume cooking with Caroline who had, thanks to her growing reputation, many offers to cook in prestigious companies with generous entertainment budgets.

'Look what's for dinner tonight, hope you didn't have much lunch,' Leonie greeted Julian one evening a few months after they'd settled into the house in Putney. He came into the kitchen where she was unpacking some delicious leftovers from one of her directors' lunches. Some of the guests had not turned up, so she and Caroline had delightedly scooped up the remainders to feast on at home. There was a delicate salmon mousse wrapped in paper-thin slices of cucumber, chicken lyonnaise and an exotic fruit salad.

'It looks wonderful, darling, but you look even better.' He took her in his arms and kissed her on her mouth, then nuzzled his face in her neck. 'You're so lovely to come home to, but what with a fabulous dinner too I am surely the luckiest husband in the country.' He laughed, linked his hands round her waist and looked adoringly into her face. She smiled back, feeling warm and happy with his love.

'I'm lucky too,' she said, meaning it, 'having you coming home each night.'

'I knew we'd be happy together,' he said, and kissed her again, this time getting more passionate, running his hands down her body pulling her closer to him.

'Let's have an apéritif,' he said huskily, undoing her skirt.

The telephone ringing cut through their ardour.

'Damn,' he said, taking his face from her.

'Leave it,' she said, pulling him back.

He kissed her again, but the telephone went on and on, and eventually he released her.

'I won't be a minute, then I'll leave it off the hook.' Pushing in his shirt, and doing up his trousers as if the caller could see his dishabille, he picked up the receiver. 'Hello . . . oh Mother, it's you.' He turned his back on Leonie and with one hand, pulled his clothes together, then raked down his hair.

Leonie felt cold, excluded, as if Anita herself were standing here in the kitchen, watching them with derision.

'But tonight . . . can't you find anyone else? I wanted to stay in tonight.'

Fury began to seep into Leonie, pushing away the feelings of love and desire that a moment before had been raging in her.

'But, Mother,' his voice was firm, 'surely someone else . . . tonight is difficult, Leonie . . .'

For a second her hopes soared again. He was going to refuse his mother, do what *he* wanted tonight. She watched his back, slightly contorted with the effort of appeasing Anita, took a step forward to be closer to him, meaning to wrap her arms round him as if to defy his mother, give him the strength and encouragement to refuse, but he said in alarm, 'You mean the car's on its way? But, Mother, I said . . . I mean, I might not have been here, we might have been going out, you can't . . .'

Leonie felt the fury take hold again, but before she could say anything, she heard him say despairingly, 'All right, Mother, just this once, but never, ever do this to me again. I have my own life now. Understand?' He snapped the receiver down.

'What does she want this time?' Leonie asked. 'What car is on its way?'

He wouldn't look at her. 'She has tickets for a gala evening at Covent Garden, Princess Margaret and all. You know they're like gold dust. Philip was taken to hospital this afternoon with food poisoning and the doctors won't let him out. She wants me to go instead.'

'If she was a *kind* person,' Leonie said, stiff with fury, 'she would have stayed in the hospital with him, and given us the tickets.'

Julian looked guilty. 'She does so adore Pavarotti,' he said lamely.

'Don't we all, but surely a lover with food poisoning comes first,' Leonie said. She felt defeated. She looked at the food on the table, set out temptingly on pretty plates. 'This won't last until tomorrow night,' she said sadly. 'It's best eaten fresh.'

'I'll have it when I get back, darling. We'll eat it together in bed,' he said, pulling off his clothes as he went to the door, but this time without passion. 'I really am sorry, but I must change. It's black tie. It starts in three-quarters of an hour.' He gave her a crestfallen look and left the room. She heard him run up the stairs.

She wanted to chase after him, shout at him, beg him to stay, but she did nothing, apathetic in her despair. She just stood there, her clothes dishevelled from their aborted lovemaking, beside the food she'd so looked forward to giving to him, to the evening spent together, filled with love.

In a while a stern detachment came over her. She was hungry; she and Caroline never had time to eat much during the day. She didn't want to eat this alone, she wanted someone to praise it, share it with her.

For a moment she thought of ringing Caroline, wondering if she too were alone, possibly eating the food straight from its boxes on her knee, sitting in front of the television, with only Nelson, her Labrador, for company. But Leonie felt a little ashamed of her situation. She could not lie to Caroline, concoct some complicated story about Julian working late, nor could she admit to her, with her rosy view of love and romance, that her husband of a few months had dumped her to go out with his mother. Instead she went to the telephone and rang her sister.

'Mel, it's me. I know you're off to New York tomorrow, but would you like to come round for dinner? Julian's had to go out unexpectedly, and I've some rather good leftovers.'

'Oh, Leo . . . well yes, why not? I've only got an apple and a dusty old piece of cheese here. But I can't be late. It's the early flight.'

'Fine, see you in a few minutes then.'

Julian came into the kitchen as she was opening a bottle of red wine.

'Darling, I'll be back as soon . . .'

'Come back when you want. Melanie's coming over to have dinner with me. She eats like a horse so I don't expect there'll be much left.' She wouldn't look at him, but picked up two glasses and walked away from him to put them on the table.

'Oh, I see.' He sounded disappointed.

She turned back, her eyes hard. 'I'm not letting your mother ruin our lives – or anyway my life. She hasn't even the courtesy to ask if I minded, just expects you to jump every time she tugs the old cord.'

'Darling . . . I know she can be a little insensitive, but these tickets cost a fortune, and were almost impossible to get.' His eyes were agonised.

'She ought to know that once that cord is cut at birth, the child is a separate person with his own life, not to be used whenever she wants,' she went on, ignoring his explanation.

There was a discreet ring at the bell.

'Oh, that's the car . . . I must go.' He took a few steps towards the door, then back towards her. 'Darling, I really am sorry. I'll be back as soon as I can. I love you.'

'Just go,' she said, turning her back on him so he shouldn't see her tears.

★ ★ ★

'I'm glad you asked me,' Melanie said, finishing the last of the fruit salad. 'This is so good. I never dare use some of this more exotic stuff – star fruit, lychees, delicious.' She smiled and wiped her mouth.

'You're lucky. We cooked for the secretaries today and they always like a pudding. There was a chocolate something, but that all went,' Leonie said flatly.

Melanie looked at her seriously. 'This is marriage for you, my dear. Once they've got you, they go back to their old life of doing what they want. Oh,' she held up her hand, seeing Leonie was about to protest, 'I grant you he's not going out with a girlfriend.'

'It seems like another woman . . . of course it is another woman, but you know what I mean,' Leonie said with a sigh.

'Jason may say the difference between marriage and living together is just a piece of paper, but when you're married you're an accepted part of the family, *both* families.' Melanie laughed and took a sip of wine. 'As a wife, even today, you have to play a certain role in those families, like tonight, and be understanding. As a girlfriend you don't. Jason's mother never asks me to do anything, or, which is more important, takes me for granted, or treads on me.'

'Maybe she's a nicer person.'

Melanie shrugged. 'I don't know, but it suits me. I don't want to be a slave to a man and his family just because I've married him.'

'But children, Mel, surely you want children?'

'I don't know that I do, Leo, certainly not in the foreseeable future,' she said, looking thoughtful. 'I like being my own boss, responsible for myself, with my own money, flat, life. I don't want to stay at home doing creative things with loo rolls and yoghurt pots to amuse tiny children. In fact,' she smiled, 'I don't want to share, always putting other people before myself. I know I'm selfish, but look at Ma.'

'What's wrong with her?' Leonie said, slightly shaken at Melanie's point of view.

'She's given up her life for Dad, for us. She's not a bad painter, but those flowers – *little*, pretty pictures. She could do so much better. If she'd had the time and the energy, she might have achieved something really good, become a serious painter, but she just frittered her life away on us.'

'She didn't . . . she wanted to. Oh Mel, she could have painted bigger, better things if she'd really wanted to. After all, we are grown up now; she has the time,' Leonie said, not wanting to think she was responsible for curtailing her mother's talents.

Melanie smiled in that rather superior way Leonie hated. 'It's just one life I don't want. I'm good at my job and I want to go to the top, which I will, on my own. I'm twenty-seven – there's plenty of time to settle down to babies later, if I want them.'

'It doesn't always work out like that. Look at those women who have been years on the pill, then in their early forties find their reproductive bits don't work.'

'I'll risk it. But you've chosen to marry. You must have known a bit how it would be,' Melanie went on.

'We were going to live in Italy, remember?' Leonie sighed. 'Then we'd have been on our own. Everything would have been wonderful.'

'What's stopping you?' Melanie got up and switched on the kettle. 'One coffee then I'm off. You've got no commitments, why don't you let this place and just go?' She glanced round the now-cluttered kitchen. 'There's a couple of men in my office who are looking for somewhere.'

'It's not so easy now Julian has this job at Christie's. I mean, it could lead to great things.' Leonie stacked the plates into the dishwasher, feeling cornered as she had as a child when Melanie pulverised her with some demand.

'I'm sure Julian could have a sabbatical, or do some work for them in Italy. You have to make your own life, Leo, or get on with the one you have, like Ma has.' She poured some boiling water on to the coffee grounds in the percolator.

'We'd be fine if Anita would leave us alone. Even though she has a man in her life, she keeps ringing Julian, wanting things from him, making him call round on her before he comes home. Tonight she could have taken Diana. I'm sure she would have loved to go.'

'Diana looked really put upon,' Melanie said. 'She barely spoke at the wedding, sort of slunk into the shadows, poor girl. Perhaps you should have asked her here tonight, got her on your side.'

'Perhaps I should have,' Leonie said, thinking how accurate Melanie's description of Diana was. She wondered if Anita would reduce *her* to that. She should be more like Melanie, tough and resilient. She wouldn't have stood any nonsense from Anita.

Melanie poured them both some coffee. 'And your stepmother-in-law is about my age and sexy with it. Really, Leonie, what a family you've chosen to marry into.'

'I know.' She decided she would only have to suffer Melanie's scorn if she told her Clemmy was Julian's ex-girlfriend. 'I didn't choose them, Mel. When I met Julian I fell in love with him. I never thought about his family. It was just he and I, no one else mattered. It was magic.'

'Magic is not real life, Leo,' Melanie said impatiently.

'But you need it. A relationship without it would be empty, monotonous, ordinary.' As she said it, she thought she was giving an apt description of Melanie and Jason. She'd never seen any magic between them. Theirs was a practical relationship, two people knowing what they wanted from life and taking it. Harry's remark about their 'finding a window' in their business-oriented lives for sex, or anyway to meet, was true.

'I love Julian,' she pushed on before Melanie could tell her to get a life, romantic love was for novels, or foolish people. 'We have so much in common, and we . . . Oh Mel, you must know how it is, sort of electric between us,' she insisted, her face, her body glowing, thinking of him. 'We were so happy in Florence.'

'Then you should have stayed lovers like Jason and me,' Melanie said archly, putting two spoonfuls of sugar in her coffee, 'kept well away from his family.'

When Melanie had gone home, Leonie thought hard about what she had said. But it was too late now – they were married, and they would stay married. Of course, she thought to herself, their situation was still quite new to both families, a novelty which would surely wear off before long.

If Julian could just make Anita see that he would not jump every time she called, she would get on with her own life, leave them alone. Until they had a baby anyway, Leonie smiled wryly. Then no doubt both families would interfere with that too.

Chapter Nine

'Of course it's none of my business,' Zinnia said to Leonie, in a tone of voice that implied that she thought it was, 'but you have been married almost three years now, and there's still no sign of a child. You shouldn't leave it too late, you know, or you'll get too set in your ways to cope with one.'

Her remark caught Leonie off balance. They were sitting in the garden on a sleepy summer afternoon, the gentle buzz of the bees working in the flowerbed beside her lulling Leonie into drowsiness.

Zinnia saw the way Leonie's face changed, saw her fight to compose it, heard her give out a strangled laugh.

'Darling, you don't mean there's something wrong?' she said. But before Leonie could answer she ploughed on, 'I mean, there's nothing wrong with you, you're regular, aren't you?' she said firmly, as if no child of hers could possibly be defective in that most natural of human functions.

'I don't know, Ma. I . . .' Leonie, having got control of her feelings, now struggled to get her mother off the scent of this latest worry in her life, a worry that she usually succeeded in hiding from everyone, not least herself and Julian.

Six months ago she'd gone to visit her old school friend, Jessica, who obviously had no trouble having babies, having just had her third.

'Henry just has to look at me and I'm pregnant,' she boasted delightedly.

They'd spent a quiet afternoon just gossiping, her mother-in-law having taken the other two children out. Jessica was holding her baby when suddenly the telephone rang and she dumped him in Leonie's arms while she went to answer it.

71

Holding the tiny, solid bundle against her shoulder, feeling his rubbery little face against her own, smelling his baby smell, Leonie was suddenly assaulted by a powerful yearning for a child of her own. The feeling was so strong that she felt a physical pain in the pit of her stomach. It both amazed and frightened her. She held tighter to the baby in case she should faint and drop him.

Of course she and Julian wanted children – were going to have children – but these last two years had just flown past without their really discussing it. Leonie and Caroline had got so much work on with their cooking. Julian too had been busy learning the ropes at Christie's – he had now moved from the front desk to working with Victorian watercolours – and what little time they had left, they spent together or with friends. They hadn't even had time to go to stay with his father and Clemmy, though neither of them had made much attempt at finding the time for that.

When she had got home that evening after visiting Jessica, Leonie told Julian about this strange, powerful emotion when she'd held the baby. 'I just couldn't believe the strength of it. I've always liked babies, wanted one, but never with that sort of powerful, almost a surge of feeling deep inside me,' she laughed. 'It was almost biblical. You remember those barren women that suddenly conceived, and their babies leapt in their wombs?'

'I think they leapt some months after conception,' he laughed, 'but, my darling,' he hugged her to him, 'it obviously means it is time for us to have a child.' He looked deep into her eyes with tenderness and concern. He said gently, 'We must take more time off for ourselves to start our family. It's what we both want, isn't it?'

'Yes,' she sighed happily, hugging him back. Her face glowed as she saw his own happiness, his love for her. For a long moment they stood there entwined, basking in the intensity of their love.

Julian broke the spell, saying, 'I'd love a little girl, just like you.'

'Not a son?' she smiled, tracing his lips with her fingertip. 'Most men want sons first.'

'The next one can be a boy, a girl and a boy,' he laughed, nibbled her finger. 'Think what fun we'll have making them.'

But the fun produced nothing. Every month Leonie felt as if she were experiencing a little death. She tried to push their failure to the back of her mind like a shameful secret, telling herself that they must have made love at the wrong time, that *next* month would be the lucky one.

Her more fertile friends assured her that 'dozens of normal, healthy women take time to conceive', and they would tell her of a friend or relation who had tried night and day with no success, then given up, and with a single, rare sexual act, become pregnant.

'What do you mean, you don't know, darling?' The thin edge of anxiety in Zinnia's voice brought Leonie back to the present. She was aware her mother feared any form of defect or illness in her family.

'I just mean that we have . . . sort of been trying, but . . .' Leonie gave a good imitation of a laugh, 'we are both so busy working, so perhaps it just hasn't happened. Wrong time of the month and all,' she finished rather lamely. She found it so much easier to talk with her girl friends about sex than with her mother.

'It can take time with some people, I suppose,' Zinnia said doubtfully as if 'some people' couldn't possibly be any of her family. 'Have you seen a gynaecologist?' Idly she put out her hand to deadhead a geranium.

'No. I—'

'Well, you must, darling.' Zinnia smiled and patted Leonie's hand reassuringly, leaving behind the faint acrid scent of the flower. 'I'm sure it's nothing. After all, I had no trouble with all of you, but it could be . . . well,' she coughed discreetly, 'it could be Julian. I mean, he is so sweet and sensitive—'

'Whatever do you mean by that remark, Ma?' Leonie retorted, looking round quickly in case Julian was near and had overheard her.

'You know, dear . . . he's not one of those tough, meaty men, is he? Which makes him so much nicer, of course, but . . .' she floundered, not knowing how to express herself without offending Leonie.

'You mean you don't think he's capable of fathering children because he's not some great hunk?' Leonie almost laughed. 'Nor is Dad.'

'No, but he . . . he's very masculine and—'

'And Julian is not. Do you think he's gay or something just because he's far more beautiful-looking than the average man? Honestly, Ma, you are the limit.'

'What's she said this time?' Harry lumbered out of the house, his rumpled shirt hanging out of his jeans, his hair hanging over his eyes, making him look rather like a Shetland pony. Her brother had been working in the wine trade since leaving university, though his sisters had laughed at his grandiose ideas of one day owning a vineyard, and told him the only thing he was good at was drinking it. He was, at this moment, much to his father's concern, 'in between jobs', spending much time sitting in trees that were in the paths of planned motorways. He existed on surreptitious handouts from Zinnia and a small income from a Trust left to him by his grandparents. He collapsed on a chair beside them.

'Nothing.' Leonie got up from her chair unable to bear any more of her family sifting through her and Julian's life and adding their bits of advice.

'Bet it was something,' Harry said, picking up one of the Sunday papers from the ground and flicking through it.

'You are deliberately trying not to understand what I'm saying,' Zinnia said, flustered now. She had always ruled the roost here, but now her children were grown up they came at her with new events, new ideas that often bewildered and unsettled her.

'Tell me. I'll explain it to Leo,' Harry said with exaggerated patience.

Leonie turned on him angrily as if *he* had made the remarks about Julian. 'Do you think Julian is too weak to father children?'

Harry's mouth dropped open, then he gave an embarrassed laugh. 'Well, I don't know, Leo, do I? I don't go to bed with him.'

'Don't be disgusting, Harry,' Zinnia said, her mouth curling as if his words left a nasty taste in her mouth.

'What on earth are you two talking about then?' Harry said indignantly.

'Ma thinks that because Julian isn't "tough and meaty", as she put it, he—'

'I only meant he may have a low sperm count,' Zinnia said with embarrassment, looking rather flushed.

Harry let out a shriek of laughter. 'Mum, honestly, do you really think you can tell that by just looking at a man? Every man who is tall and willowy and rather beautiful has a low sperm count, while

74

the tough James Bond types . . . and there we are.' He clapped his hands together to emphasise his point. 'If James Bond types are meant to have a high sperm count why aren't their films littered with screaming babies or at least pregnant bimbos?'

'I didn't mean it quite like that,' Zinnia said.

'I think you did,' Leonie said, sitting down again, 'and anyway, I don't want to talk about it. It is our business and it will work out.'

Harry said, 'I don't want children, they bleed you dry and then when you need them when you're old and batty, they've gone.'

'Speak for yourself,' Leonie said crossly, feeling hurt at her mother's strange ideas about Julian. Zinnia had always seemed devoted to him, but had she really always thought of him as a wimp? The thought infuriated her.

'I was going to tell you about my plans,' Harry interrupted her thoughts, 'if I'm allowed a few minutes of air time.'

'Help yourself,' Leonie said, leaning back in her chair shutting her eyes.

'What are you plans, darling?' Zinnia said with an attempt at enthusiasm.

'I'm leaving for Tibet next week,' he said, in the same sort of voice he might have said, 'I'm leaving for Cornwall.'

'Tibet?' Both women started up. Leonie, seeing the satisfaction in his face to their reaction, feigned boredom. 'Tibet?' she said dismissively.

'And India. I'm going to study Buddhism properly,' he said, 'see it in its proper setting, as it were. I shall be back for Christmas.'

'That's all right then,' Leonie said. 'I thought for a moment you were going to become a Buddhist monk.'

Harry flushed. 'You don't think I take anything seriously, do you?'

'No,' Leonie said.

'Children.' Zinnia passed her hand wearily over her face. 'Harry darling, Tibet is miles away and travelling there is very difficult, and there's trouble with the Chinese . . .'

'So?'

'Well, dear, do you have to go quite so far? I mean, I'm sure there are some Buddhists here in England, and the library might have books – and what about your career?'

75

'Mother,' he sprang up, scattering the dogs who flopped in the shade of the table, 'I do not want to stay in Sussex and read up about Buddhism in the Chichester Library. I go to Tibet next week. I've bought my ticket. And my career can go on hold. Once I'm settled in a job I won't be able to go anywhere like that. After all, I never had a gap year like all my friends did!'

'Does your father know?' Zinnia asked weakly.

'No, I'm going to tell him now. Ask him to get some dosh from my Trust,' he grinned. 'I see he and Julian have finished their game of tennis. He looks as if he's going to have a heart attack so I better get to him before he does.' He loped off towards them, leaving Zinnia staring after him in disbelief.

'Do you think he means it?' she said at last.

'Probably,' Leonie said, thinking how lucky he was just to up and leave.

'Perhaps I ought to get Father Bennet to talk to him,' Zinnia said. 'I mean, Buddhism!'

'Leave well alone,' Leonie said sternly. 'You know what Father Bennet will say. Better to search through all religions to find your God, than sit complacently back and think you have been saved. Or better to search than deny there is a God at all.'

'But Harry has a God already.'

'Obviously not one that satisfies him,' Leonie said wearily. 'Let him go, Mum, he'll be back for Christmas.' She got up and went towards Julian, who was coming over to her. Her father and Harry had wandered off together towards the tennis court.

'Good game?' She linked arms with him.

'Yes. He's a great player, your father. He nearly beat me.'

She laughed. 'Let's get ready to go back, shall we? I've quite a lot to do before tomorrow.'

Her mother's words had dispelled her contentment in the weekend and she was suddenly anxious to get away.

On the drive back to London she said as nonchalantly as she could, 'Do you think I ought to see a doctor about having a baby? I mean, we have been trying some time now.' She sneaked a look at him to see his reaction.

His mouth tightened, but he turned to her with a quick laugh. 'If you want, but . . . I think we need a good holiday. Plenty of time to ourselves.'

'Yes, perhaps you're right,' she said, suddenly relieved. She didn't want the intrusion of a doctor on, to her, a rather embarrassing subject, or, she admitted with a terrible fear, to hear the news that for some reason they could not have children.

'We both work so hard, especially you. Couldn't we find time to go somewhere nice together?'

'Yes, as long as we go before the run-up to Christmas. We've got quite a few business parties on.' She laid her hand on his thigh and he covered it with his own.

'Where shall we go? Are we rich enough to go to the Caribbean?' he said.

'Not the right time.'

'Stay in Europe?'

'I'd like to go further, while we can. I mean,' she laughed, feeling excited about the holiday, certain it would give them a child, 'once we have a baby, we'll have to have safe holidays, nearer home.'

'That's true.'

'We might go with Harry to Tibet,' she laughed.

'Your mother's not too pleased about that. But he's a sensible chap; he won't come to any harm.'

'I think she's more worried about his soul than himself. Nasty foreign religion, worse in her eyes than nasty foreign dangers,' Leonie said, laughing.

'Oh darling, she's not as bad as all that,' Julian admonished her.

'Yes she is,' Leonie said, remembering Zinnia's assumption of Julian's sperm count. 'She collects facts like a magpie, then adds her own outrageous ideas based on absolutely nothing. She lives in her own isolated world of like-minded people who haven't realised that people of different nationalities and cultures are not dangerous to mix with. She knows nothing about any religion except Catholicism, and not much about that I should think. If Harry did become a Buddhist, it would be because he was infuriated with her ideas.'

'Oh darling, you're not being quite fair.'

'I think I am,' she said firmly, still cross with Zinnia.

'Well, I'm very fond of her,' he smiled. 'By the way, talking of holidays, Mother's taken a chalet in Verbier for Christmas. She wants us all to go together.'

A silence dropped like a damp blanket over their good-natured bantering. Neither looked at the other.

'Will Philip be coming?' Leonie said at last, knowing that they would have to go and it was no use wasting energy on arguing.

'I expect so . . . I don't know.'

Philip was her weapon against Anita. It had come about quite unexpectedly.

For the first year or so of their marriage, despite despising herself for her weakness, Leonie suffered agonies each time they had to visit Anita.

'I can't help feeling sick as I never know what mood she's going to be in,' she had complained to Julian.

'What do you mean, darling? She's always pleased to see you,' he said.

'Not always, Julian. Last time she quizzed me for hours on nouvelle cuisine, saying what a con it was as if I had been personally responsible for inventing it. The time before it was my colour of chair covers in the drawing room. I think that blue is perfect, picks out the darker tone in the wallpaper, but she says it ought to be white. White chair covers! Does she think we live in a museum with everything covered with transparent plastic?'

'You shouldn't take it so much to heart,' he said wearily.

'Maybe not, but I do.'

One evening Julian had said in the hesitant way he had when he discussed Anita, or her plans with Leonie: 'Mother has asked us to dinner and bridge tonight. There will be just her and Philip. I said we'd go.'

'I do so like feeling wanted,' Leonie said acidly. 'What's the betting she's been let down at the last minute?'

'You like playing bridge, and after cooking all day, wouldn't you like to have Janet cook the dinner?' he said with false cheerfulness.

'I do enjoy bridge but fun bridge. Your mother takes it far too seriously. But at least I do play bridge. I *almost* passed the test as a suitable wife for you – right class, right colour, tennis and bridge.' She looked defiantly at him. 'The problem is *no one* would quite pass your mother's exacting standards.'

He looked away, hurt, and she felt mean. The prospect of spending time with Anita often made her take out on Julian the feelings of inadequacy and anxiety she induced in her.

'I'm sorry, darling.' She kissed him. 'It must be hell for you having to juggle with the two most important women in your life.' She did not add that she sometimes felt that Anita was the more important to him. She was eternally thankful that Clemmy lived so far away and was too busy with her children and her book shop to come South and add to her anxiety. One mother-in-law always made insidious remarks to undermine her, the other was so pretty *and* her husband's ex-lover.

They arrived at Anita's on the dot of 7.45. Knowing Anita would look wonderful, Leonie had taken extra trouble and put on a new black silk dress and two rows of pearls at her neck to soften the colour. Philip got her a drink, and engaged her in conversation, leaving Anita and Julian to talk to each other. He was dressed in one of his immaculate dark suits, with a blue shirt and expensive tie.

As they started dinner, Anita turned to Julian and said in her imperious voice, 'I saw that awfully pretty girlfriend of yours the other day, Sarah Bailey.' Although she was looking at Julian, Leonie felt Anita could see her too, feel her jealousy and inadequacy welling up inside her like a monstrous growth. Anita often made remarks about other people that made Leonie feel as if they were said specifically to show that *she* wasn't pretty, or clever, or whatever it was these other girls possessed in abundance.

'Her marriage has broken up, you know,' Anita went on. 'Not that that was surprising really. It's very unstable, that branch of the family she married into. Good thing they won't inherit the title.'

'Really? So how was she?' Julian did sound bored, Leonie had to admit, but he didn't look at her.

'She was very well, asked fondly after you.' Anita put down her knife and fork, clasped her hands together and looked at the ceiling in mock contemplation. 'She was *such* a pretty girl, intelligent too, and so fond of Julian.' This remark she passed to Philip.

Leonie knew Anita was trying to annoy her, to punish her after seeing Julian taking her in his arms in the hall just after they'd arrived and kissing her, but still she minded. She was fighting with herself to appear nonchalant, struggling to think up a clever, throwaway remark: 'How nice. I'd love to meet her, I'm sure we'd get on so well.' But the words stuck in her throat.

But Philip, who usually just sat there, making it his business occasionally to steer the conversation away from the rocks ahead, suddenly rescued her. 'She's missed the boat with Julian. He couldn't have found a prettier, nicer girl in Leonie.' He beamed at Leonie, who, surprised and touched at his support, flushed with delight. She shot him a dazzling smile, slightly wobbly with unshed tears of gratitude. Her look made Philip flush with pleasure in his turn and for a split second there was a flash of warm recognition between them, a feeling of being on the same side.

Anita saw the full force of these looks. Her painted mouth tightened, her dark eyes glittered. She said sourly, 'Julian had many pretty girlfriends.'

'And I had many good-looking boyfriends,' Leonie spun back, given courage by Philip's remark.

'I'll bet you did, and how lucky you two settled for each other. Isn't it, Julian?' Philip's question was a challenge to Julian to stand up for Leonie against his mother.

'Of course, very lucky,' he said and smiled at Leonie, but as he did so she saw that his eyes shifted uneasily towards his mother as if fearful of her disapproval.

When it came to cutting the cards to choose bridge partners, Philip and Leonie were together. She fanned out her cards and felt a *frisson* of excitement. Her hand was a strong one. Glancing over the cards at Philip, she saw he was matching her, a slight smile on his lips. Again she felt the quick flash of recognition between them.

She played as she'd never played before, remembering all the cards that had gone before, trumping, leading the right card for Philip to win the trick. As they won more and more, she felt the excitement curl in her, tight like a spring. She could feel Anita's controlled anger, see how she stabbed out more and more cigarettes angrily in the ashtray in front of her. Leonie looked at Philip, enjoying his smile of pleasure when she led the right card, the gleam of admiration in his glance.

Suddenly Anita studied her watch and said abruptly, 'Bed time.' She gave Philip an icy smile. 'I'll settle my debts with you later, darling.' She got up from the table, her remark sounding like a threat.

The room became suddenly cold. Leonie glanced at Philip, but his face was impassive.

'Thank you, Philip,' she said. 'That was a wonderful game.'

'It was, we make a good pair,' he said gallantly, but Leonie felt the excitement had gone. He was just plain Philip, good-mannered and good-looking, the perfect escort.

'Come on, darling, let's go home,' Julian had said, and for once made a quick exit home with her.

But since that evening Leonie had felt more confident with Anita, especially if Philip was there. She felt that Anita watched her guardedly, seeing in her a possible threat, though of course that was nonsense, for she loved Julian, was just not interested in any other man. But it was a tiny weapon and she learnt to use it, engaging Philip in serious conversation or flashing him warm smiles every time Anita monopolised Julian, or tried to belittle her in his eyes. At last Leonie was learning to fight back.

Chapter Ten

'I suppose you don't want children,' Anita said just before Julian and Leonie left for their holiday. They had gone round to say goodbye to her and she grumbled about the distance and the destination they were going to, remarking too on the expense and wondering how Julian's salary would stretch to a trip to Thailand. She seemed to Leonie to be working herself up to a frenzy of petulance and envy that they were going away to enjoy themselves, leaving her behind. She threw out the accusation of their not wanting children like a final poisonous dart.

'You young women today just want careers. We managed to do both, have children first, then start a successful career.' She didn't add that she hadn't brought up her own children, and thanks to her ex-husband's large payoff, she was able to start a business without much effort.

'We've plenty of time to have children, Mother,' Julian said wearily, 'just leave us alone.'

Leonie flashed him a grateful smile, but Anita said, 'Get them out of the way first,' as if she were talking about a tedious chore or exam, not a beloved child. 'Besides, you must have a son.'

'Why?' Leonie shot back before she could stop herself. 'Julian hasn't a title or anything. Anyway, he has two half-brothers, so the Hunter name won't die out.' She knew this remark would annoy Anita, but her anxiety at not having yet conceived a child lay like a wound inside her, making her thrash out when anyone touched it with thoughtless remarks.

Anita's expression tightened to one of menace. Julian intervened quickly with an awkward laugh.

'Let's not talk about it any more. We'll make you a grandmother all in good time, Mother. Now tell me about your new property, that dilapidated mews house off Queen's Gate.'

But Anita, once she had started on a subject, was not so easily shaken off. 'Do you want children?' she demanded of Leonie. 'I know Julian does, but men,' the way she said 'men' Leonie knew referred to Tony, 'can have children for far longer than we can. You must not be selfish about your career, a career which, after all, is only a domestic service, hardly of enormous value.' She smiled pityingly. 'You cannot put off having children until it is convenient, or you may not have any at all.'

Stung by her impertinence, hurt by the pain and disappointment of not yet having a child, Leonie leapt up from her chair. 'It is none of your business, Anita. We will have children *if* and *when* we want to. It is entirely up to us.' She stormed out of the room before she said something ruder.

She heard Julian behind her bleating, 'Oh darling, don't go, please don't get so upset.' Then: 'Honestly, Mother, can't you leave her alone? It is none of your business.' But she didn't want to put up with any more. She swept through the hall, opened the front door and slammed it behind her, not wanting him to follow her, dreading skating round the hurt they both suffered but which was too painful to share – the terrible suspicion that they could not have a child.

'I will not see that woman ever again,' Leonie swore despairingly to herself, fighting tears and knowing that short of leaving Julian, she couldn't escape her.

Still in the drawing room, Julian was furious. 'Honestly, Mother, why do you do it? Sometimes I think you try to upset Leonie on purpose,' he stormed at Anita, and made to leave the room to follow Leonie. He felt the familiar sinking sick feeling these rows induced in him, hating his mother for hurting Leonie, hating himself for not being able to protect her.

'These things have to be said,' Anita said firmly. 'Having or not having children is a very important decision in marriage. It is something that can't wait indefinitely and I think it's only fair of me . . .' She dropped the brisk almost defiant tone of her voice, adding warmth and tenderness to it. 'I care so much, you know. I don't want to see this marriage fail.'

'It's not likely to fail, especially if we can be left alone to make our own decisions,' he said, still angry with her and helplessly torn between wanting to run after Leonie, who by now had probably got on a bus or in a taxi and gone, and appease his mother.

If only she could give him her love and approval unequivocally, without tormenting him by holding it out temptingly one minute only to snatch it away when she was displeased.

Despite knowing her tricks, he felt the edge of his anger soften as he began to be mollified by her new tone of voice, her words willing him to believe that she really loved him and wanted the best for him.

'Darling,' her voice now caressed him, 'I know it's a touchy subject, but it's one that must be faced. Do you want children or not?'

'Of course we do . . .' he said quickly.

'Well then,' she touched his hand, 'is there a problem in that department? Would you like me to pay for you to see a specialist?'

For a moment he was drawn in by her charm, believing that she loved him, wanted everything to work out for him. He was about to admit to her that they had been trying but no child had come, that they both felt so afraid that they couldn't have children they had hidden the truth away from each other, just making excuses to themselves each disappointing month.

But before he could speak she said in the slightly acid tone he dreaded: 'After all, you married a Catholic and they don't believe in contraception, do they? Look how your father was caught by that ruse. I'd have thought you'd have at least two babies by now and another on the way.'

His anger and impatience with her seared again. He felt guilty that he had almost let Leonie down by confiding his fear of their childlessness to his mother, who would use it like a weapon against them, against Leonie. He felt an overwhelming sense of loss, knowing that again he had failed to get her genuine love.

Guessing she could lose him if she went too far, Anita squeezed his hand and purred, 'Darling, I understand. Have a lovely holiday. That is sure to give you a baby.'

It was on the long flight back from Thailand that Leonie discovered that she was not pregnant. She slumped in the tiny lavatory on the plane and wept.

Fate made a mockery of the last few days, laughing at her expectation of conceiving a child. She and Julian had been so close these last two weeks, alone again, quickly restoring the old magic of their time in Florence when there was no one in their lives but each other.

After lovemaking, in the darkness of night, the new light of morning or the golden warmth of the afternoon, they had laughed, joked about who the little being was who had surely been conceived and was now, smaller than a pinhead, growing into new life. But it had all been in vain. Anita was right: she was a failure, she couldn't even conceive a child.

Leonie sat in the tiny, plastic washroom, completely dejected. She thought of the years ahead without children, of Anita's cruel jibes which would, surely, in the end, turn Julian against her, break up their marriage.

Then she thought of her own mother and her thoughtless remarks about Julian being the infertile one. It was odd, she thought, that even in the 1990s, well-meaning people like Zinnia, who would rather die than hurt her, made stupid and thoughtless remarks about fertility. Both women, in their own way, were being cruel to them.

I can't go on sitting here, she thought, catching sight of her blotchy face and red-rimmed eyes in the mirror. She washed her face and, blowing her nose firmly, went sadly back to Julian. He saw at once that something was wrong and when she told him she was not pregnant, she sobbed again, hiding her face against his shoulder.

'Oh darling,' he said, 'are you sure?' He was fearful of going into more intimate details, especially in such a public place, though fortunately they were the only people sitting in their row.

'Yes, I am sure. I do feel such a failure.'

'You're not, oh darling, never think that,' he said frantically, making the people across the aisle look at them curiously. He caught their look, and said more quietly, 'Maybe we tried at the wrong time. Look, we'll go to Dr Wharton when we get home. He'll know what to do.'

Dr Wharton, middle-aged and fatherly, was their GP. Leonie liked him, but then she'd never really had anything wrong with her, just an occasional sore throat, once a septic thumb. She was afraid now of embarking on painful tests and embarrassing treatments, and – the worst horror of all – being told that they could not have children. She felt dull with misery, empty as a hollow fruit, barren.

Their homecoming was subdued. They were tired from the long flight and jet lag, and this time there were no flowers or groceries waiting from Anita. In the pile of letters Julian found one from his father.

'They're coming down in a fortnight as the boys are to be pages at a friend's wedding,' he said cheerfully, trying to lighten her mood.

'It will be good to see them,' she said mechanically, then feeling that she must push off this leaden feeling before it destroyed her, added, 'Why don't we have them to stay? I mean, we have all these empty bedrooms.'

Julian looked surprised, then delighted. 'Do you really want to, darling? We only have one spare bed, but I suppose the boys could bring sleeping bags.'

'Yes, why not? I'd like to see your father again.' She thought of Tony's warmth, like her own father's, though without the closeness that would make talking about difficult subjects, like infertility, too painful. She thought too rather wryly of pretty Clemmy and how she'd been to bed with Julian. *She* had no trouble with her fertility. But she must stop thinking like this, Leonie told herself firmly, or she would destroy both herself and Julian. Quickly she pushed the images of Clemmy huge with child, Clemmy in bed with Julian, from her mind.

'If you're really sure, darling.' Julian came over and hugged her. 'The boys can be quite a handful.'

'They're only children, what do you expect?' she said, wriggled out of his arms and went upstairs quickly before he could see her tears. Why shouldn't they come here? she thought. They might be the only children that ever do.

Caroline noticed Leonie's sad mood the next morning as they worked together in the kitchen in a merchant bank off Threadneedle Street.

'Didn't you have a good holiday, Leonie? I mean, you look great, lovely and tanned, but did you get hit by one of those dreadful tummy bugs?' she said sympathetically.

'We had a wonderful time . . . but . . . oh Caro,' she sighed, her voice wobbling, 'we went hoping to start a baby, convinced that a holiday would give us one. But the minute I got on the plane home, I started the curse.'

'Oh, I'm sorry . . . but maybe it was the wrong time . . . or . . .' Caroline floundered, throwing out as many kind and encouraging remarks as she could think of.

'I'll have to go to the doctor, and God knows what horrors that entails. I can't help feeling such a failure. It's ridiculous, isn't it?'

'Yes, it is rather,' Caroline said, fiercely cutting up the vegetables that were going into a ratatouille. She resolutely went through life smiling. It would destroy her if she started to think of herself as a failure. At least Leonie had a husband.

Leonie suddenly realised that she was being tactless. She knew, though she'd never spoken about it, that Caroline longed for a husband and family, but had probably not even had an affair, let alone a marriage proposal. She knew too that she must pull herself together and do something constructive about having a baby, or forget about it altogether.

'Sorry, Caro,' she said, 'I didn't mean to moan. I'm jet lagged, finding it difficult to get back into the swing of things again.' She gave her a wobbly smile. 'Everything seems much worse when you're tired, doesn't it?'

Caroline grinned with relief that Leonie wasn't going to go on in this way. 'Yes,' she said, 'it does. I've heard,' she continued understandingly, 'that the more you want a baby, the more difficult it is to start one. If you forget about it, one just comes. I mean, look at all these unwanted pregnancies.'

'I expect you're right,' Leonie said, though she was not convinced. 'Now this meat, do you think I've threaded enough fat through it? We don't want it to be too greasy.'

Caroline examined the lump of meat with the fat like white ribbons threaded through it. 'I should think that's enough. What's the time? Should it go in yet?' She bustled on, determined that Leonie should cast aside her worries, at least for a few hours, and

Leonie, aware of the rules of this game, managed to pretend that she had.

'How lovely to see you and how pretty you look, my dear,' Tony greeted Leonie with two great kisses on each cheek.

'Leonie, how sweet – and brave – of you to have us all to stay.' Clemmy kissed her too. 'Now, boys, say hello.'

Ben and Tom stood rather silently by their mother, staring at Leonie. They were both blond like Clemmy. Ben, the elder, was light-boned like her too, Tom, the image of Tony.

'Well, give her a kiss, she is your sister-in-law,' Tony said laughing.

'Yuck, do we have to?' Tom said, then seeing Leonie smile, coloured a little, but smiled too.

'You will not be rude, Tom,' Tony said, 'or next time we'll leave you at home with a nanny.'

'Don't worry,' Leonie said, 'I hated kissing my relations too when I was his age. There was an old cousin of my father's that had prickly whiskers on her chin that tickled dreadfully.'

Ben giggled.

'Whiskers like a rat's?' Tom asked.

'A bit. Now come and have tea. I expect you're hungry.' She led the way into the kitchen. 'Or anyway the boys will be hungry. We'll sit them down at the table, then I'll show you your room.'

'It's such a pretty house,' Clemmy said, looking round. 'I love the colours.'

'Anita did it all . . . except the furniture,' Leonie said shortly.

'Oh, I see.' Clemmy smiled sympathetically. 'Pity she has such good taste. It would be expensive for you to re-do it all.'

'How is Anita? Still giving you hell?' Tony said. They were sitting round the laden table in the kitchen. Having got advice from her friends with children, Leonie had spent a fortune on Jaffa Cakes, chocolate-covered marshmallows, animal biscuits, crisps and Coke. She took out some sausages and fishfingers from the oven. She had made some scones and a sponge cake for the adults.

She sighed. 'She's not easy. I . . .' She smiled wryly. She wished she could confide in Tony, tell him all her grumbles about Anita, but she knew she couldn't. Instead she laughed and said, 'I don't see too much of her. It's Julian she really wants to see.'

'Still? But she's had this man for some time now. I should have thought he'd take some of the pressure off Julian, though my poor Diana still puts up with a lot from her,' he sighed. 'It was sweet of you to ask her for dinner tonight. I really must see what I can do about getting her a flat of her own. It really is time she left home.'

'I'm afraid I don't see much of Diana. I'm just so busy with the directors' lunches. We're doing so well, I cook five days a week sometimes, and the occasional Saturday if we're doing a wedding.' Leonie felt a pang of guilt that she hadn't asked Diana round more.

'I'm glad your job is successful, but don't you worry, you can't do it all. In fact, you're a darling to have us to stay.'

'I wish you'd come to us in Scotland,' Clemmy said. 'I know,' she threw a quick glance at Tony, 'why don't you come for Christmas?'

'Oh, we'd love to, but Anita's taking a chalet in Verbier and . . .' For a moment Leonie's hopes rose. Perhaps she could persuade Julian to stay with his father for Christmas, instead of his mother.

'Don't tell me, I understand. You've had your orders.' Tony grimaced. 'Well, come to us for New Year. Will you be back by then?'

'I do hope so. I love skiing. We used to go every year when we were children, but . . .' She grimaced, then laughed and said, 'Oh well, I expect it will be all right.' She didn't say how she was dreading a week stuck in a chalet with Anita. Visions of being snowed in for longer rose up in the dark hours of the night to haunt her further.

Tony guessed her feelings. 'If you're lucky she'll have a big house party, and you can be off skiing most of the day. But come and stay with us for Hogmanay. Entertain us with how awful it was!' He grinned at her.

Tom, lurching forward to grab a Jaffa Cake, fell off his chair. Ben giggled, squashing his hand over his mouth in a vain attempt to hide it.

'Ow, don't laugh.' Tom picked himself up off the floor and thumped him. His glass of Coke spilt, the brown liquid fizzing through the crumbs round his plate.

Clemmy jumped up. 'I'm so sorry, Leonie,' she said, grabbing a cloth from the side and dabbing at it.

'You boys will leave the table at once!' Tony thundered.

There was the sound of a key in the front door and Julian walked in. He laughed, picked up his small brothers and playfully smacked them. 'Been naughty already?' he said. 'We'll put you in the garden for the night, let the cats get at you.'

Leonie watched him as he greeted Clemmy, trying not to imagine them in bed together. They kissed each other, slightly stiffly she thought, on the cheek. Julian turned away immediately and began to talk to his father, and the boys went to play in the drawing room. Clemmy helped Leonie clear away the tea, chatting comfortably about what a handful the boys were, and how she supposed boarding school would sort them out, though she dreaded their going.

'They can't be going yet, surely?' Leonie said, thinking *if* she ever had a child, she certainly wouldn't send it away at eight.

'Ben goes in September, when he's nine,' Clemmy said. She dropped her voice even though they were alone in the kitchen. 'I don't want him to go at all, but Tony is a different generation. He went, Julian went and really I have to accept that. Some of them do enjoy it, after all. Tony is so much older and they do tire him out dreadfully, sometimes.'

'I suppose they do, but he adores them,' she smiled sympathetically. She couldn't help but like Clemmy. She wished she could kick her jealousy of her having once been Julian's lover, and his first one.

'He does. Not that he doesn't love Diana and Julian, but they had a full-time nanny. Anita could only cope with them for five minutes, apparently, and then they had to be clean and quiet.' She raised her eyebrows at Leonie.

'I can quite imagine it,' Leonie said.

'But I can't bear those droopy girls mooning about in the house,' she laughed. 'So the poor darling is hands on with all the dirt and muddle most of the time.'

Before they got to say any more, there was a thump, followed by another one, then a scream. Both women ran into the hall to see the boys, a tangle of legs and arms, fighting at the bottom of the stairs. Clemmy picked them both up by the scruffs of their necks as if they were puppies, and shook them.

'Can't you behave for a second?' she said wearily.

91

'Perhaps they'd like to watch television?' Leonie said, not knowing what else to do with them.

'Just for half an hour then, but if there is any more naughtiness there will be great trouble,' Clemmy said angrily, though neither boy seemed at all concerned by her threat.

Despite protests about not being at all tired and wanting to watch television, because 'everyone else at school stays up until midnight and it isn't fair, we aren't babies,' the boys were finally sent to bed, or rather to their sleeping bags laid out in the small room at the top of the house.

Just as they were going up, Diana arrived looking exhausted. She seemed quite relieved that Clemmy was taking the children away already.

'I'm so glad you've come, Diana,' Leonie said warmly, as they went to sit down with Tony. 'I'm sorry I've been so bad about asking you here, but time just seems to fly.'

Diana flushed. 'Oh, I know,' she said eagerly. 'I've been so busy too. Janet's been ill and I've been cooking for Mummy and . . . Philip. I'm not very good and—'

'I'm sure you're wonderful at it.' Leonie would have offered to help them out if it had been anyone else but Anita. Even though Leonie had a cooking diploma probably higher than Janet's, Anita would have found fault with her efforts.

'Philip says I am.' She flushed again. Leonie saw a gleam in her eyes, a little smile play round her mouth as she said his name. 'Philip's so kind, though. He eats anything . . . even,' she giggled, 'my mistakes.'

'He is nice,' Leonie agreed, and before she could say any more, Tony said, 'I really would like to find you a flat of your own, Diana. You might like to share it with friends. Would you like that?' He had his hand on the back of her chair, sitting looking at her fondly.

Diana started. 'Well . . . I hadn't thought. I mean, I have plenty of room with Mummy and—'

'I know, my darling,' he said patiently, 'but I thought now that you are older, you might like your own place. Your mother's hardly the easiest person in the world to live with, and I'm sure she keeps you running here and there doing errands for her, keeping you from getting on with your own things.'

Diana bit her lip, 'I know, but now she has Philip . . .' Her eyes shot up again to his face, then down, back to her hands twisting distractedly together in her lap.

'She's easier when she has some poor bastard to boss about, I grant you. But wouldn't you like to be independent? Or go on a course abroad, like Julian did, or Leonie?' He laughed. 'Have a love affair with a handsome Italian?'

Diana blushed, then laughed as if it were expected of her. 'Daddy . . . I . . . As you know, I've got my china mending and thanks to Julian I'm doing things for Christie's now and then, and other people too, of course.'

'I know, darling, you're very clever, but you could put it aside for a while. I don't see you much, being in Scotland, but I want you to be settled, happy, and I thought a flat would be nice for you. I'm afraid, though, it won't be very big,' he smiled a little shamefacedly, 'now I have the boys to educate.'

'It would be lovely, thanks, Daddy, it's just . . .' She gave him a quick, nervous smile, hunting for the right words to explain her reservations to him.

'You could share it with a friend, if you don't want to be alone,' Clemmy, returning, broke in encouragingly, suspecting, rightly, that Diana felt scared of being too independent.

'I know. I . . . well, at the moment I'm quite busy. Janet's been ill and I've had to cook—'

'My dear, you should not be your mother's slave. It wouldn't do her any harm to cook for herself,' Tony said sharply. 'You must get out more, Diana. Life is for living. You're young, pretty, intelligent, you should be out with friends of your own age, not stuck at home with your mother.'

Diana hung her head. Leonie saw her lower lip tremble. Clemmy saw it too and jumped in.

'Well, it's only an idea, Diana. Sleep on it, and if you want a flat, let your father know.'

Diana gave her a grateful look. 'I will, thanks,' she said.

Later Diana helped Leonie stack the dishwasher. Ben had

appeared saying someone was in the cupboard in his room, and Clemmy had gone upstairs to settle him. Julian and Tony were drinking port in the drawing room.

'I can't leave home at the moment,' Diana said abruptly as if the words had flung themselves from her. 'Daddy, not being here very often, can't possibly know how busy I am.'

'But surely you'd like to have a place of your own, have parties, your own friends? I mean, I don't suppose your mother likes noise and disturbance,' Leonie said, wondering suddenly if Diana did have any friends. She'd never seen any, not that she'd seen much of Diana, but she certainly wasn't the type to have riotous parties.

'I don't much like parties,' Diana confirmed. 'But you see,' she went on earnestly, 'I'm quite a help to Philip. He's inherited some beautiful china from his aunt but a lot of it is broken and stained and I'm mending it for him. He thinks I've done them wonderfully.' Her face took on a glow as if she were describing a lover.

Leonie's heart sank. Oh no, she said inwardly, she can't be in love with Philip. What chance will she have against Anita?

Later that night she confirmed her fears to Julian.

'Oh nonsense,' he said flippantly. 'She's always having crushes on people, poor thing, but Mother's love dramas have rather put her off the real thing. She should leave home, lead a normal life with men of her own age, away from Mother. I agree with Dad over that. I'll take her out to lunch next week and talk to her.' He settled down to sleep.

Lying awake, Leonie thought of Diana. Anita would never let her go while she needed her. It was hardly surprising she had a crush, if that's all it was, on Philip. He was attractive and kind, so likeable, lovable even. She wondered how old he was. He was certainly quite a bit younger than Anita, who must be in her late fifties, though she looked younger, but he was surely the only attractive man in Diana's life.

Leonie was so tired she slept later than she'd intended, then, leaving Julian still asleep, crept downstairs to make herself some coffee and put out the breakfast things. As she went down she noticed to her amazement that all the white doors in the house were crudely painted with thin, wobbly, red crosses. She went into the drawing room. The two boys were busy wrapping up the sofa and chair cushions with drying-up towels. Ben looked up at her.

'Bring out your dead,' he said and went back to his task.

'What?' She caught sight of an empty bottle of her nail varnish on the carpet beside him. A little trickle of varnish had escaped on to the pile.

'Bring out your dead. It's the plague,' Tom explained helpfully.

'What the hell is this?' Julian's voice cut through the air. He ran on down the stairs. 'These crosses – they've ruined the white paint. Who . . .?' he took one look at the pile of cushions roughly wrapped in cloths and shouted, 'What are you doing?'

'Playing the plague,' Ben said nervously.

Leonie bit her lips to stop a sudden whirl of laughter that threatened to engulf her.

Julian looked horrified, saw her suppressed laughter and shouted angrily, 'Don't you see the mess they've made? They've ruined the paint and the carpet. What will Mother say?'

'Damn your mother. This is *our* house. She gave it to us, remember?' Leonie retorted, wheeling round and going into the kitchen, leaving him to deal with the cleaning up.

Chapter Eleven

Leonie arrived at Anita's chalet in Verbier alone, two days before Christmas. She did not feel well. She and Caroline had been working all out these last few weeks. She hadn't even been able to travel out to Switzerland with Julian, as she'd had a large drinks party to organise yesterday.

'But we're all going out together on the twenty-second,' Julian complained when she'd told him, his face taking on that irritated look that she'd begun to dread, whenever she couldn't fit in with his mother's plans.

'I know, but I have a big do at Hill Samuel that night. I can't leave Caroline to cope with it on her own.'

'But, darling, you have other staff now.'

'Only people to serve and wash up. I must be there.' She'd been firm, determined not to let Caroline down, relieved too that she would not have to travel out with Anita.

'I'll be there the next day,' she smiled, and kissed him. All the time she was thinking: how tired I am of this endless emotional juggling I have to do to please everyone.

When she arrived at Geneva airport she looked eagerly round for Julian, but she could not see him. A middle-aged, florid-faced man, wearing a bright skiing jersey that clashed with his complexion, came up to her, smiling hesitantly.

'Leonie?'

'Yes.'

'I'm David Knight. Anita sent me to meet you.' He took her case from her and smiled again. 'The others are out skiing. The conditions are marvellous.'

'I see.' She squashed down a stab of disappointment that Julian hadn't come to meet her. She'd been looking forward to the drive to Verbier alone with him, finding out about who was staying, being together for a precious hour or so before Anita took them over.

'The snow's been wonderful, but it's a bit icy in the mornings,' David went on. 'Yesterday we all went over to Mont Fort. It was so cold at the top, we all had to have a shot of Williams before we set off.' He laughed as if he thought it was rather daring to drink alcohol so early in the day.

Leonie smiled rather sickly at him. She prayed it wasn't going to be one of those drunken house parties where raucous men, and girls too, drank too much and boasted about it, as if opening a bottle of alcohol and consuming it was an enormous achievement.

David spent the whole journey telling her heartily about the snow conditions, the ski runs, both here and at other resorts he had stayed at over the years. Leonie didn't have the heart to stop him, as she felt that he thought it was good manners to 'entertain her', and it would be churlish to tell him just to shut up and leave her alone with her thoughts.

'To be really truthful, I don't much like skiing,' he astonished her by saying as they arrived at last at the resort. 'But my wife, Rosemary, does and being such a friend of Anita's we couldn't turn down her kind invitation.'

'I suppose you couldn't,' Leonie said, wishing that she could. She felt leaden with boredom. David, she suspected, did and liked whatever he was told to.

Julian was waiting for her at the large chalet when they arrived. He came out when he heard the car, still dressed in his skiing clothes, wet marks from the snow round his legs. He greeted her with enthusiasm: 'Darling, I've missed you so.' He hugged her to him tightly.

'I only saw you yesterday morning,' she said, slightly irritated at his show of affection here, when she'd have much rather had it at the airport, and had him to herself on the drive from Geneva.

'I know. I'm sorry I didn't come to meet you, but . . .'

'Don't tell me,' she sighed. She felt so tired, it must be all those lunches and parties she'd catered for these last few weeks, not to mention David's monologue on the drive here. She couldn't face another round of Julian's excuses, made up to cover the real truth – that Anita had wanted him here.

'My dear, you look terrible,' Anita greeted her cheerfully, kissing her warmly in front of her other guests. 'You've been working far too hard, but in this lovely bracing air, you'll soon pick up.'

'You do look tired, darling,' Julian said as if he hadn't noticed before.

'Don't you start,' Leonie hissed at him before sinking down in a chair by the fire and thankfully taking the cup of tea Diana offered her.

'I expect it was the journey. Did you feel sick coming up that winding road to here? I always do,' she said kindly.

'I do rather,' Leonie admitted, smiling at Diana. She was looking pretty. Her heavy-knit green jersey, with a glimpse of a frill of a white shirt under it, suited her.

She looked idly round the room. The curtains and chair covers were cherry red and dark green, the walls pale wood, dotted with hunting prints, the riders in green and pink coats. It was bright and cosy against the snow outside. From the window she could see the dying day, dark clouds coming up the valley through the fir trees.

Philip sat by the fire reading. He had greeted her with a social kiss on each cheek as he had taken to doing now each time they met. He was elegant as always in designer jeans and a pale blue polo-necked jersey. Every so often Leonie caught Diana giving him surreptitious little glances, looking up from the piece of tapestry she was working on. Philip, engrossed in *The Bonfire of the Vanities*, seemed oblivious to her.

Julian appeared from their room, changed into beige cord trousers and a blue shirt. He looked healthy and beautiful, and despite her exhaustion she felt a surge of desire for him. He came to sit on the floor at Leonie's feet. David and his wife, Rosemary, a horse-faced woman who had made the best of herself by a good haircut and expensive, well-chosen clothes, came in with a cocktail shaker which they put down on the side, taking out some glasses from the cupboard below.

'We had this in Jamaica,' David announced to anyone who was listening. 'It's called Yellow Bird and it's a mixture of—'

'It sounds very good, David. I hope it's not too strong.' Anita cut him off firmly, looking up from a French magazine on interior design. She sat in a high-backed chair, every so often looking regally round at them all.

Leonie's already low spirits plummeted further. She could see by now exactly what kind of a Christmas this was going to be.

Leonie skied the next day and found, to her surprise, that she was a stronger skier than Julian, more on a par with Philip, who did a couple of runs with them, then went off on his own to higher mountains, promising to join them later. Anita was in wonderful form. She skied elegantly, laughing as she came down the slope, playfully racing with Diana, even kissing her and praising her when she won.

'You do ski well, Leonie, better than any of us, even Julian,' she said smiling, and before Leonie could get over the shock of this new side to Anita, she turned away and began to praise the beauty of the mountain.

Leonie had never seen her so relaxed, so charming to everyone. It's going to be all right, she thought with relief. It must be living in London, the tensions of her job that make her so different back home.

They got back to the chalet about tea time. Julian went out to do some shopping for Anita, and Leonie, tired but feeling more relaxed after all the fresh air and the light-hearted atmosphere, was enjoying a rest on her bed with her book when she heard Anita's voice outside in the living room.

'We'll leave here for the midnight service about twenty to, which should give us time to find a place to sit. The church is quite small and we don't know how many people are out here. Do you think that's early enough, Philip?'

Leonie sat up in shock. She'd been so disorientated and fraught, she'd quite forgotten it was Midnight Mass tonight. She didn't, like her parents, go to Mass every Sunday, but Christmas and Easter were sacrosanct.

The last few Christmases had been easy. Either they'd been with her parents and Julian had happily gone with them, or they'd been in

London, gone together to her church and then Julian went again with Anita, *if* she had wanted to go, which she didn't always.

The others would naturally go to the English church, but she ought to go to the Catholic one. Surely Anita, in her new pleasant mood, would understand that. She went out into the sitting room. Philip was doing the crossword in *The Times* she'd brought from London yesterday. He looked up, pen poised in his hand, and gave her a smile.

She said: 'Anita, I must go to Midnight Mass at the Catholic church. It's that big white one up the road, isn't it?'

Anita, who was writing letters at the table, put down her pen and looked at her as if she'd confessed to a desire for human sacrifice. 'Aren't you coming to church with the family?' she said coldly, as if Leonie had breached a serious rule of etiquette.

'I'll come with you all tomorrow. There must be another service at your church,' she said as pleasantly as she could, but feeling suddenly sick. Where was the pleasant Anita she'd been with all day?

There was a leaden silence. Then Philip spoke behind her. 'I'll come with you, Leonie. I haven't been inside a Catholic church for years.'

'What *do* you mean, Philip? You can't just go into another person's church,' Anita said, her eyes glittering dangerously.

'It's not another person's church. I was brought up a Catholic.'

'But you never said,' she spat. 'You never go to church unless you come with me.'

'I know, my dear,' he said pleasantly. 'I suppose I should describe myself as a lapsed Catholic. I've hardly been inside a Catholic church since I was in my early twenties.'

'Then there's no need to start now,' Anita barked.

'I feel like it, I don't know why. It's Christmas Eve and if I am to go to church, it might as well be the one I was baptised into,' he said.

Anita shot Leonie a look of such hatred she almost flinched. It was a glance that said: Look what you're doing, you're trying to get him into your church, take everyone from me.

Philip, thinking about his crossword, didn't see this shot of hatred. 'Do you know what time Mass starts?' he asked Leonie.

'N-no,' she said, afraid that at any moment Julian would come in and she would suffer that awful guilt at seeing his pain and irritation as she floundered through this crisis, brought on entirely by herself.

'I'll ring and find out.'

As Philip was telephoning, Leonie stood awkwardly by the window, feeling utterly vulnerable as if she were alone in the room with Anita and that at any moment she would shoot her down. She found herself bracing her body for the bullets of venom. It scared her too that Anita could change her personality so quickly. She'd seen a little of it before in London, but today she had been so charming and fun on the slopes, she'd thought it would last the whole holiday. To her intense relief Rosemary and David came in.

'My, it's cold out there,' David said jovially, rubbing his hands and beaming at everyone. He reminded Leonie of a large, friendly dog, running at everyone, tail wagging, tongue out, longing to be loved. She was surprised he hadn't sensed the murderous atmosphere in the room.

Rosemary said, 'We saw the Lawsons in the wine shop. They asked us all over for a drink tomorrow evening.'

Anita said nothing, and only then did Rosemary and David pick up the dark vibes that rolled round the room like the threat of a storm.

Rosemary laughed brightly, embarrassed as if she'd mistakenly lurched into an intimate scene. 'Anything I can do before I change for dinner?'

'No, thank you, Rosemary,' Anita said, writing her letters with such fury that Leonie could hear the squeak of her pen on the paper.

There was a clunk of glass on the stone floor in the entrance outside. Julian came in. 'I've got the champagne. Heavens, it's expensive if you think in Swiss francs.' He stopped, felt at once the atmosphere and looked anxiously from his mother to Leonie and back again. For a second Leonie wondered what his childhood had been like. Had he constantly worn that worried frown, always wary of his mother's changing moods?

At the same moment Philip put down the telephone and said, 'Our Mass starts at midnight, but there are carols for half an hour before. Of course they'll be in French. Will you know them?' he addressed Leonie.

'Philip has decided to go to the *Catholic* church with Leonie,' Anita said, as if insinuating they were going to worship Lucifer.

Julian swallowed, shot Leonie an agonised glance. She pretended not to see it. Trust Anita to build this unimportant issue into something significant and threatening.

'Each to their own, I always say,' David boomed cheerfully.

'We can leave at the same time as everyone else,' Philip said pleasantly and with the newspaper under his arm, left them and went to his bedroom.

'Yes, thank you for finding out, Philip,' Leonie called after him, and went back into her room, not looking at anyone.

Julian came in a few minutes later.

'I don't want to talk about it,' she said firmly, feeling the now familiar surge of guilt at his anxious expression.

'But it's Christmas, and as a family we should go together,' he said, looking rejected.

Leonie knew that if it had just been the two of them, there would have been no difficulty as to which church they attended. But she had gone too far now to turn back, and she did not want Anita to have the satisfaction of winning. She could not tolerate the cheerful defiance Anita always assumed in the endless times she did win.

She knew too that Julian would not come to church with her while he was with his mother. 'I'll come with you tomorrow,' she said, picking up her hairbrush and vigorously brushing her hair.

She felt very sick for the rest of the evening. Over dinner, Anita pointedly ignored her. Even Diana, who had become quite friendly with her, shot her troubled looks, and only spoke to her if Leonie asked her something. Leonie realised that her decision had probably spoilt the mood of the whole Christmas for the party. She felt irritated with all of them: with the way Julian and Diana were so easily affected by Anita's wishes and moods; with Anita who tricked her, tricked them all, with her charm, making her think that she liked her after all, before turning so quickly to acrimony.

We walk on ice, she thought, never knowing what will trip us into the freezing water of Anita's displeasure.

She wished suddenly that she were at home among the light-hearted squabbles of her family. For an instant she felt such a wave of homesickness it brought tears to her eyes. She spent the rest of the meal in miserable silence, pushing her food round her plate. Once or twice she caught Philip's eye on her, but she ignored it. Only David, bulldozing on with trite and cheerful remarks and Sam, the chalet girl, who knew nothing about the row and anyway wanted to talk about her boyfriend, kept the storm clouds at bay.

Julian did not speak to Leonie as they left for their respective churches. The main party were to drive, even though it wasn't far away. Philip and Leonie were going to walk up the hill to the large, white, modern church that looked over the village.

When the cars had gone and Philip and Leonie were halfway up the hill, she said, 'We, or rather I, have caused rather a lot of bad feeling over this church business.'

Philip laughed. 'It will soon blow over. You know Anita likes everyone to dance to her tune. She's just cross because we want to do something different.'

'I don't know how you stick with her,' Leonie blurted out before she could stop herself, adding at once, 'I'm sorry, Philip. I shouldn't have said that.'

He took her arm. The night was sharp and cold, the white of the snow throwing up a ghostly stillness under the moon. Little chinks of light shone from some of the chalets between the trees. The church bells pealed above them, calling them in.

'I know it's difficult for you,' he said, 'being married to her only son. I don't think she likes her own sex very much, unless they're plain like Rosemary, or useful like Janet. But she's a very beautiful, warm woman, you know, intelligent too. There's a lot of qualities in her that I like.'

'I saw a bit of that side of her today. To be honest I was surprised, but she soon changed back. But you must get a great deal of her better side, or you wouldn't have stayed with her,' Leonie said awkwardly, noticing that he hadn't said 'love'. 'I don't know her as well as you do, and she doesn't like me . . .'

Philip squeezed her arm. 'Try to understand her, Leonie. Her father, who was quite old to be a father when she was born, gave her everything she wanted. He died when she was seventeen, leaving his money to her mother. This would have been fine, if her mother hadn't then married a man with two older daughters. In a few years, all the money had gone – one daughter had a drunken or ill husband, I forget which. The money was spent on them, not her. In the end they had to sell the house she adored.'

'Cinderella, but she got her prince in Tony. She could have stayed with him,' Leonie said sourly, then added, 'Worse things have happened to people, and they've got on with it, tried to be kind to other people.'

Philip laughed. 'You don't like her, Leonie, so you don't give her a chance, but I do admit she's not good with you either.'

They had arrived at the church, people pouring in from all around.

'Why doesn't she let Diana go? Though I suspect she would if she were beautiful like her. Too bad her looks came from Tony.'

'Leonie, don't be bitchy, it doesn't suit you,' he said. 'Anita works very hard, you know. Everything has to be perfect in her houses. I think she gets rather impatient with people, especially her children, if they don't achieve so much.'

'But she hardly gives Diana a chance. She keeps her at home, having destroyed any self-confidence she might have had, like a Victorian girl. If she had her hair done differently, dressed in more modern clothes, she'd be very attractive. She looks great in the clothes she wears here, don't you think?' She did not add, 'Don't you see she's in love with you and that in the end will destroy her?'

Philip smiled. 'Yes, she does, but you exaggerate, Leonie. She had a very good education, and now is building up quite a business with her china mending, which she's very talented at. She could easily get up and go. Her father's even offered her a flat, I understand. You can't expect Anita to do everything,' he said. 'But you're happy with Julian, just concentrate on that. That is what really matters.'

Leonie looked at him under the light from the church. She knew so little of him, who he was, where he'd come from. He'd just been a relief to her, 'the poor bastard' as Tony had put it, to keep Anita out of their hair. He was good-looking, charming, surely he had the pick of any woman he wanted? Did he love Anita? She found it hard to believe. Was it just sex? She didn't believe that either.

'Were you ever married?' she asked him suddenly.

He paused, gave a quick, bitter smile. 'Yes I was. My wife died.

I . . .' he dropped his eyes, his mouth working.

Leonie put her hand on his arm. 'Oh Philip, I'm so sorry, forgive me. I didn't mean to intrude.'

'It's all right. I can't come to terms with it. It just ruined my life . . . I seem to drift here and there with other women . . . women completely unlike her, but without her . . .' His eyes glistened with tears. He glanced at the church through its open doors as if it were a malevolent force.

'Forgive me,' he touched her arm, 'but I don't think I will come after all. I'll meet you at the end though, walk you home,' and he was gone.

Leonie was left being gently jostled by the streaming mass of happy people going into the church, feeling utterly alone.

As good as his word, Philip was waiting outside at the end of the service. Taking her arm, he said cheerfully, 'Your French good enough to understand the sermon?'

'Not really,' she smiled, sensing that he wanted to forget the scene before Mass. 'How much skiing do you think we'll get in tomorrow?'

'I don't know. Would you like to do Mont Gelé with me? The snow's great.'

'Love to. When shall we go?'

'Better play it by ear. We don't want any more ructions.'

'No,' she said, 'we don't.'

The next morning instead of just feeling sick, Leonie was sick. She kept it to herself, assuming it was the late night and the tension with Anita beforehand.

After breakfast everyone opened their presents. Julian had spent ages trying to find something Anita would really like. In the end he had bought a beautiful and expensive book on the interiors of several houses in Europe. Leonie had drooled over the pictures of the rich furniture, the clever effects, the artful use of colour, light and textures. She watched as Anita opened it.

Julian stood beside her like an excited, expectant child, waiting for her praise. He was so pleased with his choice of present, he had found it difficult to wait the few weeks to Christmas to give it to her.

She opened the paper, glanced at the shiny, luxurious cover, put the paper over it again, put it on the table and said, 'Lovely, thank you, darling,' without even looking at him.

Leonie felt she would cry. The look of crushed disappointment on Julian's face smote her like a physical blow. She suddenly realised with a shock that Anita did not love him, did not love him with that all-consuming love of a mother for her son. If she had been overpossessive and jealous because of her love for him, Leonie would have understood. But not to love him, and not to let him go and be loved by someone else, that was unforgivable. She was the spoilt child, sated with toys, who though bored with them, clutched them tightly to her, refusing to share.

In that moment Leonie hated Anita for her selfish cruelty. She saw a quick look of distress pass over Diana's face, as if she understood his feelings exactly. Leonie picked up the present Julian had bought for her and ran to him, taking him in her arms and kissing him.

'I'm going to open this one first.' She forced a smile.

He put his arm round her, needing to feel the security of her love. Then, with an effort, his face cleared as if he were resigned to this put-down by his mother, and would have to try harder to please her next time.

Leonie opened her present. It was an old print of Florence. She stared at it, wishing with sudden passion that she was there, that they were both there, alone among its magic. She looked up, and saw the same feeling in his eyes.

'Thank you, darling,' she said. 'How I wish we were there.'

There was a silence in the room. She laid her head against him and looked out of the window at the snow-clad trees.

'Florence stank like a sewer when I was last there,' David said cheerfully. 'Lovely picture, though, pretty frame,' he added kindly, not understanding when Leonie suddenly rushed into her room.

Leonie did not tell Julian about Philip's wife. Somehow it never seemed the right time, and anyway, she felt it was such a private thing, something he may now have regretted telling her.

'We must have our ski, Leonie,' Philip said while they were all lunching. 'We thought we'd go down Mont Gelé if it's open, Julian. You can come too, of course,' he said affably.

'I think I'll be too slow for you two,' Julian said laughing. 'Really, darling, you're so good at skiing, I'm very impressed.' He grinned at her, blew her a kiss. 'Yes, go and enjoy it. I'll come another day if you'll wait for me.'

'You're not that bad,' Leonie said. 'Of course you can come with us.'

'Not as good as you, and I know what hell it is being held up by someone slower.' He stretched across the table and took her hand. 'Will you go when we've finished lunch?'

Philip looked at his watch. 'We're eating late. It might be a bit cold, and there could be a long queue for the lift to get back. What do you think, Leonie? Shall we do it first thing in the morning?'

'If you like. We'll have more time. We might even do it more than once,' she said brightly, aware that Anita was eating her food with exaggerated nonchalance, but that every fibre of her being was listening to the exchange between them.

Leonie was sick again the following morning. This time Anita caught her coming out of the bathroom.

'Are you pregnant?' she said, 'I can't help noticing you being sick every morning, and you don't look at all well.'

'I . . . I don't know.' Leonie stood there in front of her, clutching her dressing gown round her, the word 'pregnant' ricocheting round her head. They had been so busy these last few weeks, her yearning for a baby had receded to the back of her mind.

After her holiday she had been to see Dr Wharton, who, having asked her a few questions, had patted her shoulder and said cheerfully, 'Babies don't always come to order, my dear, but I expect you'll get one soon. At your age there's plenty of time to sort things out if we need to. It's ladies ten years older than you that we have to worry about. If nothing's happened by after Christmas I'll send you to a specialist. But above all,' he winked, 'don't worry, enjoy yourself.'

'You must know your own body,' Anita said bossily.

'It's just I've been so busy and . . .' Her mind fumbled for the date of her last period, but she couldn't remember it. Could she be pregnant? The thought made her feel weak. But it shouldn't be like this – Anita interrogating her as if she were at fault. It should be a private thing between her and Julian, a secret joy to nurture just on their own before telling everyone else.

'I'd go to a doctor if I were you,' Anita said sharply. 'Anyway, it puts paid to your skiing. It wouldn't do for you to go throwing yourself about the mountains. Quickest way to a miscarriage.'

'Yes,' Leonie said feebly, knowing it would please Anita that now she couldn't go off skiing with Philip on slopes out of Anita's range.

She went into her room. Julian was dressing, he looked up.

'You all right?'

'I don't know.' She sat down on the bed. 'I've been sick for the last two mornings, and felt rotten before. Your mother wondered if I was pregnant.'

'Oh darling, are you?' At once he was beside her, kneeling on the floor, his arms round her.

'I don't know. It sounds so stupid, but I've been so busy I've hardly thought of dates, except for which party's on which day. I just can't remember when I last—'

'Nor can I,' he said, then after a moment: 'Yes I can. It was that weekend we went to stay with Miles and Sophie. You said it was early.'

'That was . . . six, seven weeks ago.' She looked at him, a long smile beginning to creep on to her mouth, her heart beating faster. 'Do you think . . . oh darling, do you?' She clutched at his shoulders, her eyes begging him to confirm it.

'It sounds like it. I mean, what else makes you sick and miss periods? Oh darling, you must be so very careful. You'd better not ski any more, and must give up your work and—'

'But, Julian, I'm not an invalid,' she laughed.

'But you mustn't ski. Even though you're so good you might fall, or someone might knock into you. Some people ski so fast, not looking where they're going.'

'I won't ski,' she promised him, laying her cheek against his, 'but I'll die if it's a false alarm.'

Chapter Twelve

'They never said it would hurt so much in the antenatal class,' Leonie moaned, still holding herself tense from the last contraction. 'The nurse there only looked about fourteen anyway, so she obviously knew nothing about it. She said it might be uncomfortable. Uncomfortable. It's agony!'

'Oh my poor darling, do try and relax. They said that would help. I'll rub your back,' Julian said anxiously, his face ashen, fear in his eyes. Ever since Leonie had gone into labour that morning, his emotions had swooped from excitement to fear, and recently to anguish at her suffering. He pulled back the bedclothes and tentatively rubbed her back.

'Oh, do leave me alone,' she snapped, pushing his hand away. She'd been here for hours, and she'd had enough. She wanted to get up and go, leave this baby business for another time.

'I'm sorry, darling.' He backed away, his large eyes watching her reproachfully from the corner of the small hospital room. 'I just wish I could help you.'

His look annoyed her, but she bit down the words of irritation she longed to hurl at him. She felt out of control, her body and mind enemies instead of friends, taken over by some alien force. A contraction bit again, and she cried out, knowing just how much it was going to hurt and feeling she couldn't bear to suffer it all over again.

The door opened and a nurse came in. She smiled, came over and said breezily, 'Another contraction, Mrs Hunter?'

'If it's not a contraction, I don't know what it is,' Leonie retorted, then relaxed briefly as it loosened its hold and faded

111

away. She knew that at any moment there would be another one and another, and goodness knew how many more before this child would be born. She didn't think she could stand it and said so in no uncertain terms.

The nurse laughed. 'You're doing well,' she said. 'I'll just examine you.' She glanced over at Julian who, giving her a nervous smile, shot from the room.

'I'll get the anaesthetist in to give you the epidural,' she said. 'You're well into the first stage of labour now.'

'If that's the first stage I dread to think what the last is like,' Leonie said, feeling better now she knew that help was on the way, and that she had not been forgotten and left to writhe in agony by herself.

With the epidural in place and the pain numbed, Leonie felt more relaxed. She lay on the narrow bed in the delivery room, holding Julian's hand, her irritation with him quite forgotten. Every so often she was told to push, and was heaved up by a nurse and Julian on either side of her. She felt like a vast beached whale.

'Just a couple more pushes and we're there,' the gynaecologist said, and suddenly she felt the sensation, mercifully without pain thanks to the epidural, of something bursting then sliding out of her.

'Here we are, a lovely baby,' the gynaecologist said, holding it up.

Relieved, curious to see the identity of the person she'd been carrying all these months, Leonie looked towards it with wonder, with excitement. Her heart froze. The baby's face was the image of Anita. Tiny, red, but unmistakably Anita. For a moment it stared, then it crumpled up its face and cried and the image was gone.

'Oh darling, she's wonderful.' Julian was almost in tears. His face was shining. He kissed her and when the child, wrapped in a towel, was put in Leonie's arms, he put his arms round both of them and gazed at them in amazement and love.

'A lovely little girl,' the nurse said. 'However much I see it, I still think of birth as a miracle.'

'Well done, Mrs Hunter,' the gynaecologist said. 'She's a beauty.'

Nervously, fearful of seeing Anita's likeness again, Leonie looked closely into the tiny, crumpled face. She was overtaken by a surge of love. The baby seemed so small, so vulnerable. The fleeting horror that the child had looked like Anita, receded in this moment of wonder, along with the other pains.

'She looks like you,' she said to Julian.

'I think she's like you,' he said and kissed her again.

They felt bound together in love and triumph. At last, they had the baby they longed for.

'She's such a darling,' Zinnia said when she visited the following day, holding the baby reverently as if she were priceless porcelain. 'And Eleanor – I do like that, plain but pretty.'

'You look well, darling,' George said, his face flushed with pride and pleasure at becoming a grandfather, but appearing rather out of place at this intimate scene. He was afraid Zinnia and Leonie would launch into the gory details of childbirth, and would really much have preferred to see them both at home, Leonie fully dressed, far away from the earthiness of birth.

'I love these dresses,' Leonie said, opening the parcels her mother had brought her, spilling out the tiny pink and white garments on the bed.

'I got them at Peter Jones so you can change them if you don't like them,' Zinnia said.

'I adore them,' Leonie said, folding them back again into the tissue paper.

Someone opened the door and Anita swept in. At once she took in the family scene and her cold, beautiful face opened with a smile.

'How lovely,' she said, 'all us grandparents together.'

'She is the dearest thing, do look.' Zinnia held Eleanor out to her.

Anita's dark eyes flickered briefly over Leonie, making her feel as if a predator had entered the room. She had a sudden urge to snatch her baby back to protect her.

'Sweet,' Anita said, barely glancing at the sleeping child. She did not put out her arms to take her.

George pulled up a chair for her, but she declined to sit down.

'Philip is waiting for me in the car. We couldn't park anywhere,' she said, 'but I just had to pop in. I see you got my flowers.' Her eyes inspected a huge basket of orchids and green leaves.

'They are lovely,' Zinnia said, 'so jungly.'

'Yes, thank you, they're beautiful,' Leonie said, though she found them a little sinister, much preferring the prettier pinks, white and pink delphiniums, and roses that other people had sent.

Leonie, seeing these three grandparents all together in the room, realised that now they had Eleanor she must make more effort with Anita, try to encourage a more united family for her child. She said tentatively, 'Would you like to hold her, Anita?'

'Of course she would,' Zinnia said, getting up and making to put the child in Anita's arms.

Anita gave a strangled laugh. 'I . . . well, just for a moment.' She took the child awkwardly, then almost straight away gave her back to Zinnia. 'Sweet,' she said again. Then with a smile, her dark eyes boring into Leonie, she added, 'Funny, I could have sworn it would be a boy. Still, there's next time . . .'

'I started with two girls and thought it the right way round,' Zinnia said. 'They're precious whatever they are.'

'But a man likes to feel his family name will continue, doesn't he, George?' Anita turned her full gaze on him, her melting eyes lingering on his mouth, then moving slowly to look deep into his eyes, her mouth sensuous with a smile.

George flushed, his eyes sparkling in response. 'Well, Anita, I—'

'I've never seen anyone love girls as much as George,' Zinnia said firmly.

'Quite so,' George said, reluctantly tearing his eyes away from Anita. 'As long as they're all right, that's the main thing.'

'Julian wanted a girl first,' Leonie said, wishing suddenly that he were here to stand up for her. She felt quite weak and weepy. She wished Anita would go.

Her wish was soon granted. Anita flashed a pitying look at her remark and, saying goodbye, explained how she had to rush and see a house she hoped to buy to do up.

'I really dislike her,' Leonie said when she had gone.

'Oh darling, she's all right really, just a little thoughtless. You know how she likes to be the centre of attention. But now we have this little darling, she'll steal the limelight from her. She'll adapt, you'll see. After all,' Zinnia tucked Eleanor back into her cot, 'she is the grandmother of this little love too, you know.'

'She's a good-looking woman,' George said, still feeling warm

114

from her look. Then, seeing his wife's sharp glance, coughed, and asked after Julian.

It was Diana who seemed the most affected by Eleanor's birth. She arrived nervously at the hospital clutching a blue and white teddy bear and a large bunch of pink flowers. She hovered at the door of Leonie's room as if unsure of her welcome, yet drawn by a compulsion to see her new niece.

'She's so tiny,' she said shyly, looking down with wonder at the baby sleeping in her cot. Her face was glowing with more pleasure, more emotion than Leonie had ever seen in her before.

'Would you like to hold her?' Leonie asked her.

'Oh . . . I . . . well, I'll wake her.' Diana's expression was half fearful, half amazed that Leonie had even suggested it.

Leonie felt a pang of tenderness for her. All her life, seemingly, Diana had been pushed into the background, her own feelings ignored. Now she was overcome at seeing this tiny child, yearned, yet was afraid, to touch her.

'It's nearly time for her feed anyway.' Leonie picked her up and put her in Diana's arms. She could almost touch the feeling of love and awe in Diana's expression. It seemed as if from that moment, Eleanor became the most important person in Diana's life.

Leonie had arranged to work three days a week with Caroline, and to prepare various dishes at home when needed. At first she took Eleanor with her in her carrycot, but as she got bigger and noisier, she shared a nanny, a large placid girl called Cheryl, who looked after a neighbour's small boy who spent his mornings at nursery school. Cheryl took them both out in the afternoons. Any evening they wanted to go out, Diana baby-sat.

'It's so sweet of her, but I feel she should be going out herself, not hiding here night after night with a baby,' Leonie said to Julian one evening as they drove off to a dinner party.

'She's no one to go out with,' he said. 'I mean, she has a few girl friends from school that she sees sometimes, but she loves Eleanor, and she's better than some strange person from an agency. After all,' he smiled at her, 'we do want to go out together still.'

Leonie didn't answer. A new baby was bound to cause some

changes, but lately she felt that Julian had become more demanding of her. He adored Eleanor, there was no doubt of that, but he kept urging her to come out with him: 'There's a film I want to see,' or 'Let's ring some friends and go out to dinner at that new restaurant written up in the *Evening Standard*. I'll ring Diana.'

If she protested, complained she was tired or, trying a different tack, said they must not take advantage of Diana, his beautiful face would cloud over, and he would say sulkily: 'You never want to come out any more.'

'But can we not stay in sometimes? We never used to go out so much before Eleanor was born,' Leonie said, trying not to sound cross, or whiny, or to show her irritation at this new side to him. When they were alone, or going out together, he was easy and loving, but when he had to share her with Eleanor he would start on about going out. 'And I don't want to curtail Diana's chances of spending her time in more amusing company,' she added.

Even as she said this, Leonie knew that Diana was happy as things were. Looking after Eleanor was an excuse not to have to take these chances. Also, she could get away from her mother, a move with which Leonie thoroughly sympathised.

Leonie never knew a child would so absorb her. Wherever she was in those first months after Eleanor's birth she felt the baby was with her. As Eleanor grew plumper, her little face wreathed in smiles, her round body wriggling in pleasure whenever she saw Leonie or Julian approach, Leonie loved her more. She had Julian's wonderful eyes, but the rest of her features were more like hers. So, to Leonie's great relief, she did not look much like Anita. But the fright of that first glimpse of Eleanor's face, when she had looked exactly like her, sometimes came back to haunt Leonie in the night, making her afraid that the child might become like her grandmother. After all, she thought fearfully, we are not surprised when children look like their immediate family – why should they not have some of their personality traits too?

Leonie also knew, though she would hardly admit it, that Julian was now in second place in her heart. Feeling guilty about this, but telling herself it was surely natural, as babies needed a mother's care to survive, she rather apprehensively gave in to his request to spend a weekend with Tony and Clemmy in Scotland.

Their grey stone house was austere from the outside but the colour and warmth inside gave it a welcoming atmosphere. As soon as they entered, the boys crowded round to admire their tiny niece.

'She's a bit small,' Ben said, dismissing Eleanor at once. Tony laughed. 'You boys are her uncles, would you believe?'

'I don't want to be an uncle.' Tom burst into tears.

'Oh darling, why ever not?' Clemmy ran to him, throwing an apologetic glance at Leonie.

'Because I'll be dead like my uncle is,' he cried bitterly.

'Silly chap,' Tony said, ruffling his hair. 'You're much younger than my poor brother, John. He was ten years older than me, after all.'

Tom regarded him solemnly. 'Will you be dead in ten years?'

'Not if I have anything to do with it,' Tony said, looking sober for a moment.

Leonie went into the kitchen to purée some vegetables for Eleanor's lunch. Julian and Clemmy were talking intently together. Clemmy had something in a pan on the stove, Julian was standing close to her, his dark head almost touching hers. For a long moment, they didn't see her. Leonie felt jealousy knot tightly in her stomach. Although they were not touching there was an air of intimacy between them that made her afraid.

When Clemmy turned round and saw her, she frantically prodded whatever it was in the pan and said brightly: 'Eleanor all right? You will help yourself to anything you want for her – fruit, milk, whatever – won't you, Leonie?'

Julian darted away from the stove as if he had been burnt.

'Is she asleep?' he said quickly, not meeting Leonie's gaze.

Before she could answer a sharp cry from Eleanor pierced the room. With relief Julian ran out. Leonie followed close behind.

Eleanor's pram, which had been put in the scullery for her to sleep in during the day, was piled high with toys. Tanks, trucks, guns, a few books and a load of Lego were packed haphazardly on top of her.

'What the devil?' Julian ran and pulled things off her frantically, tossing them on to the floor.

Leonie reached down and picked her up. Eleanor hiccuped,

117

stopped crying and gave them a watery smile.

'What have you boys been doing?' Julian thundered when he found the boys sprawled in front of the television.

'When?' Tom didn't take his eyes off the screen.

'Putting all those things on top of Eleanor in her pram.'

'Daddy said to share,' Tom said.

Clemmy came in. 'What's happened?'

Leonie, her emotions stretched with jealousy and fear for her baby, snapped, 'The boys nearly suffocated her, piling all their toys on top of her.'

'They didn't hurt her, thank goodness, but she could have swallowed something,' Julian said.

'I'm so sorry.' Clemmy looked horrified. 'You boys were told not to disturb her. Babies need lots of sleep.'

'We thought she'd get bored,' Ben said, 'sleeping all the time.'

'Eleanor is little, she could easily be hurt. You must not give her anything without asking us first,' Julian said.

'She's only a girl,' Tom said, 'and we don't have any dolls and things like that. So we can't share really,' he added with relief.

'Oh heavens,' Clemmy said, turning to Leonie, 'I'm so sorry. They're not used to babies.'

Tony came in and everything was explained again. He took the boys and Julian off to buy some fish for supper. Leonie was left behind with Clemmy.

They sat in the huge, untidy playroom with a mug of coffee and Eleanor on a rug between them, talking about the time and the energy babies and small children drained from them. Leonie found herself wondering if there was still a spark of desire, of love, between Clemmy and Julian. Clemmy was pretty, slim in her leggings and large jersey, her blonde hair looped back behind her ears, making her look very young. Attractive and kind though Tony was, he was nearing sixty and she might long sometimes for someone nearer her own age. Leonie wondered why Clemmy had married Tony and not a younger man, why she had let herself get pregnant by him.

She was hit suddenly by the malicious thought that Clemmy had got pregnant by someone else and married Tony to solve the problem. Then rather ashamed of herself, she dismissed it. There was no doubt that both boys were Tony's.

As she sat and batted small talk back and forth with Clemmy, she wished she could just like her, feel comfortable with her, not always be worrying that Julian still loved her.

Leonie got very tired with her work and looking after Eleanor. At night all she wanted to do was sleep. She loved being with Julian, liked being held close, but her body seemed to crave for rest, not for sex, and this caused problems between them.

'I love you more than ever now we have Eleanor,' she had said in bed one night. 'I just don't feel very sexy at the moment.'

'You mean you don't find *me* sexy any more?' he said, in a hurt voice.

'No, I do, it's just me. Maybe having a child . . . your body lays off it for a while,' she said frantically, wishing he wouldn't take it personally, would be more sympathetic.

'Perhaps you should go to a doctor, have a tonic,' he said, as if her loss of libido was a fault that could be quickly righted.

'It's fairly normal after having a baby,' she said, having asked some of her girl friends, and knowing that she'd be far too embarrassed to go to a doctor about it.

'I hope it won't go on for too long then.' His tone of voice hurt her. She wished she could discuss his new demanding behaviour with someone, but she didn't know who to turn to. Zinnia would be impossible, and she'd rather die than admit to any problems to her girl friends. She just hoped it was his way of adjusting to being a father and that things would work out on their own.

They did make love sometimes, but to her shame, and not a little despair, Leonie had to force herself out of the beckoning warmth of sleep when once she would have desired him as much as he did her. This added to her guilt and anxiety. She felt that yet again she was struggling all on her own to keep the family boat on an even keel, but this time, with darling Eleanor as extra ballast.

She knew too that her guilt made her jealous. Julian was attractive, and all her girl friends liked him. Sometimes she caught the occasional look of flirtation darting between them. But Clemmy, she thought, giving her a covetous look from the depth of her chair, was different. She had been his lover. His first lover.

★ ★ ★

When they were in bed later that night, Leonie asked Julian why he had looked so guilty when she had come upon them in the kitchen.

'Guilty? Don't be silly, darling. We were just gossiping.' He did not take his eyes off his book.

'What about?'

'I don't remember, nothing much,' he said, turning to her with a smile. 'Darling, she is my *stepmother*.'

'And your onetime mistress.'

His face hardened. 'Forget it, Leonie. She is my father's wife.' The way he said it made her ashamed, but also wary.

'Why *did* she marry your father?' she asked him, determined suddenly to have all the ghosts pulled out of the cupboard.

'She loved him, of course,' he said impatiently, turning a page deliberately as if reminding her that he was trying to read.

'I mean, why didn't she marry someone nearer her own age? He's great, your father, I'm very fond of him, but he is so much older than she is,' she persisted.

There was a heavy silence. Julian stared hard at his book and she thought he wasn't going to answer her. Then he said with a resigned sigh, 'A man . . . before me, hurt her dreadfully, she . . . well, she threw herself into affairs and then she met my father. He calmed her down, gave her the security, emotional and financial, that she needed.'

'And the baby, was it a genuine mistake or did she really set out to trap him?' she said, suddenly rather spiteful. Then seeing the expression on his face she knew she had guessed right. She said more gently, 'He knew the age gap was too much, didn't he, thought it wrong to marry her, so she trapped him by getting pregnant?'

'Yes,' Julian said heavily. 'She was desperate for stability. She thought she would have it with my father. He loved her, was besotted with her.' He gave a sour laugh. 'It's hardly surprising. You have to admit she's a great girl.'

'Yes, she is,' Leonie said, trying vainly to squash the jealousy that rose up in her again.

'She's made him very happy, she loves him very much,' he said defiantly.

120

'Do you still want to go to bed with her?' she asked, fearful of his answer.

'Of course not, you silly darling.' He put down his book and took her in his arms. 'I love you, you and Eleanor. There could never be anyone else.'

He started to make love to her and she forced herself to respond, although her heart wept.

In front of other people Anita was the doting grandmother. At Christmas and birthdays she gave Eleanor the most lavish presents, especially beautiful smocked dresses that she always drew attention to, making sure that everyone knew she had given them to her.

The dresses had to be hand-washed, and were hell to iron, so Leonie only used them for special occasions. But when Anita saw Eleanor wearing something she hadn't given her, she would say scathingly, 'I don't like her in trousers,' or 'that colour', or whatever else she could think of. 'What a pity you didn't put her in that pretty *new* dress I gave her.'

'I don't want her to spoil it in the garden; grass stains are impossible to remove,' Leonie would say, certain that Anita had never had to care for children's clothes.

But when no one was there to impress she never hugged her or made much of her as Zinnia did. However, she was pleased to use Eleanor as an excuse to keep Leonie at home, especially if Philip was around.

'I've asked Julian over this weekend, but I know dear little Eleanor will get tired so I quite understand that you'll want to stay at home with her,' she said with a bright, *understanding* smile.

But Leonie found this arrangement suited her too. She would much rather visit friends or take Eleanor for walks along the tow path, pointing out the boats bobbing on the Thames, or watch the sculls, like huge water beetles, being rowed up to Barnes, or feed the geese that waddled by the edge, scrounging food, than put up with Anita.

It was plain by now that Anita was never going to make an effort to accept Leonie, and in return Leonie had just about given up the struggle to meet her halfway. It was easier to admit to herself that she loathed the woman, and to avoid her whenever she could.

Chapter Thirteen

It was Eleanor's third birthday and Leonie planned a party for her. 'She's old enough to enjoy it now,' she said to Julian. 'We'll have the grandparents, Toby across the road, Jessica and Sophie's children and some from the nursery school, and of course Diana.'

'Sounds enormous,' Julian laughed, 'we'll have to have a marquee in the garden. And what about Melanie and Harry for good measure?'

'Mel's in New York and I don't think it's Harry's scene, do you? Especially if he's got one of those anorexic girls in tow.'

'Don't let him come with one of them. I couldn't bear another lecture on all the poison we're eating and drinking.' Julian clutched his head with mock horror, remembering a weekend with his in-laws, when a thin girl called Skye sat on the floor in flowing garments, meditating or lecturing them on pollution, when she wasn't cooking up little messes of lentils and seeds. 'What I've never been able to understand is why people who profess to eat "properly" look far iller than those of us who consume all this so-called poison.'

Leonie laughed. 'I won't ask him, but I'll remind him it's her birthday.'

Eleanor had just started nursery school and had already been invited to quite a few parties.

Caroline, who was her godmother, made a cake in the shape of Winnie-the-Pooh. Zinnia said she'd come, Anita didn't answer the invitation.

'I'll arrive about six, drinks time, if that's all right, darling?' George said.

On the morning of the party Leonie and Cheryl laid the table with

Winnie-the-Pooh paper plates and cups. Leonie made tiny sandwiches and cakes decorated with Smarties and Dolly Mixture. Cheryl had bought masses of crisps, popcorn and mini chocolate Swiss rolls in silver paper.

'They much prefer shop stuff to home-made,' Cheryl said as she ripped open yet another box of cakes. 'It's hardly worth making things.'

'You know I'd much rather Eleanor didn't eat junk. Goodness knows what chemical rubbish is in it. Chocolate, strawberry flavour this and that, that has never been near a cocoa bean or a fruit,' she said, thinking she sounded like Skye.

'But they don't like fresh these days,' Cheryl said.

Leonie, knowing small children didn't have much chance to know what they liked as nannies like Cheryl hated cooking and much preferred to buy ready-made food, changed the subject. 'Funny Diana hasn't come yet. She was so looking forward to helping.'

'Probably held up, traffic's awful,' Cheryl said, forgetting Diana would be coming by tube.

'I expect her mother's found an excuse to keep her,' Leonie said darkly. Cheryl had had a few clashes with Anita, who'd asked her why she wasn't wearing a uniform, as surely jeans and a none-too-clean black jersey were hardly hygienic when one was working with children.

Julian had promised to come home early. Cheryl fetched Eleanor and Toby from school and took Toby home while Leonie fed Eleanor and put her to bed for a nap before the party.

'I want party now,' Eleanor said petulantly.

'When you've had a sleep. All your friends are sleeping,' Leonie said brightly.

'I not.'

'Come on, darling, you want to look pretty.'

'Don't.' She stuck in her thumb and began to fiddle with the door handle. Leonie knew that if she insisted on Eleanor going to bed she'd only scream and then she'd be all hot and bothered for the party. And, if she didn't sleep, she'd probably be bad-tempered. Either way she couldn't win. She glanced at her watch. Julian should be home any minute, or Diana would come, they were both wonderful with her.

She heard the tick of a taxi slowing down outside in the street, and her heart lifted, waiting to hear Julian's key in the lock, but the taxi revved up again and passed on.

At a quarter to three, neither Julian nor Diana had come. Leonie telephoned Julian's office to be told that he had left. Relieved he was on his way she washed and changed Eleanor, putting on a pretty green and white smocked dress that Diana had given her.

The door bell rang and the entertainer, a Mr Perky, who looked at least seventy, his white hair dyed a violent orange, grinned at her, showing very white and plastic-looking teeth. At half-past three Cheryl and Toby, unnaturally tidy with his hair slicked down, arrived, soon followed by Jessica and her children, Zinnia and the rest of the guests. There was still no sign of Julian or Diana.

'Where is he?' Leonie asked Zinnia in alarm, her mind conjuring up pictures of ghastly road accidents or sudden heart attacks.

'He'll be here, darling. You know he wouldn't miss his little girl's party for anything. He's probably fetching his mother.'

'She never said if she would come or not.' Leonie felt edgy with apprehension and irritation. If Anita had done something to spoil this day, their daughter's birthday party, she would never forgive her. Surely, she thought desperately, Julian would not stand for any of Anita's nonsense today.

Mr Perky, now dressed in a suit striped like a candy stick, a red nose over his own, was entertaining the children with two dog puppets and a huge green caterpillar. The children sat transfixed on the floor. Eleanor didn't seem to notice that her father hadn't arrived.

He still hadn't come when Mr Perky told her it was tea time. He was red and perspiring freely and was obviously in need of a cup of tea, if not something stronger. Leonie, swept up in seating the children, making the tea and showing them the way to the loo, forgot about Julian for a while. The telephone rang just as she was putting a plate of hot sausages on the table.

'Oh heavens, the phone. Don't burn yourselves. Cheryl, can you cope?' she said, going to answer it.

'It's me.' Julian sounded a hundred years old.

125

'Where are you, don't you know it's Eleanor's—' she began, her worry and anger at his not being here making her sharp.

'I know, darling . . . It's Mother. She—'

'When isn't it your mother?' she said furiously.

'She's ill. She . . .' he sounded exhausted, as if he hardly had the strength to form the words, 'she's got cancer.'

Chapter Fourteen

Anita needed an operation to remove her ovaries and womb, where the cancer was. Zinnia insisted on staying with Leonie for a few days. 'So that you can give your entire attention to Julian,' she said briskly, having not much to do at home and feeling that in the face of crises, 'keeping busy' was the best solution.

But Julian did not seem to need Leonie. When he'd returned home later that evening after Eleanor's party, Leonie was shattered at the change in him. He was as pale as paper, his eyes wide with fear and anguish. She scooped him up into her arms and held him, but she felt she was holding an empty husk of a person, not the man who was her husband and lover.

'I didn't know she was ill,' she said at last, not really knowing what else to say to him, how to reach him in this moment of shock.

She had not seen Anita for a few weeks, but she'd heard no hint of such a catastrophe. Leonie imagined that if Anita was suffering from something as serious as cancer, Julian, or anyway Philip, would surely have noticed that something was wrong.

'She found out about the results of some tests on Monday, taken after a routine visit to her gynaecologist,' Julian said, pulling the words out of himself as if each one were an effort.

'Monday? But today's Thursday,' Leonie said, vainly trying to squash the question as to why Anita had chosen to tell them on the day of Eleanor's party. Surely if her gynaecologist had suspected something that needed tests Anita would have had time to plan when to tell them.

Her thoughts made her feel immediately guilty. Now that Anita had cancer, Leonie was going to have to excuse her a lot of things and force herself to be nicer to her.

Both Julian and Diana haunted the hospital when Anita went in for her operation, but Philip, who had offered to put off a business trip, had been firmly told by Anita to go ahead with it. She told him that she did not want him to see her at her worst.

'Let me come to the hospital with you, darling,' Leonie said to Julian one morning after Anita's surgery, afraid of this new, shattered person.

'No, it's better that just Diana and I are there at the moment,' he said, leaving the house without kissing her goodbye.

'I know it's difficult, darling,' Zinnia said, having just put down the phone from her daily call to her cleaning lady to enquire about the dogs. 'Cancer always frightens people like mad, but nowadays it's not necessarily a death sentence. You know how close Julian is to his mother. When she's over this operation, he'll be better.'

'But she doesn't love him!' Leonie burst out, feeling suddenly the injustice of Julian suffering so dreadfully for someone who didn't love him. She told Zinnia about his Christmas present in Verbier and other small incidents she'd seen over the years.

'She probably cares in her own way,' Zinnia said. 'I think it must be hell to be so beautiful and have men making fools of themselves over you all the time when you're young, then suddenly realising, like all of us, that in the end time catches up and spoils one's looks. She's jealous of other women, I think, though why, when she's so much better-looking than most of us, I can't say. But I suppose if men have poured love on her without expecting any back, she's got out of the habit of giving out affection to other people.'

'*If* she ever had it. But, Ma, I can't bear seeing Julian give so much, go through so much, for someone who doesn't love him – who just uses him,' Leonie said, slumping in a chair.

'Buck up, darling,' Zinnia said. 'You know what men are like with their mothers. She is seriously ill, after all, and it's come as a great shock to him . . . to all of us.'

'I know, I keep telling myself that. But why do you think she waited until the afternoon of Eleanor's party to tell them? I mean, if it had happened to you, or Dad, you would have waited until after the party, or told us before so we could cancel it, wouldn't you?'

'I'd have tried to hang on until after darling little Eleanor's party . . . yes,' Zinnia said. 'But then you never know how this sort of news will take you. After all, it is something we all dread.'

'I wish Julian would let me share his worry.'

'Darling,' Zinnia gave her a quick hug, then began to pick up Eleanor's toys that were scattered over the floor, 'as women, wives, mothers, we have to weather many storms. We're emotionally stronger than men, remember that. Just stay there for him. He'll need you more than ever now. Conserve your energy for that.'

'What do you mean, Ma?' Leonie said impatiently, not feeling in the mood for one of her mother's fanciful ideas.

Zinnia put a handful of wooden animals and a baby doll into the basket by the sofa. 'Some men spend their whole lives looking for the love they should have got from their mothers. I think Julian is one of them.'

'But I don't love him as a mother . . . He's my—'

Zinnia sat down on the sofa. 'You remember that talk we had about need, on the way back from the airport after you'd first met him?'

Leonie frowned. 'No . . . oh yes, you asked if I thought he needed me too much.'

'Exactly. You know we women have so much power, we can muck up a son's whole life, and the people in it.'

'Anita certainly can.'

'He loves you, you and Eleanor, and he'll come back,' Zinnia said convincingly. 'He'll realise that you can give him the love he's been looking for.'

'But only if she dies,' Leonie said without thinking, and realised suddenly, with a sickening horror, that death was the only way that they could all escape from Anita.

But Zinnia did not like to dwell on the dark side of life. 'Nonsense, darling,' she said briskly. 'She'll probably get better. They've made marvellous strides in conquering cancer these days, but this illness will make him realise that his mother will not be there for him for ever. He should put all his energy and love into his family, the family that loves him.' She got up and began to briskly tidy away the newspapers.

129

'Will it, or will it bind him closer to her?' Leonie said sourly.

'His family will be the most important to him in the end, you'll see,' Zinnia insisted. 'After all,' she added brightly, 'it's time Eleanor had a little brother or sister. *That* would keep him occupied.'

Leonie, feeling she'd had enough of her mother's theories for one day, did not want to tell her that she had been trying for another child. Her libido had thankfully returned, but it seemed to be Julian's that was now waning. She did not want to voice her fear that he no longer desired her.

Leonie took her mother's advice and waited with patience for Julian to need her. She cooked delicious light suppers to sustain him and suggested that Diana come and stay, not liking to think of her alone in the large house in Kensington, worrying about her mother.

'Thank you so much for thinking of it, Leonie,' Diana said, 'but Philip comes back tomorrow and I must look after him. And I'm not alone – Janet is there.'

'But I thought Philip had his own flat?' Leonie said. Although Philip and Anita were 'living together', Philip had kept on his flat.

'The builders are in it. The whole block's been found to have major structural damage,' Diana said.

'But Janet—'

'Mummy needs Janet. She says if she's going to get better she needs a special diet. Janet has to cook it and bring it in each day.'

'I see,' Leonie said, wondering why she minded the thought of Diana and Philip being alone together under the same roof. Diana may be in love with Philip, but she was hardly the seducing type, Leonie thought, looking at her sitting at the table, her plain face without makeup, dressed in a simple pale yellow blouse and a full denim skirt. Or was she? She was, after all, Anita's daughter.

Once she would have suggested this to Julian in a jokey way. Now he was so edgy and abrupt with her, she kept away from any subject that might upset him.

'But it's good news that she's getting better,' she said cheerfully one evening when he had returned from his vigil. 'Are you sure she wouldn't like me to visit her? I'd take Eleanor but she is rather noisy at the moment.' She didn't add that Anita probably didn't want to see the child anyway.

'She does want to see you, actually,' he said suddenly. 'Why don't you go tomorrow?'

'Of course I will.' Leonie tried to hide the surprise in her voice. Perhaps, she thought charitably, Anita's illness had made her decide to be nicer to her. 'Can I take her anything?'

'I don't think so.'

She got up and went to sit next to him on the sofa. 'It's been a terrible ordeal for you, darling,' she said, and put her arms round him. He laid his head on her shoulder and burst into tears.

'Oh darling,' she held him, rocked him, 'she'll get better, won't she? She's such a fighter.'

He didn't say anything, but after a while he stopped crying and got up, blowing his nose. 'I'm sorry, darling,' he said, not looking at her.

'Don't be. I know how upset you are about her. Cancer gives everyone such a fright,' she said.

'I just wish . . .' he began desperately, then shrugged as if matters were quite out of his control. 'I'll go to bed, if you don't mind. Try not to wake me if I'm asleep when you come up.'

'OK,' she said, feeling a sudden pain of rejection, wishing he wouldn't shut her out. They had barely spoken this last month, in the time building up to Anita's operation and the weeks after it. It was as if he were deliberately distancing himself from her, as if it were he who was about to leave this earth, and was halfway there already.

Julian lay miserably on his back in bed listening to Leonie clattering about downstairs. He rather wished she'd come up, get into bed beside him so he could feel comforted by her warmth. But then again he wanted to be asleep when she came. He knew she didn't like Anita and although she was trying to say the right things over her illness, he was sure she didn't mean it.

This cancer terrified him. Surely it would kill his mother, eat her away with devastating power, destroy her looks, her dignity, and he could do nothing to help her. The thought of her pain and suffering ahead poleaxed him. He knew nothing of the disease except that cancer was a word spoken with dread. But the doctor had seemed optimistic – almost too optimistic, Julian thought – that he could help her, though his choice of words was strange. He kept talking about the 'quality' of life, not the length of it. He would not say he could cure her, but talked instead of remission. Julian had not dared question him further, fearful he would admit that his mother was dying.

Diana couldn't talk about it either. It was as if they were both shell-shocked. They had always clung together when Anita was difficult, never saying anything, as if putting their feelings into words would somehow make matters worse, make true what they hoped to deny. They each knew what the other was going through, both damaged by her, yet both craving her love, grabbing hungrily at any scraps she occasionally threw them. Every time either of them had tried to leave her she had pulled them back to show them that she did love them, needed them.

They were, Julian thought suddenly, as fearful of the illness as they were of her displeasure, afraid that somehow it was their fault it had struck her, that she would blame them for it, but they couldn't say it to each other.

He could never tell Leonie all of this, she wouldn't understand. She didn't think Anita was worth loving and she would tell him to pull himself together, smother him with words of trite comfort to paper over his terror, to prove that he didn't need to give his mother so much of his time. He felt cross with her now, and he let his annoyance with her squash the guilt that he'd looked for comfort elsewhere. But he couldn't help it at a time like this, finding someone who understood.

He heard Leonie coming upstairs and he quickly turned over and shut his eyes, feigning sleep. He wondered why his mother had demanded that Leonie come and visit her as soon as possible, and hoped desperately that she was going to make her peace with her and the two of them would grow to like each other. It would make life so much easier if Leonie got on with Anita. He felt so tired, so isolated, helpless against the severity of her disease. With the desperation of a child he wished he could wake up and find some good had come from this cancer, bringing them all closer to each other, instead of pushing them further apart.

The following day, armed with some flowers, Leonie went to the hospital. She felt sick with trepidation. She hated illness and disliked Anita, and the combination of the two brought on such an attack of nerves, she had to keep rushing to the loo.

She arrived at the hospital, went to the loo again, then firmly braved Anita, not knowing what state or mood she would find her in.

Anita lay propped up in bed. She was pale, but her face was made up, her hair clean. She wore a lacy nightdress that showed off her still magnificent bosom. Leonie felt a surge of admiration for her. Ill and in pain she might be, but she'd made the effort to look her best.

'Oh Leonie, how nice,' she said unconvincingly.

Leonie forced herself to put on a bright smile. 'How are you feeling?' she said nervously, approaching the bed with the flowers.

'Bloody awful, but I'll live,' Anita said firmly. 'I'm not letting this cancer get the better of me.' Her tone of voice implied that if Leonie had something to do with it, she'd better realise at once that she had failed.

'I'm sure you won't,' Leonie said. 'Here's a card from Eleanor. She drew it for you at nursery school.' Proudly she put the large, bright drawing with 'Get well, Granny,' obviously written by a teacher, with Eleanor's wobbly attempt to trace over it, on the bed by her hand.

'Thank you, put it on the side for me,' Anita said, hardly looking at it. 'Lovely flowers. Give them to a nurse and ask if they've got any vases left.' Her eyes flickered round the room, filled to bursting with flowers, her expression implying there couldn't possibly be a vase left in the whole hospital, let alone this floor. Leonie felt her flowers were superfluous.

'Now,' Anita said, clasping her hands and looking directly at Leonie, 'I want to know why Julian's father's wife feels she should be down here.' Her dark eyes bored into Leonie, who had no time to disguise the flash of surprise in her face.

'Wh-what do you mean?' she bleated feebly.

'I mean,' Anita said coldly, 'that this woman has taken it upon herself to come down to London, saying she is being supportive to Julian and Diana. I would have thought that was your job.'

'I didn't know. I did ask Diana to stay, and Julian has taken the news of your illness very badly – he's still shocked.' Leonie heard the words pouring out of her. She felt like a child being reprimanded.

133

Then the surge of the unfairness of this remark rose up in her.

'No one has told me she has come down, and where is Tony?' she demanded.

'Why should I know where he is? *I'm* not married to him,' Anita said coldly.

'No one told me Clemmy was here. She certainly hasn't told me,' Leonie repeated wildly, feeling sick because Julian hadn't told her.

'I know why she's here and she must be sent packing immediately. *Your* job is to look after Julian – and Diana if necessary. You will see to it,' Anita commanded, with enough strength to chase away ten cancers.

'I'll ask Julian why she is here.'

'Don't ask him, *do* something yourself. She's here to get her hands on Philip, and I won't stand for it.'

'Philip?' Leonie said weakly.

'I noticed her making eyes at him at the wedding, and at the christening too. Not content with taking one man off me,' she continued, as if her love affairs had not been responsible for Tony's defection, 'she's after the next one. She's far too young for Tony, and he can't be up to much now at his age,' she said dismissively. 'She's after Philip while I'm stuck in here. Get her out.'

Leonie had come to expect trouble from Anita, but nothing had prepared her for this.

Chapter Fifteen

Leonie went straight round to Christie's to confront Julian. She asked the girl at the reception desk to call him, and went upstairs to the salerooms to wait for him.

She wandered aimlessly round the collection of furniture and pictures waiting to be sold. She often wondered about the life story of some of the furniture. Was it a much-loved piece sadly being sold by its owner to meet a financial crisis? Or was it hated by a new wife or girlfriend, or didn't fit into a modern shoe box house, and who would love it in the future?

She tried to concentrate her thoughts, admire the beautiful workmanship of light brass round a French table. To wonder how one craftsman could make it look so delicate, so perfect for the piece, when another had quite ruined a bureau with such heavy decoration it looked as if it were being attacked by barnacles.

Usually she could lose herself, let her problems diminish in the sheer beauty and skill of a certain picture or piece of furniture, but today, she found it impossible. Why was Clemmy here, and why hadn't she been told she was here? Were Julian's tears last night grief for his mother's illness or guilt for his behaviour with Clemmy?

She examined a dark oil painting of a pastoral scene. There were two lovers, or she supposed they were lovers, sitting by a stile in the corner of the picture. She wondered what had happened to them. Had they loved each other constantly or had some flaw like an impossible mother-in-law eaten away their happiness?

How had she and Julian allowed themselves to drift to this state of uncommunication? she wondered. It was as if some insidious poison had crept into their once-warm love and silently eroded it, almost

135

without their noticing it. The seeds of it had always been there, she now saw, but she hadn't known the damage it would do through Clemmy, Anita and now this dreadful illness that seemed in danger of devouring them too.

'Oh darling . . . there you are.' She could tell Julian spoke with false brightness, no doubt to benefit any colleagues who might be listening. He kissed her, a social kiss. 'Do you want lunch? I've got half an hour.'

'I'm not hungry. I . . .' She glanced round. No one was within hearing distance. 'I want to know why no one told me that Clemmy was here.'

'Oh,' he laughed awkwardly, 'I'm sure I told you. She's down visiting her sister and her new baby.'

'You did *not* tell me,' Leonie said firmly, feeling as if there were a wall of glass between them, and that though they were speaking to each other, they were not making any contact.

'Oh darling,' still, she noticed he was playing to the imaginary crowd, 'it must have slipped my mind, with everything else at the moment. She's in Richmond, where her sister lives.'

Leonie looked closely at him. His face, a little heavier now, was still beautiful. He looked so elegant in his grey suit, his blue striped shirt and red and blue silk tie. His dark-lashed eyes flickered round the room as if he were expecting someone, a colleague, even Clemmy, to arrive. His mouth curved in a polite, charming smile, but there was no warmth in it.

'Your mother thinks she's after Philip.'

'Philip?' His laugh was wary.

'Yes, he is after all attractive, charming and rich.'

'That's ridiculous. The drugs must be making Mother . . .' He gave her a look to suggest that Leonie had made this up.

She said quickly, 'Your mother is as lucid as ever. She may, it is true, feel edgy about not being able to keep her eye on Philip from her hospital bed, but that is what she believes.'

'She's wrong. I'll speak to her.' He took her arm and propelled her towards the door. 'Let's go out and find a snack. I'm starving.'

'It's Diana your mother should be worrying about with Philip – not that I said anything about her, of course.'

136

Julian laughed. For a split second he reminded her of Anita, thinking that Diana was too insignificant to worry about.

'Anyway, how did Anita, stuck in hospital, know Clemmy was here and I didn't?' Leonie said, slowing her pace as they reached the stairs. She felt that if she stayed here with him he would answer her questions, but once she had him away from people he might know, he would clam up and say nothing.

'Don't be silly, darling. Diana's just happy to worship him from afar. Mother knows that,' he said, ignoring her question.

Leonie stopped. 'I want to know why no one told *me* Clemmy was here, and what your father thinks about it. Where is he?'

'Hello, Leonie . . . Julian.' A distinguished-looking man passed them on the stairs.

Leonie nodded at him. Julian gave him a quick smile and said earnestly to Leonie, 'My father is working. She's only down for a few days, just helping out while her sister recovers. Hardly Dad's scene.'

They passed a few more people he knew, then almost before she realised it, they were out in King Street, walking towards St James's. The further they walked away from Christie's into the bustle of St James's, the further Leonie felt from the answer she was seeking.

'Is she supporting you in her stepmother role, or that of ex-mistress, or perhaps . . . current mistress?' she asked bitterly.

'Leonie,' his mouth was hard now, 'why do you go on like this? She is my father's wife.' He said the words like a bad actor saying the lines he'd been given, his eyes skittering off her face.

Leonie stopped in the middle of St James's, outside one of the elegant buildings. She held tightly on to his arm as if she were afraid he would disappear. She had to confront him now or she'd lose her chance for ever. 'You don't love me like you used to. Oh Julian, think what we had, where has it all gone? I can't help feeling suspicious, jealous when you won't talk to me any more, won't even share your grief at Anita's cancer. Then I found out through your mother that Clemmy is here comforting you. How do you think that makes me feel?'

For a second he looked shaken, contrite, then he said, 'Don't be silly, Leonie. Of course I love you, you and Eleanor.'

'Not as you used to,' she said sadly.

'Darling,' the word did not sound like an endearment, 'of course we've changed since our carefree time in Florence. We're a family now. You've changed,' he said accusingly, 'now you've got Eleanor—'

'You love Eleanor. She's our child, naturally we love her more than anything else, but that's different from us. I don't feel you love me like you did,' she cried out, making an elderly gentleman, on his way into the sanctity of Boodles, turn round in horror. His look made her bite back a further torrent of pleas. She surprised herself with her outburst, but it was what she needed to say – to point out the slow disintegration of their love, knowing now that it mattered to her more than anything else.

Julian took a hold on himself. He said reasonably, 'It's been a terrible last few weeks with Mother's illness. It's knocked me sideways, I don't mind admitting. I naïvely thought other people got cancer, not someone like Mother who takes such care of herself. The strain on all of us has been dreadful. We're all saying, thinking, things quite out of proportion.'

'Are we?'

'Of course we are.' He smiled his charming smile, the one he used when he was trying to please. 'I'll tell Clemmy to ring you, or you can ring her.'

'I thought our love for each other was tough enough to cope with anything,' she said sadly, 'even two mothers-in-law at once. I want to like Clemmy, but I just don't trust her.'

'You're being very silly, Leonie. She's been very supportive over Mother's illness.'

'You never gave me the chance to be supportive. Every time I tried you turned away,' Leonie retorted, as if he had accused her of rejoicing in Anita's cancer.

'You're so busy with Eleanor, and your job, you haven't time to cope with me,' he said defiantly.

'My mother came to stay to look after Eleanor so I would have time for you, only you weren't there.' She turned away from him, feeling that whatever she said now, he would contradict it.

'Don't let's fight,' he said suddenly. 'Look, let's go and have lunch.'

'I'm not hungry,' she said, suddenly not able to bear any more of this. He was a stranger – a different man to the one she'd loved so passionately in Florence, to the father of her child – and she felt the once-rich fabric of their marriage was tearing, worn through by Anita's acid tongue and Clemmy's sensual one. Could it ever be patched up and made loving and trusting again?

'Come on, Leonie, don't make a thing of it,' Julian said anxiously, seeing her expression.

'You must go and tell your mother she needn't worry about Philip,' she said, not wanting to pursue the condition of their marriage any further. 'I must go to Fortnum's to get some things for the party we're doing tomorrow. 'Bye.'

She didn't kiss him; she just walked away, feeling quite empty inside. She was both relieved and saddened that he did not try to stop her.

Later, feeling quite drained with the emotional drama of confronting him, Leonie slumped in a chair, trying to read the newspaper while Eleanor and her best friend, Mandy, played mummies and daddies.

'I'll be the mummy,' Eleanor said, snatching up a Cabbage Patch doll, whose face, Julian had remarked, would surely put most little girls off having babies for ever.

'All right,' Mandy said reluctantly.

Eleanor was too demanding, Mandy too amenable, always falling in with Eleanor's commands. Leonie found herself wondering how much of Anita was surfacing in Eleanor, and often went out of her way to make her give in to her friends. But today she felt too weary to interfere.

The girls played on, Eleanor talking to the baby while she dressed it and pretended to feed it with a pink plastic spoon.

Mandy, wanting to join in, said, 'Here's the daddy, home from the office.' She stumped up close to Eleanor, kissed her and then the doll.

'You can't come yet, you're at hospital,' Eleanor said bossily.

'Why? I aren't ill.'

'Daddies are at hospital,' Eleanor said.

'My daddy isn't.' Mandy stayed firmly where she was.

'Mine is,' Eleanor said, holding the doll tightly to her and turning away.

139

'Darling,' Leonie got down on the floor with them, 'let Mandy have a turn with your doll.'

'She can't, she's in hospital.'

'Don't want to be in hospital,' Mandy said, her lower lip trembling.

Leonie put her arms round both of them, her heart heavy. She knew small children just took things as they were in their own lives. She wondered how Eleanor would have played if she'd known her father was with Clemmy. Would she have assumed that daddies visited attractive women without telling their wives? It frightened her to think how much damage, even unwittingly, could be done to Eleanor.

Eleanor dropped the doll, put in her thumb and nuzzled her face into Leonie's neck. Leonie felt a huge surge of love, of need to protect her. She took her arm from round Mandy and hugged Eleanor tightly to her.

Whatever happened she would put her first. She must preserve her marriage at any cost to herself, give her child love and teach her to give love back, so she would not suffer like her father did. She remembered with sickening clarity Zinnia's words, 'Some men spend their whole lives looking for the love they should have got from their mother.' Was Julian looking at Clemmy for that love? Was he not able to cope with Leonie herself being so absorbed with Eleanor? She was certain now that there was something going on between them, but how deep and how serious it was she could only guess.

If only she could talk about it with someone. Zinnia would irritate her with her complicated theories. Melanie would ask her in a disdainful way what she had expected from marriage. Her friends, however sympathetic, would seize upon her confession with delighted horror, and would not be able to resist passing it on. After all, it made a juicy piece of gossip – a husband going off with his young stepmother, a story straight from Greek mythology. In other circumstances, Tony would be the best bet to confide in, but how could she tell him about her suspicions?

'Why are you taking my dolly's clothes off, Mandy?' Eleanor perked up suddenly.

'Bath time,' Mandy said firmly.

'Not it's not.' Eleanor thrust out her hand to take the doll.

'Come on, darling,' Leonie said wearily. 'You've got lots of dolls. Let Mandy borrow that one.'

The telephone rang and, leaving them squabbling, Leonie went to answer it.

'Hello, my dear, Tony here.'

'Tony . . .' She blushed as if he knew about her suspicions of Julian and Clemmy.

'I'm coming down next week, Thursday. I wondered if I could cadge a bed?'

'Of course,' she said as brightly as she could, her stomach plummeting. Was he coming to snatch away his wife from his son's arms?

'I'm very sorry for Anita and this cancer business, but the time has come for me to take a stand over Diana,' he continued.

'Diana?' Didn't he mean Clemmy?

'Yes, Diana. I understand from Clemmy that her mother's using this illness to keep her away from her job, and any friends she might want to see. I also understand that she's alone in the house with this boyfriend of Anita's and is in love with him. Do you know anything about this, Leonie?'

'Well . . .' There were screams from next door. Leonie craned to hear if they were bad enough for her to drop the phone and go and deal with the trouble.

Tony mistook her hesitation for appeasement.

'Please tell me, Leonie. I won't have her in danger. She's not got the social skills she should have at her age, and I don't want her getting into trouble with Philip and getting hurt. Can you imagine how Anita will react to her daughter being involved with her boyfriend?'

'Julian tells me she just has a crush on him.'

'Clemmy thinks otherwise. I'm coming down and I'm going to see for myself. Anita has a perfectly good housekeeper and if she needs nursing care, she can well afford to pay for it. I'd like to send Diana abroad. I've a few ideas, but I must get her away now. I should have done it before, but . . .' he sighed, 'you know how it is, time rushes past.'

Leonie didn't dare say she thought Diana was all right, it was Clemmy he should send away.

141

'How are the boys?' she said, to steer him away from such dangerous waters.

'They're enjoying prep school, but Clemmy misses them dreadfully. I do too, naturally, but a bit of old-fashioned discipline will do them good,' he said briskly.

'I'll send them a postcard,' Leonie said, thinking: so Clemmy is searching for comfort too.

'They'd like that. Clemmy's coming back tomorrow, thank goodness,' he laughed. 'I expect you've seen her. She had to help out a sick friend.'

'I thought her sister had had a new baby?'

'Baby? Yes, that's right, last year. I'll see you Thursday then, my dear. About eight, dinner time? OK?'

'I look forward to it,' she said, forcing a smile as if he could see her, while her heart was being wrenched apart.

Chapter Sixteen

There had been an uneasy truce between Julian and Leonie since her outburst in St James's. Now Tony was expected the following evening and Leonie was wondering how Julian would behave with him so soon after Clemmy's 'support' over Anita's illness.

'I wonder if your father will succeed in getting Diana to go abroad now Anita's out of hospital,' Leonie said, to get on to the subject. She put a fluffy herb omelette in front of him, then went back to the stove to cook one for herself.

Julian had played a riotous game of tigers and lions with Eleanor before bed time, but he now seemed almost comatose. He slumped at the narrow kitchen table, flicking through a Christie's catalogue.

'I don't know, doubt it, he hasn't succeeded before. Now, excuse me a minute, darling, while I just check on something. I'm sure that Munnings of a bay and his stable lad I saw today came up a couple of years ago.'

'Have you discovered an exciting fraud?' Leonie said, hoping to stave off the feeling of apathy and gloom that kept descending upon him since his mother had returned home and Clemmy had gone back North.

'No, it just intrigues me.' He continued to pore over the pages as if his life depended upon it.

Leonie was not fooled. She knew that such information could be quickly found in his office on a computer. She continued talking to him about Tony, folded her omelette on to her plate and sat down opposite him.

'It is time Diana left home, started her own life,' he said, mechanically digging his fork into his eggs.

'But there is no truth in anything between her and Philip is there, Julian? I thought he looked very depressed yesterday when we went round to see your mother.'

'Of course there's nothing in it. Not how you mean, anyway. But it is becoming embarrassing. Clemmy says—' He stopped, choked, took a large gulp from his wine glass. Leonie waited, becoming uneasy seeing his discomfiture.

'Clemmy says what?' she said at last, when he seemed to forget what he had been saying to her and his eyes had gone back to his catalogue.

'Nothing . . . it really isn't anything.' He gave her a quick smile, stretched across the table and curled his hand over hers.

'Isn't it?' It was his sudden smile, meant to appease, that irritated her. She said, 'I want to know exactly what happened when Clemmy was down here. I know she's missing the boys dreadfully, but you told me she'd come to help her sister who'd had a new baby, though Tony told me she was helping an ill friend. Which of you is speaking the truth?'

'Oh darling . . . you know Dad . . . He never takes things in. Babies, friends – it's all the same to him.' He smiled again, bending forward and lifting her hand quickly to his lips.

'Well, which one was it?' Leonie kept her voice even, her eyes on him. She saw his expression shift, a wariness come into his eyes.

'What do you mean?'

'You know exactly what I mean, Julian. I do love you still, despite your making everything very difficult with running to your mother one minute, your stepmother the next. Well, I'm not having you going after Clemmy. I've been thinking hard these last few days. What happened before we married, and your father married Clemmy, is past. You are not starting anything up with her now.' She flung his hand away, got up and roughly pushed a salad at him. 'Eleanor is not going to be hurt as you and Diana were, do you understand?' Her eyes flashed at him. She felt furious seeing him sitting there, pretending to study his omelette, trying to think of something to say.

'Of course I wouldn't hurt Eleanor, or you, and anyway, Leonie, I don't know what you mean—'

'Oh yes you do,' she said. 'I'm sorry your mother mucked up your life, but you're not letting the same thing happen to Eleanor.'

'She didn't muck up my life. Leonie, how can you be so unkind, especially when she's so ill with cancer?' She saw the fury clench round his mouth. She knew it was caused by anger at being found out, not at what she had said about Anita.

'She was like it from the beginning, and you know it, long before the cancer.' She stood beside him, bending down close to him, so he would take notice of what she was going to say. 'We love each other, remember. We made serious vows in church. Now we have Eleanor, whom we must love and protect. We should have another child to keep her company. If you won't do your best to make our marriage work, keep our family together, I'll . . . I'll leave you.' She heard herself contradicting her previous promise to herself, to make the marriage work at all costs. But suddenly she felt that was the only threat she had, the only threat she could hold over him to make him take their marriage seriously.

His eyes wide with fear, he looked at her aghast. 'You wouldn't? Oh darling, I know you're angry but—'

'I would,' she said, knowing she couldn't retract now. She stood tall and defiant over him. Seeing his fear she felt a small burst of power. He still loved her, didn't he? Or did he only want her to stay because his mother had let him down so often in his life, and perhaps Clemmy had too, marrying his father instead of him? She and Eleanor were all he had left, but unless he treated them properly, he must see that he would lose them too.

'It's been such a difficult time . . . Mother's illness . . .' he started.

'You could have turned to me,' she said firmly.

'But you . . . you don't like her . . .'

'I can't imagine Clemmy does much either.'

'She understands—'

'Don't you dare!' she shouted, making him start in surprise. 'Don't you dare start along that track. You won't give me a chance to understand, retreating into yourself with your anxiety. Unless you come back to us, in every way, put us first in your life, Eleanor and I are leaving.'

Her words provoked a silence. She went to the door, then stopped, turned round and looked at him. He stayed sitting at the table as if moulded to his chair, his agonised face lifted to her, his eyes like a bewildered child's, searching her face, his expression a little hopeful that she didn't really mean it, that she would take him in her arms and hold him, telling him everything was all right.

Leonie did not move. The anger left her, replaced by an aching sympathy for him, knowing how dreadfully Anita had let him down when he was a child. But she wouldn't yield to it. She felt that if she held him now, she would lose. He would slip back into scavenging for love from Anita and from Clemmy while her and Eleanor's love for him shrivelled and died. He assumed that she and Eleanor would just be there, without any effort on his part.

Besides, just now she didn't feel she wanted to hold him. He was so selfish in his emotional needs. Instead of using his longing for love as a reason to enrich their marriage, he used it as an excuse to destroy it. Perhaps he couldn't help but ruin the life of his own child, as his mother had done with him and Diana.

Perhaps that was why Diana loved Philip in her platonic, safe way. He was so out of her reach there would never be any danger of putting a full-blooded relationship to the test of commitment.

'What happened with Clemmy?' Leonie said into the silence. 'Did you go to bed with her?'

There was a pinched look round his mouth. 'No.'

'Are you sure there is nothing between you?'

He looked at her, his huge eyes deep with pain. 'It's a terrible mess,' he said. 'She no longer loves my father, not in the way she should. You know . . .' he looked acutely embarrassed as if she were not his wife, the woman he had shared the most intimate moments and actions with.

'I don't know.' She tensed herself for what else he was going to say, what he was going to confess to.

'I mean the . . . bed bit isn't working,' he said, shamefully as if it were he who could not perform.

'I see.' She almost said, 'So she wanted it to work with you,' but she did not dare, terrified he would confirm it.

'She misses the children dreadfully and felt she must get away. She came down to stay with a friend and rang me. It was just after I'd heard about Mother's illness. We both sort of stumbled together.'

146

'You mean into bed?' Her voice was sharp. Funny how beds often seemed to appear conveniently to stumble into when people were looking for comfort, she thought bitterly. She held her breath for his answer.

'Not as you think.'

'How then?'

'Nothing happened.'

'If you mean you didn't have sex, what were you doing in bed together?'

'Just comforting each other. We knew it was wrong so all we did was hold each other. I promise you, darling, that's all that happened. I love you, you must believe me. It was just a weakness, two unhappy people trying to comfort each other.'

'You mean you couldn't make love to her, so you think it's all right. If you had, you wouldn't have told me.'

'No. We just clung to each other, we were just so unhappy. It really has nothing whatever to do with how I feel about you. You must see that. I didn't want to tell you; I knew you wouldn't understand. I just hoped you would never find out. That's why I didn't tell you she was down here.'

There was a cry from upstairs and Leonie went up at once, relieved to get away. She took the stairs two at a time, terrified now that Eleanor had heard their raised voices, heard her father admit to going to bed with another woman. She felt numb, quite unable to grasp his story.

Eleanor was sitting up in bed flushed pink with sleep, her bed-clothes on the floor.

'What is it, darling?' Leonie took her in her arms.

'Piggy,' Eleanor said, putting her thumb in her mouth.

'I'll find him.' She put her back into bed, finding Piggy among the tangle of duvet and sheets on the floor. 'Here he is.'

Eleanor grabbed Piggy by his tail, pulled him to her face and fell straight back to sleep while Leonie tucked her in. She stood looking down at her for a long moment, the chubby pink cheeks, the long lashes curled on them, the soft mouth distorted by her thumb. If only her only worry in life would be finding Piggy when he'd fallen out of bed.

She heard a step on the landing and Julian came up behind her.

'Is she all right?' he whispered.

'Yes.' She walked past him and went downstairs to clear up the dinner. He went into Eleanor's room and it was some time before she heard him come out again.

Julian went to bed early with a pile of Christie's Yearbooks. Leonie stayed downstairs and made a couple of vegetable terrines for a directors' lunch the following day. He was asleep when she went up. She lay awake a long time, thinking. She had taken her own childhood and her parents' relationship for granted. The house, her parents, Melanie, Harry and assorted pets and relatives had always been there, the one stalwart against the problems of boarding school, work and broken love affairs. It must have been hell for Julian not to have had that, never to have been loved by his own mother, only used by her as an accessory, a toy, a slave even. However annoying Zinnia could be, she would stand up for her children to the death. To her last breath she and George would be there for them. Leonie had always instinctively known it, but never really thought about it, had never known how hard their struggle to keep this continuity had been. There had been rumours of her father with other women – how much had her mother suffered over these *if* they had happened? It would not be fair to ask Zinnia how she had coped, nor did Leonie want the idyll of her childhood shattered. She needed the safe, rosy memories of those years intact if she were to win this battle of Julian and Clemmy 'comforting' each other.

The next morning, Julian spent a lot of time helping Eleanor eat her egg, chanting 'Humpty Dumpty' to her so many times, Leonie thought she'd go mad. Eleanor was too old for this sort of game, but she joined in with exuberance, getting far too excited. Leonie knew he was trying to make amends, so she said nothing. He kissed them both goodbye with affection.

'I'll be back early,' he said, his eyes not quite meeting hers.

Leonie was relieved when he had gone.

'That was an excellent dinner, my dear,' Tony said, wiping his mouth with gusto. It was the second night of his visit. 'You're a lucky chap to have a wife who is both beautiful and a good cook. I hope you never forget it.'

148

'I won't, Dad.' Julian's eyes flickered over to Leonie and he smiled at her.

Leonie wondered if Tony knew what was going on between his son and his wife, and whether indeed it had been just an act of desperate comfort, not the resumption of a full-blown affair. She'd come to the conclusion that she must accept his word and force the incident out of her mind, not let the thought of it fester away, destroying any love that was left. For Eleanor's sake their marriage had to succeed.

'So what have you decided about Diana?' Leonie said, to move on to a safe subject.

'A friend of ours in Scotland has a relative who works in the Limoges factory. He said he could arrange for Diana to work there in the painting room,' Tony said.

'That would be wonderful. What does she think?'

Tony smiled. 'She'd love to go really. Painting is the part she finds the most difficult and if she got a bit of training there she knows it would help her enormously, but . . .' he shrugged, 'I suppose it's understandable but she's a bit daunted by the plan.'

'Of course she will be at first, but it's a great idea,' Leonie encouraged him. 'And she can improve her French. Where would she live?'

'With my friend's relative's family. The wife is Scottish, the husband French. They have young children, so she can help with them.'

Julian said nothing throughout all of this. He drank his wine, fiddled with his knife.

Leonie said, 'Just what she needs, isn't it, darling? A new start.'

'If she'll go,' Julian said. 'There have been other good ideas before, but she wouldn't go.'

'I think she's definitely been persuaded to go this time,' Tony said. 'Your mother is very demanding—'

'She's very ill,' Julian reminded him.

'She has always been demanding, Julian. Now, if you take my advice, which I'm sure you won't, you'll take Leonie and Eleanor off on a holiday, get away from any flack over Diana's departure. Anita is making a good recovery. She has plenty of people to care for her and she must not use this illness to take over your lives.'

'That would be lovely. I'm sure Caroline could cope a week or so without me – we're not very busy at the moment.' Leonie jumped at the idea. They hadn't had a holiday this summer, apart from going for a few days to her parents in Sussex. Getting away, alone as a family, would give them the chance they needed to start again.

'She's only just got out of hospital—' Julian started.

'She's been out over a week, and I understand from Diana that she has Janet, a nurse, whom she doesn't really need, her long-suffering boyfriend, and her friend, Rosemary, among others. I think she'll be all right for a week or so.'

'Let's go then,' Leonie said, 'to the sea. Eleanor loves the sea. What about Santa Margarita, or the South of France?'

'Lovely at this time of the year, the end of the season and not too many crowds,' Tony said. 'Take your family there, old chap, give yourselves a break.'

Julian looked dubious.

Leonie said, 'So when will Diana go?'

'Next week. She'll be a paying guest with the family and I sent the first month's cheque off this afternoon. If she really doesn't like it there after a month she can come home, but I'm hoping,' he winked at Leonie, 'that once she's away, doing something she really likes, she might stay, or anyway have the confidence to live in a flat of her own.'

'You were very clever to persuade her to go,' Leonie said. 'You only saw her for lunch and this afternoon.'

Tony looked a little awkward.

'What did you say to her?' she teased him, fascinated.

'Oh, nothing that wasn't the truth,' he said.

'Like what?'

'It's time she fell for a man nearer her own age.' He looked rather embarrassed. 'I know it's difficult for her when I've married someone so young, but Diana needs to have a proper relationship with a man, not a crush, going nowhere, on her mother's boyfriend.'

'But doesn't she find a crush going nowhere safer?' Leonie said, hardly imagining Diana bounding into a full affair with a man nearer her age.

'It's unhealthy, and a waste of her emotions,' Tony said firmly.

'But you've said all that before. Why did she take your advice this time?' Leonie said.

150

'Leave it, Leonie,' Julian said.

'I'm just interested,' Leonie replied. 'I mean, why is she suddenly agreeing to go to France, stay with people she's never met . . .'

'It was Clemmy's doing really,' Tony said. 'She must take the credit for it. I suppose being nearer Diana's age, she understood her better.'

'Oh, I see . . .' Leonie looked at Julian, who got up and went to open another bottle of wine.

'How clever of her. I wonder what she said.' Leonie could not leave it alone.

Tony smiled. 'I think she just reasoned with her. Told her Philip would feel proud of her if she went, explained that it was embarrassing for him having her keen on him when he was her mother's boyfriend.' He laughed, finished his glass of wine so Julian could refill it. 'Clemmy has a good way of putting things, making people see sense.'

'I bet she does,' Leonie said, forcing herself to smile, wishing she hadn't liked her so much. 'Well, I'll look into our holiday tomorrow, Julian. We'll leave at the end of next week. You'll square it with Christie's, won't you?' she said determinedly.

'OK.' His face cleared suddenly and he looked almost happy. 'I should like that, see what Eleanor thinks of a foreign seaside. Get some brochures and we'll decide tomorrow.'

They decided to go to Juan-les-Pins. The following week, Leonie bought Eleanor some new clothes, trailing her round the children's department at Peter Jones, trying to distract her from the woolly jerseys with fluffy animals on the front. There was not much selection of summer clothes now it was the end of September.

'Will Mandy come?' Eleanor said, unpacking her new clothes when they had returned home.

'No, it will be just us. It will be lovely and warm and neither Daddy nor I will be working so we can play with you all day.'

'Make sand castles?' Eleanor's eyes shone as she tried to imagine it. The days this summer that they'd gone to the beach in Sussex had been cold and the tide hardly out.

'Yes, and swim and perhaps go in a boat.'

'I'll take my arm bands. Will you buy some for Piggy? Piggy will come, won't he?'

151

'Of course Piggy will come, but he'll stay in bed. Look, here's Aunt Diana.' Leonie saw her approaching the house and ran to open the front door.

Diana had come to say goodbye. She was leaving in the morning and Philip had promised to take her to the airport.

'We're going to the seaside. Are you coming?' Eleanor announced.

'No, but you'll send me a postcard, won't you?' Diana smiled, handing over a carrier bag of books. 'I brought these for you to read on the beach.'

Eleanor tipped the bag on to the floor and fell on the books.

'Read to me,' she thrust one at Diana.

'Not now, Eleanor, and say thank you,' Leonie said.

Eleanor looked crestfallen. 'Thank you.' She jumped on Diana's knee with a book, turning the pages, and leaning back against her.

'It's so exciting you're going to Limoges,' Leonie said.

'I'm rather scared,' Diana admitted.

'Why are you scared?' Eleanor picked up the word.

Diana looked down at her, gave a forced laugh. 'Well, not scared really, it's just a new place, new people.'

'We'll see new people. I'm not scared,' Eleanor said, getting off her knee and sitting on the floor to look at the other books.

'No . . .' Diana looked awkward, her pale face leaden with inertia.

Leonie said, 'Once you're there, and in the painting room you'll be fine. You speak French well enough, don't you?'

'Not the technical stuff.'

'You'll soon pick it up. After all it's such a chance.' She pushed on encouragingly.

'I just feel leaving Mummy . . .'

'But she's got a lot of people to help her, and her illness is under control now, isn't it?'

'Yes, it is. I just feel guilty.' She was grinding her hands in her lap.

Leonie was certain that Anita was working overtime to make Diana feel guilty. She had tried it on them the other evening when she and Julian had gone round.

'My children are going off to enjoy themselves just when I come home from hospital having undergone major surgery and nearly died with cancer,' she'd exaggerated, closing her eyes and lying back against her chair as if she were about to die at once.

'You've been home several days, and you're up and about again. You've even been to visit friends,' the private nurse had said briskly. She had told Leonie that she felt herself superfluous here, and was glad she had a proper nursing job to go to the following week.

'We'll only be gone ten days and Rosemary, Janet and Philip are here with you,' Julian had said to Anita.

'Anything can happen in ten days. I suppose children today don't have the same feelings . . .' she'd started again.

'You'll be fine,' Philip had said, rather sharply, Leonie thought.

Now Diana broke in bravely. 'I'm not far away, Mummy, if you should need me. I can be back in a few hours.'

She'll find a reason to need you all right, Leonie thought privately.

There was some crisis at the office so Julian was caught up the whole of their last day before their holiday. He rang Leonie, sounding exhausted.

'Pack for me, darling. I don't know when I'll be back, but we'll get there, I promise you.'

In the early evening a woman rang the house.

'Could I speak to Mr Hunter, please?'

'He's not here. Can I take a message?'

'Can I reach him anywhere? I've tried the office but there's only the answerphone.'

Remembering his exhausted voice, Leonie said, 'No, he's terribly tied up with his work and I expect he has turned off the phone. Can I help you?'

'Well,' the woman sighed, 'Mrs Maitland told me I must speak to him personally. I'm the nurse looking after her. She wants him to come . . . I think she's taken a turn for the worse.'

Leonie felt her heart sink. 'Has she?'

'She has pains everywhere and—'

'Has the doctor been called?'

'I'll call him when Mr Hunter—'

'Leave it with me,' Leonie said and put down the phone. Why, if

Anita had been ill for ages, did not Philip, Janet or Rosemary ring them instead of the brand-new nurse?

Leonie's eyes caught the suitcases stacked in the hall, ready for an early flight in the morning. Was it just coincidence that Anita, who had shown such courage and determination to fight this disease before Diana and Julian had announced their plans to go away, had had a relapse? Or had she managed to persuade this new nurse that she was ill enough to need her son at once?

She closed her eyes. If she told Julian, he would stay and Eleanor would be let down. She was so excited about going on holiday, having her parents just to herself. Leonie felt she couldn't bear to disappoint her, and knew if they did, she would hold it against Julian. It would be another nail in the coffin of their marriage.

But what if Anita really was worse? What if Leonie said nothing to Julian and his mother died while they were away? That would surely kill her marriage stone-dead.

God, she thought, how I hate Anita. I know she's doing this to spite us. I just know it.

She dialled Anita's number and Philip answered.

'It's Leonie, Philip. Is Anita really ill – too ill for us to go away?'

'Oh Leonie . . . where is Julian?' He sounded depressed. Leonie wondered if she really was on her deathbed.

'He's got a crisis at the office. Look, Philip, we're about to go away. Eleanor is so looking forward to it, and we . . . well, we badly need time together as a family. Please tell me if Anita really needs us to cancel the holiday, or—'

'Go.' Philip's voice was firm now. 'I'm sure she's fine, nothing we can't handle. If I were you I'd just go. Wait a few days, then tell Julian, say the nurse exaggerated, that you spoke to me and she's fine. Your number's here, *if* I should need it.'

His answer surprised her. 'But is she worse?'

'She's deteriorated very quickly since tea time, apparently. I've only just got back from the office myself. Julian phoned much earlier to say goodbye, but she was out and he hasn't rung again. I don't think it's fatal. The doctor has not been called.'

'But shouldn't he be?'

'My dear Leonie, you know she likes to be the centre of

attention.' His voice was weary. 'Just go, and do enjoy yourselves. Your marriage is worth preserving.'

He rang off, leaving her asking the empty room, 'Why did you say that, Philip? What do you know about preserving my marriage?'

Chapter Seventeen

It was a dismal end-of-autumn day, and Leonie went round to
Anita's house with some curtain tiebacks she'd been told to pick
up for one of her houses.

She parked the car at a meter just off Kensington High Street,
knowing that if Anita saw the car outside the house she would insist
on being taken somewhere, not caring a bit that Leonie would then
be late picking up Eleanor. She walked up the road of comfortable
houses which always, to her, gave off an aura of security, of cosy,
plain family life being lived out behind their solid fronts. Her
grandmother had lived in such a house in faded elegance. She
remembered tea time with the silver teapot, the delicate bone china
cups, covered dishes of buttered toast triangles, the firm,
no-nonsense Victoria sponge. All that had long gone, she knew, the
occupants now probably sprawled in front of the television, eating
frozen chips and lurid coloured bought cakes. Once these houses had
epitomised respectable family life, though no doubt there were as
many scandals hidden behind the heavy front doors then as there
were today.

She turned up into Anita's street, the feeling of nostalgic security
receding. She still hadn't got over the sick feeling of tension each
time she had to see her, but over the years she'd made herself ignore
it.

To everyone's surprise, Diana had not come dashing back from
France when Anita was ill, and Leonie had taken over some of the
errands Anita used to expect Diana to do for her.

'There are rumours,' Tony said, one evening when he came down
on business, having left Clemmy behind, 'that she's friendly with a

widower who has two small children, but don't, for goodness' sake, tell her mother.'

If this news were true, Diana was telling no one. Her letters and occasional telephone calls were all about her work, and the family she was staying with. Leonie hoped desperately that she had found someone of her own to love and would make a life for herself. She half envied her finding a Frenchman who had no doubt made his home there and would keep her there, out of Anita's way.

The drama of Anita's sudden relapse on the eve of their departure to France had never been completely explained to Leonie. Philip, true to his word, had written to Julian explaining that his mother had felt ill for a short time, but that this was put down to the new drugs and was not serious. Leonie had not pursued it, thankful that Julian had accepted this news without insisting that they curtail their holiday. But, although she felt mean about her thoughts, Leonie could not help but wonder if Anita really had felt worse, or if she had tried on one last scene at the eleventh hour to try and stop them going away after all.

Since then, Anita's health had not been too bad. Her hair had gone after the chemotherapy, but she wore beautiful silk turbans, which enhanced her striking looks. Leonie had to admit, she had shown enormous courage over her ordeal.

She rang the bell and Janet opened the door.

'Hello, Janet. How are things?'

'Not too bad, thank you. Mrs Maitland is resting at the moment. She's going out this evening.'

'I just brought these round. I hope they're the right ones.' She thrust the packet at Janet.

'I don't know.' Janet peered into the tissue paper at the cherry and cream cords. 'Stay for a cup of tea. She should be down soon.'

Leonie would have liked to refuse and leave, but she knew if they were the wrong tiebacks, Anita would only ask her to return to change them. Besides, Eleanor was having tea not far away with a friend and short of wandering round the shops until it was time to fetch her, Leonie had nothing else to do.

'Thank you, if it's no trouble, though I'm sure you're busy, Janet.'

'Of course it's no trouble. Now, how's that little girl of yours? We haven't seen her for ages.'

'She's fine. I'll bring her round soon.' Anita soon tired of Eleanor, but Janet loved her and often took her into the kitchen to feed her chocolates and let her make pastry, Eleanor's passion.

'I've lit a fire upstairs, if you'd like to go up,' Janet said.

Leonie walked upstairs to the small cosier drawing room on the first floor. The family used this book-lined room, which also housed the television and a stereo. Leonie went in and saw Philip sitting by the fire, an open briefcase by his side, a stack of papers on his lap.

'Philip, I haven't seen you for ages. No, don't get up, or let me disturb you.'

'You won't disturb me. These reports are boring me rigid anyway.' He gave her a smile. 'Come to see Anita?'

'Just doing an errand for her. Janet is making me some tea while I wait for her to appear.' She sat down in a dusky-pink armchair opposite him. 'How are things?'

He looked up at her as if gauging whether her remark were one merely of politeness or of more depth. 'So-so.'

The door opened and Janet came in with the tea tray. 'I thought you'd like one too,' she said to Philip while he got up and moved a tapestry stool in front of the fire to take the tray.

'Janet, you're a mind-reader,' he said.

Leonie saw Janet's dough-like skin flush and her eyes sparkle with pleasure. Diana, she thought, is not the only one in this house to have a crush on him.

When they were alone again and she had poured the tea, Leonie said, 'Have you been working here all afternoon?'

'No, but I'm off to New York tomorrow and I just wanted to complete these before I went.'

'You seem to be gallivanting off almost every week,' she joked. 'You must be exhausted, I know I would be. I get jet lagged just visiting my parents in Sussex.'

Janet had drawn the curtains against the damp dusk outside. The only lights in the room were from table lamps and the glow of the fire. Philip's face was slightly distorted by shadow, but she sensed he was watching her, thinking deeply.

Slightly thrown by this almost uncomfortable silence, she said, 'I meant to thank you for insisting that we went on holiday in September.

And for your letter to Julian, telling him about his mother's health. It was so important that we went just then and we did have a wonderful time.'

'Good.' He smiled briefly. 'So things are back on an even keel now?'

'What do you mean?'

'Your marriage. I thought it was going through a lumpy patch, that you needed the time together.' He put away his papers with great care, making sure each page was exactly on top of the one below.

Leonie didn't know how to take this. She blurted out, 'But how did *you* know? I mean, I didn't tell anyone.' She wondered for one terrible moment if everyone knew, had always known about Julian seeking comfort from Clemmy.

He smiled. 'You didn't need to, Leonie. I saw what was going on. It was clever and courageous of you to stop it in its tracks like that, though. Also it did do some good because Diana got away.' He bit off a chunk of shortbread and leant back in his chair, regarding her intently.

Cold clutched at Leonie's stomach. She'd tried so hard to banish images of Julian and Clemmy in bed together, even though 'nothing' had happened, had forced herself to be understanding and forgiving, to accept Julian's word. Their holiday had been wonderful and to a certain extent their love for each other had been revived.

She said, 'Tell me what you mean, Philip. Please.'

'Oh heavens, I haven't said anything you didn't know, have I?' He bit his lip.

'Is it about Clemmy?'

'So you do know?' He looked relieved.

'Yes, Julian told me.' She jumped up, paced the room in her disquiet. 'I understand what a hell of a life Anita has given him, and I want to believe that he and Clemmy – who has problems of her own – did just fall into bed together for comfort, but that they didn't make love. Please . . .' she turned to him, her face white, her eyes large with pain, 'please don't tell me I'm just being naïve. I don't want to ruin Eleanor's life by breaking up our marriage. She needs us both.'

'My dear,' Philip said, 'my poor, brave Leonie. You've had a lot to put up with. Julian's a nice chap, but I admit he's weak. He's been so manipulated by his mother I suppose he just jumps whenever a woman calls him. But no, I don't think there was much between them. Nothing bad enough to end a marriage.' He smiled. 'Forget it. Forge on with the good things. You're right, Eleanor deserves the best.'

'I keep patching things up,' she smiled wryly.

'Marriage is never easy . . .'

'But yours was,' she burst out before she could stop herself.

He gave her a sad smile. 'We weren't married long enough to make any cracks to paper over. There would have been some eventually, I dare say, but we knew we had something special enough to keep going. As you and Julian have.' He gave her a quizzical look, as if he expected her to deny it.

'Yes, we have,' she said, remembering their holiday and the joy they'd shared over being with Eleanor, watching her pleasure as she splashed in the sea, her curiosity over trying new foods, her funny jokes and remarks. But without her, Leonie thought suddenly, would we have enough to hold us together?

Philip reached out and took her hand. 'A relationship must move on and change or it will die,' he said. 'You and Julian were young, abroad, away from your families. You shared a love of art and, after all, met in one of the most romantic of places. Even if you had lived out there you couldn't have stayed like that. Something – a job, or lack of it, money, someone else—' he smiled, 'something would have happened that would have changed your relationship. You have Eleanor. She has changed your life, enriched it.'

'We might not have anything without her,' Leonie said quietly.

Philip shrugged. 'That I don't know. Sex, love even, is not always enough. You have to build a relationship brick by brick. That's why people who stay together for a lifetime are so solid together, invincible against the rest of the world. But today people are too impatient, want everything perfect at once.'

She let her hand slip away from his and walked over to the window, pulling open the curtain to look down on to the street in the glow of the streetlights. 'You're right, of course. I've my own parents' marriage to prove it. I know it's not meant to be easy, but I feel I've had more than my fair share of difficulties. You must admit,' she turned back to him with a wry smile, 'Anita is not the easiest of mothers-in-law, and Clemmy is so pretty and sexy and his one-time girlfriend!'

'But you've coped marvellously.' His smile was warm.

'I can't help thinking of Julian and Clemmy in bed together,' she suddenly cried out in anguish. 'What does it really matter what they actually did if they got in there anyway? You can have very loving intimate moments without sex.'

'Your imagination has probably gone far beyond what really happened,' he said. 'It was a moment of madness. I've had quite a few myself, I can tell you. They don't mean much, not compared to the real thing.'

'But if you know all about this, Anita must know too,' she continued desperately, wondering when she would start taunting her with it.

'No, she doesn't. I only know because Diana and I saw them together at the Italian restaurant down the road. We often ate there during Anita's illness when Janet was out. They were just sitting together at a table. Diana asked them rather sharply what they were doing, why they hadn't told her Clemmy was down South.'

'What did they say?'

'They looked . . . well, I have to say guilty, but Diana did rather go for them. She's mad about her father, as you know, and she'd hate him to be hurt. She told me about Clemmy being Julian's ex-girlfriend.'

'So Clemmy got Tony to send Diana away?'

'I think she did, but not because she wanted to carry on with Julian. Anyway, you dealt with Julian, then you all went on holiday, and a crisis was prevented—'

'If Clemmy sent Diana away, it was surely because she wanted to continue the affair?' Leonie broke in despairingly.

'Leonie,' his voice was gentle, almost loving, 'don't torture yourself. Your marriage is fine, keep it that way. The shock of Anita's cancer made Julian a little mad for a moment. It was nothing important, believe me. I know he loves you; it's in his face every time he looks at you.'

'Clemmy doesn't love Tony any more,' she said to point out that Clemmy was still ricocheting around.

'That is not Julian's problem. Remember, she adores her sons so she'll probably settle down again. She seems quite a restless person to me, but then no one is perfect to live with, you know.'

'Your wife was,' she said quietly.

He smiled a lost smile that made her want to go to him and hold him in her arms. 'I thought she was and sometimes I feel cheated and angry that we had so little time together.'

'How long did you have?'

'Four years.'

'It must make it very difficult for any other woman in your life,' she said, telling herself briskly that her pain was nothing compared to his. 'What was her name?'

'Helena.' The name hung like an idol between them.

Leonie stared out on the dark street a long time, pain worming round her guts. Julian had been so loving on their holiday. She'd thought that he had heeded her words, been determined to make their marriage work. She must remember that, she told herself, give him a chance. But then, insidiously, another thought squirmed through her acceptance. What if he could only love her when they were away, out of reach of his family?

'Perhaps Julian and I are only truly happy when we are abroad,' she said. 'Reality makes him less loving.'

'He's probably got some mixed-up feelings about his mother, guilt about loving you when she's close by.'

'Do you think that?'

'I'm not a psychiatrist.'

'I thought marriage, children, would lessen her hold on him, but her cancer has just increased it,' she said, thinking how Anita used it to make him feel guilty and do what she wanted him to.

'I may not be here *next* Christmas, whereas I'm sure your family will, so you can spend this one with me,' she'd said to them last week. It was remarks like that that panicked Julian, made him rush instantly to her side.

'You could move away, even to Florence where you originally planned to be, if you thought it would help things between you and Julian,' Philip said.

'I don't want to educate Eleanor abroad. She's very settled here, a real London child, and I want her to be happy. I'm prepared to put up with a lot for that. I've learnt to live with Anita after a fashion.' She gave a brave smile, knowing this to be untrue.

'There's too much emotion sploshing about in this family,' Philip said. 'I've never seen another to touch it.'

'What do you mean?' She came to sit down again in the chair opposite him.

'You've been in it long enough,' he said with a heavy sigh. 'Everyone playing everyone else off against each other. Diana did it, thinking she was in love with me; Julian dying to escape but never quite managing it, so messing you up; Clemmy getting pregnant to get your father. All this with Anita in the middle, like a giant spider, drawing us in.'

'I thought you liked her,' Leonie said, surprised.

'I did, I found her extremely attractive, cultured – great fun to be with. Away from her family she's a different person,' he smiled, 'strange that, I didn't really think of it until we were all together in Verbier. But when she's with a group of friends she's the life and soul and I enjoyed being part of it, especially as my life had lacked fun for so long. It was never a great love match, but it's fun to be with someone who enjoys the same things . . . going to plays, exhibitions, going abroad, eating well. She attracted amusing people to her wherever we went, we shared a lot of good times, but now . . .' his voice died and he stared into the fire for a long moment. Then slowly, so quietly she had to crane forward to hear him, he said passionately, 'I hate illness. I hate operation scars, upset stomachs, pain . . . all of it. I want to leave her, but I know I'd be a rat if I went now, deserted her when she really needs me. She's very brave, does her best to look good, puts up with a hell of a lot from this damnable illness without grumbling.' He laughed sourly, looking across at Leonie.

'You know, when she's not trying to manipulate people by using her illness, you'd be amazed at her courage.'

'Did . . . did Helena die of cancer?' Leonie wondered if this was why he hated illness so.

'No, car crash. I was away – business again.' She saw the angry twist to his mouth. 'No, I'm just squeamish. I can't bear illness, even in myself. Fear, I suppose, of losing dignity, losing control. And this feeling of . . . revulsion,' he spoke the word as if it were obscene and would shock her, 'has exaggerated Anita's bad side to me. If I'd really loved her, as I did Helena, I'd have supported her to Hell and back, but as it is, I long, more than anything, to escape.' He looked ashamed.

'So is that why you've been on so many business trips?'

'Yes.' He leant forward. 'Leonie, you are the only person I can tell this to. The only person who will really understand. I mean, you might think badly of me . . . I feel bad about it myself.'

'Oh, no, I do understand.'

'Tony calls me "that poor bastard". I know he's glad – perhaps you are all glad – that I'm around to field her from you. I'm told by Janet she's far worse without a man.'

'Apparently so.'

'I'll get no sympathy if I leave, will I?' He gave her a sardonic smile.

'Oh yes you will, Philip, from me anyway. I don't know how you stayed so long, even though you enjoyed the lifestyle . . . even before her illness. I mean you're attractive, charming—'

He laughed. 'Are you suggesting that only hunchbacks from Notre-Dame should apply as her lovers?'

'No, of course not,' she giggled. 'I didn't mean to sound patronising.'

'But something is, no doubt, lacking in me not to have a relationship with a warm, beautiful, kind woman. Is that what you meant?'

'I meant someone like you must have so many choices, and there are so many beautiful and kind women about.'

'Like you?'

She blushed, taken aback by this remark and by the warmth that danced in his eyes. 'You know exactly what I mean.' She tried to look severe.

'I think Julian is mad not to love you more, to stay only with you, however stressed and unhappy he might be.' He sighed. 'No one knows why one chooses a certain person, or why one doesn't. Different stages of life, different moods. It's just luck if you find the right person, and . . .' he stared into the fire, a look of such sadness on his face, it smote her heart, 'luck how long you keep them.'

She wished she could think of something to say to comfort him about Helena's death. She leant forward, almost out of her chair, nearly touching him in her desire to wipe away the sadness in his face. The door opened and Anita came in.

'Oh Leonie, what are you doing here?' she said, looking sharply at Philip and then back at her, as if they had been discovered in a compromising position.

'I brought round the tiebacks you wanted.'

'Oh yes, where are they?' She held out her hand impatiently.

'Janet took them. I think they are in the hall. I'll go and find them.' She sprung up from her chair and fled from the room. She felt cold as if she'd been warm in a cocoon with Philip and Anita had cut them apart with icy knives.

When she came back upstairs, Anita was sitting opposite Philip, in the chair Leonie had just vacated.

She was saying rather tartly to him: 'I don't know why you keep having to go to New York. Surely a more junior person can go?'

'No, they can't,' Philip said, not looking up when Leonie returned. 'I'll be back as soon as I can.'

'I thought we'd go to Marrakesh,' Anita said, 'get some sun before the winter sets in here.'

'Oh . . . when were you thinking of going?' Philip threw a wild look towards Leonie, then hastily curbed it.

'Next month sometime.' Anita took the bag from Leonie, pulled the tiebacks out of their tissue paper and held them up to the lamp.

'Is that cherry or tomato, would you say?' she demanded of Leonie.

Leonie knew that whatever colour she said, Anita would say it was the other one.

'I'd say cherry. What do you think, Philip?' Leonie said.

He glanced over to them as they hung limp in Anita's hand. 'Hard to see in this light – cherry, crimson, what colour are they supposed to be?'

'Neither of you is any help whatsoever,' Anita said, crumpling them up, stuffing them back into the bag and tossing them on the floor.

Leonie, seeing with relief that it was time to pick up Eleanor, made her excuses and escaped. She was convinced that it was not their inability to name colours that Anita minded, but the fact that she felt they had been too close together in this cosy room.

Driving home with Eleanor, half listening to her chatter, she thought of Philip and his confession. She could hardly blame him. It must be hard enough facing up to the failing body of someone you loved, almost impossible in someone you'd begun to dislike.

There'd been a desperation about him that she understood. They were almost two of a kind, the thought hit her suddenly, both outsiders, caught up in this family's web.

Chapter Eighteen

'Come round this evening. Julian is taking his mother to a concert as Philip's away,' Leonie said to Melanie, when she rang sounding rather desperate. 'Nothing's happened to your job has it?' she added knowing how many of her friends were facing redundancy.

'No, thank God. See you about eight then. 'Bye.' The phone was put down quickly as if someone were listening.

''Bye,' Leonie said into the unresponding receiver.

'So who wants to see you on your own?' Julian said, looking up from his breakfast. He had on a half-smile, not quite making a joke about it.

'Melanie. She sounded as if something were wrong. It's not her job. I hope it's not Ma and Dad,' she said anxiously.

'Why should it be? If anything terrible had happened to them she wouldn't wait to tell you until this evening.'

'Must be her love life . . . Goodness, I hope she's not pregnant.'

'What's pregnant?' Eleanor said, looking up from dipping soldiers of toast into her boiled egg. She had crammed in two and was prodding the opening in the egg with a third.

Leonie exchanged a look with Julian. They always tried to answer Eleanor's questions truthfully at a level she could understand, but telling her now that 'pregnant' meant having a baby would surely lead to the complicated and embarrassing questions of 'Is Aunt Melanie having a baby then? When is she having a baby?' and so on, until she confronted Melanie with it this evening.

'It means full,' Julian said quickly.

'And stop putting so many bits of toast into your egg,' Leonie said,

169

taking one from her hand and wiping her fingers on a napkin. 'What a mess you're making.'

'My egg is pregnant,' Eleanor said happily, 'pregnant with toast.'

'That's enough, Eleanor, eat up or you'll be late for school,' Julian said, trying not to catch Leonie's eye and burst into laughter.

When Melanie came round that evening she looked terrible. Her hair hung lank against her unmade-up face, her suit looked as if she'd slept in it. She dropped her briefcase heavily in the hall. She'd come straight from the office and hadn't even bothered to freshen herself up.

'Are you ill, Mel?' Leonie said anxiously as she kissed her. Then added quickly, 'Eleanor's waited up specially to say good night to you,' to warn her not to say anything she might not want Eleanor to hear. Eleanor bounced into the hall and hugged her.

Melanie kissed her, and tried to smile while Eleanor grabbed her hand and pulled at her. 'Read to me . . . *please.*' She caught Leonie's look. '*Please*, read to me.'

'Not tonight, love,' Melanie said. 'I've had a hell of a day.'

'So have I. Miss Jane was cross with me,' Eleanor announced grandly.

'That's enough, darling. It's bed time, anyway. Pop up and I'll come and tuck you in.'

'Don't want to,' Eleanor crossed her arms tightly over her round little chest and stood there defiantly staring at them both.

Melanie walked past her into the drawing room. 'Can I help myself to a drink while you deal with madam here?'

'Of course. Ice and lemon in the fridge, or white wine if you'd rather. I'll take her up at once then join you,' Leonie said turning back to Eleanor.

'Don't want to,' Eleanor stood her ground.

Leonie was sure that Eleanor sensed something was wrong and was determined not to be banished upstairs to bed and miss it. But she and Melanie could not talk about anything serious with the child hanging on to every word, and besides it was past eight, and she should be in bed anyway.

'It's very late and Aunt Melanie is tired, and you are tired so let's go up and find Piggy.'

'I aren't tired.'

'It's bed time. I have got to get Aunt Melanie's supper so she can go home to bed.' Leonie went on as cheerfully as she could, taking Eleanor's tight body in her arms and trying to carry her upstairs.

'Won't.' Eleanor squirmed away, arching her back and digging her knees into Leonie.

'Stop it at once,' Leonie put her down. 'It is bed time now, this minute.'

Eleanor looked at her from Anita's beautiful eyes. Her mouth went firm. 'Won't!' she shouted. 'Won't, won't, won't!'

For a second she was like Anita, stubborn and in control. Leonie felt cornered. Something in her snapped. She smacked Eleanor's bottom hard, and when Eleanor opened her mouth to scream in surprise and rage, she picked her up roughly and hauled her up the stairs to bed.

'Don't you dare come out!' She shouted at her, when she'd dumped her in the middle of her bed, quivering with anger and shame at herself.

'I hate you!' Eleanor screamed, grabbing Piggy and throwing herself on to her pillow. 'Go away, I hate you!'

All Leonie's anger left her. She felt appalled at what she'd done. She knew she hadn't hurt Eleanor but she felt mortified that she had been so rough, so impatient with her. It had been her eyes that moment when she had looked just like her grandmother that had made her overreact.

'Darling,' she went over to the bed, yearning to take her small, heaving body in her arms. 'I'm sorry I was cross, but you must go to bed when you're told.'

'Won't,' Eleanor gulped into her pillow. 'Go away. Piggy and me hate you.'

Leonie went heavily downstairs, feeling shattered. She went into the drawing room where Melanie was sitting on the sofa, a half-full glass in her hand.

'I smacked her, Mel. I feel so dreadful about it.'

'She probably needed it, she's jolly disobedient. She's getting quite spoilt, you know. You must be firm with her.' Her voice was slightly slurred, and Leonie suspected she had had more than one drink.

'I shouldn't have smacked her,' Leonie said again, feeling rather resentful at Melanie's remark about Eleanor being spoilt. She poured out a drink for herself. 'Small children seem to know exactly how to make you cross. She knows we want to talk without her, so she's determined to be difficult,' she said, 'but sometimes she looks like my dreaded ma-in-law, and that makes me furious and afraid. I'm so terrified she'll turn out like her.'

'You're paranoid about that woman, Leo. But as she's Julian's child and he looks just like his mother, it's hardly surprising she does too.' Melanie sighed heavily, gulped down her drink and got up to get a refill from the vodka bottle. 'At least I shall be spared a mother-in-law.'

'Oh Mel, tell me what's wrong.'

'It's not that important,' Melanie said resignedly, her eyes dead and her whole body slumped in dejection.

'Of course it's important. Tell me, I'm listening,' Leonie said anxiously, doing her best to put Eleanor from her mind and concentrate on Melanie.

'Jason's left me,' Melanie blurted out. 'He's found someone else. He had her, would you believe, in *my* flat when I was away. Can you beat that?'

'Oh Mel, the bastard! But why in your flat? Doesn't he still have his own place?' Leonie was horrified.

'Oh yes, but it gave him a kick, I suppose, or he wanted me to find out, being too wet to tell me straight out himself.' Tears ran down her face, but she made no heed to wipe them away. 'He wants to marry her.'

'Marry her? But I thought he always said marriage was just a certificate?'

'It seems he's changed his mind. He used to say our relationship was perfect because I didn't go on about wanting to get married.' She got up to refill her glass, then sat heavily down again on the edge of the sofa, her feet planted firmly on the floor. 'I still love him,' she admitted. 'Oh God, I wish I didn't. I know he's not worth it.'

Leonie came over and sat beside her, putting her arm round her. 'When did it happen?' She didn't know quite what to say. She wanted to say she wasn't surprised that a relationship slotted in between board meetings and business trips was difficult to sustain. Relationships needed so much nurturing, as she knew to her cost. But these views were hardly fair on Melanie. High-flying careers needed total commitment too, and broken relationships were, no doubt, part of the price.

'He told me at the weekend. I went on working, stayed late, to try not to think about it, but I have to face up to it. Oh Leo, I am so lonely. You don't know how lonely.' She put her head in her hands and wept bitterly.

Leonie rocked her, muttering words of comfort, wondering how to handle this. She'd never seen Melanie, calm, controlled Melanie, like this before. It was probably the first time in her life she hadn't got what she wanted. That in itself would be a hard lesson for her to accept.

'Is there no hope that he'll ditch her, come back to you? After all, you've been together some time,' she said at last.

'No,' Melanie smiled bitterly. 'She doesn't have a proper career, not like mine. She'll stay at home, or work part time. He'll soon get bored with her. He used to glaze over when couples talked about their babies or schools or whatever, but that's his problem. I couldn't take him back after this . . . but it still hurts like hell.'

'Do you never want to be a wife?' Leonie asked, relieved that she had stopped her dreadful weeping and now seemed to be pulling herself together. 'Have a family?'

'No, Leo. Not at the moment, anyway. That's what Jason threw at me. After loving me for not wanting marriage, he now dislikes me for it. But it's true, I do put my career before him. I'm in line for promotion, which means more responsibility, more money, company car. I enjoy the buzz of meetings, of making decisions, meeting people, making deals. I really don't want to sit at home and make decisions about who to have for a dinner party, or organise a school run, or whatever.'

'Marriage, having a family, is much more than that.' Leonie felt she had to defend her position.

'It suits you. But I don't want it. I thought Jason felt the same but all the time he wanted some little wifey,' she sneered over the words, 'polishing and cooking for him back home.'

If Melanie had not been so obviously unhappy Leonie would have argued with her, told her that most people who loved each other wanted to make a home together, needed their quota of love and caring, and that human relationships couldn't fit into timetables and schedules like a business could. But perhaps that was why Melanie liked her work so much. She had always been a very practical, organised person, and work, unlike relationships, could be neatly parcelled up and kept in compartments, kept under control. Perhaps also, she had not loved Jason enough to make sacrifices for him.

'I hope you won't always feel like this about having a family, Mel,' she said vaguely, knowing that Melanie certainly wouldn't put up with difficult in-law relationships.

'Why shouldn't I? You know that saying, he travels the fastest who travels alone.' Her voice was strong now, her tears dried on her cheeks. 'I'll miss the sex,' she said suddenly, the alcohol making her brazen now instead of maudlin. 'He was good at that. But there's plenty of that around if you look for it.'

'What about love?' Leonie said.

Melanie gave her a pitying smile. 'It's a hell of a price to pay for one's personal freedom.'

'What about loneliness, then? You said you were lonely.'

'I am, and it's hell, but I bet you're lonely too, Leo, sitting here baby-sitting while Julian is out with his mother. What would you be doing this evening if I hadn't come round with my problems? Washing your hair, colour coding your bath towels in your linen cupboard, tidying your undies drawer?'

'I've lots to do,' Leonie said defiantly, not wanting to admit that in a way Melanie was right. She was perfectly happy without Julian during the day, but in the evenings, when Eleanor was upstairs asleep, she didn't feel quite complete unless he was in the house too. To hide her discomfiture and because she still felt ashamed of smacking Eleanor, she excused herself and ran upstairs to check on her.

Eleanor was asleep, her face flushed and sticky, little sobs every so often escaping from her. Leonie bent and kissed her, hating herself for her anger, wishing that Julian were here so that she could tell him about it.

'Get me a taxi, I'll leave the car here. I'm far too drunk to drive,' Melanie said when Leonie returned to the room. She got up and walked unsteadily through the hall to the downstairs loo.

'You can stay here. Anyway, you haven't had anything to eat,' Leonie said when she returned, not wanting her to go back to her empty flat alone.

'What would Julian say? Surely he doesn't want to find his disruptive sister-in-law putting ideas of going it alone to his wife?' Her smile was almost jolly.

'Of course he won't mind. Do stay, the spare bed's made up,' Leonie said, not adding that she found this picture of her sister struggling to pull herself together utterly tragic and it didn't fool her a bit.

Melanie was undoubtedly shattered by Jason's departure. She'd work all hours now to hide the yawning emptiness, the raw pain of rejection, pretending she didn't care. Her realisation of Melanie's suffering added a spur to Leonie's determination to keep her own marriage going.

Chapter Nineteen

'Eleanor needs a brother or sister, she's far too spoilt,' Anita said one Sunday afternoon, when they'd all been there to tea. Eleanor had wanted to watch something on television and had screamed when she was told she couldn't. For good measure she had thrown herself on the carpet and drummed her feet on the floor. Leonie had hurriedly bundled her up and taken her out to the garden. Janet, seeing them from the kitchen window, had come out to play with her.

'It's just her way of protesting,' Philip said mildly as Leonie came back again looking harassed, and Julian shot her a reproachful look, as if she had orchestrated the scene especially to annoy his mother.

'Poor spoilt little girl. But she's quite big now and unless you hurry up and have another child the age gap will be too large,' Anita went on.

Leonie tried to ignore her remarks although they hurt her deeply. If Anita only knew how much she wanted another child, lots of children. She and Julian were playing an elaborate charade at hiding their pain from each other at not conceiving another child. Without putting it into words Leonie suspected, when she allowed herself to think about it, that they both imagined that 'next month' another baby would be on its way. When, yet again, they were disappointed, they made silent excuses. They had been too tired, too busy that month to catch the correct time of ovulation.

Both of them were trying hard in their own way to keep their marriage stable, using unconsciously their love and pride in Eleanor as a mutual concern, an interest imperative to each other. Neither wanted to upset this arrangement at this time by unleashing such an emotive subject as their possible infertility.

177

Leonie had asked her gynaecologist about it at her last checkup, and he had found nothing wrong with her. He suggested she could have her tubes 'blown' and that Julian should be tested for a low sperm count before they took further measures. She was waiting for the right moment to broach this with him, knowing he would not be able to face Anita's ridicule if he should be found wanting.

'I think we should leave Julian and Leonie to decide on how many children they want for themselves,' Philip said firmly. 'Now, if you'll excuse me I must go round to my flat. I've got some work to see to.' He got up from his chair and went over and kissed Anita briefly on her cheek.

Anita said, 'I don't know why you keep going back to your flat to work. There's a perfectly good study here.'

'I've just got it all laid out there,' he said pleasantly, 'with no Janet to tidy up for me.'

Anita ignored this remark. Before he'd got to the door she said loudly in Julian's direction, 'I understand that your father has marriage difficulties.'

The suddenness of her remark gave Julian no time to conceal his shock. Leonie sat on the edge of her chair, waiting for Anita's final thrust. Philip stopped in his tracks, turned round and caught her eye. His steady gaze calmed her.

Anita ignored the effect her remark was having on everyone. She selected a new strand of wool for her tapestry and continued: 'Of course, he was a fool to marry such a young girl, let her trap him with the oldest trick in the world. But as they say, there's no fool like an old fool.'

'So what's happened?' Leonie, feeling strong with Philip there, dared to call Anita's bluff, not sit there miserably waiting for her ridicule.

'She's gone off with a writer . . . or someone connected to her book shop.'

'How do you know this, Mother?' Julian cried out. Leonie tried to ignore the pain in his voice.

'Betsy Campbell told me. I saw her at a lunch party last week. She often stays with her sister who lives in Scotland near them. It's the talk of Inverness.'

'Why hasn't Tony told us, *if* it's true? Anyway, I'm sure she wouldn't leave the children,' Leonie said, though she remembered with disquiet Julian's tortured account of Clemmy not loving Tony any more.

'He's hoping she'll come back, fool that he is. Though of course his trump card is his money. Shouldn't think this writer has any – they don't, do they?' she said dismissively, as if money were the only thing Clemmy was interested in. 'It may be just a fling, but he should have expected that, taking a young woman up there, living in the wilds, miles away from everything. I suppose he thought he could hide her from other men,' Anita went on, her long fingers passing the needle in and out of her tapestry as if she were inflicting pain on someone and enjoying it.

Julian looked pale, his mouth drawn in with tension.

Philip said, 'I don't think we should discuss it until we know for sure. These stories often get exaggerated.'

Julian got up from the sofa looking agitated. 'I must ring my father. Come on, Leonie, fetch Eleanor.'

'There is a telephone here, you know,' Anita said sarcastically.

'I'd rather ring from home,' Julian answered her distractedly.

Anita gave him a long look. 'Don't start overreacting,' she said. 'Surely you knew it was bound to fail? She was one of your girlfriends, after all, and you know how restless she was. It amazes me that they stayed together for so long.'

Leonie ran downstairs to the garden to fetch Eleanor. When she came back in, Philip was in the hall. He came close to her and said in a quiet voice, 'Don't let her upset you. There may be no truth in it.'

'Poor Tony, he's devoted to her. Poor little boys, but you don't think it's Julian she's after really, do you?' She glanced quickly at Eleanor, who was playing hopscotch on the squares of the carpet.

'No, Anita was certain it was someone up there. It may blow over. Don't panic until you have to.' He smiled, kissed her cheek, resting his hand on her shoulder a moment. ''Bye.'

''Bye, Philip.'

''Bye, Eleanor.'

''Bye.' She didn't stop her hopping.

As he left, shutting the front door firmly behind him, Leonie felt utterly alone. She could still feel the gentle weight of his hand on her shoulder, and she wished she could have gone with him to escape the evening ahead with Julian sunk in deep depression over this news.

He came down the stairs and picked up his coat without speaking to her. She took Eleanor's hand and they followed him out to the car, Eleanor hopping first on one leg and then on the other. Leonie envied her her cheerful innocence.

'I do wish your mother didn't always find something to upset you,' she said sharply as they drove towards Putney.

His mouth clenched and she saw a tic twitch in his cheek.

'I don't know how she knows all the dramas before anyone else does. I mean, if it's not true, it's a pretty awful thing to say.' Her voice rose, transferring her anger at Anita on to him, for yet again disturbing the precarious harmony between them.

'I don't want to talk about it.' He kept his eyes straight ahead, even though they had stopped at the traffic lights.

'What don't you want to talk about?' Eleanor picked up his words.

'None of your business, and Eleanor . . .' his voice had an edge to it, 'you are not to scream at your grandmother's house. There will be no more television today.'

Eleanor, who didn't know if she wanted any more television that day or not, started to scream at the tone of his voice.

'Shut up!' he shouted. 'Mother's right, you are far too spoilt.'

'Don't you dare take it out on her,' Leonie hissed, feeling Eleanor grab her hand and pull her arm almost out of its socket towards her at the back of the car.

'I will not have this screaming,' he said, moving over to the curb. 'Eleanor, if you don't stop at once, I shall smack you. I can't drive with this noise.'

Eleanor gulped, sniffed and stopped. They drove on in silence, Leonie hating him, but remembering with guilt how she had lost her temper and smacked Eleanor herself, the night Melanie had come. She did not want to think that perhaps it was true that Eleanor was spoilt. After all Melanie had said the same thing. If only they could have another child. It was difficult for Eleanor being the only one, especially as they both doted on her so.

Once home, Julian shut himself in his study in the small room at the top of the house to call his father. Leonie bathed Eleanor and then read to her. She heard the door of the study open, and Julian come out and go downstairs. She finished the book, tucked Eleanor up and said good night.

'It's true,' he said, slumped in a chair in the drawing room, his head in his hands.

He looked so dejected and miserable that she put her arm round his shoulders.

'What exactly happened?'

He sighed. 'It's a local writer, a Scotsman, her age. She's having an affair with him, but she doesn't want to lose the boys.'

'Poor Tony. How is he taking it?'

'Pretty cut up, but . . . well, he sort of expected it. He's being quite noble at the moment, rather hopes it will blow over, that they can reach some sort of compromise in their marriage.'

'Then there'll be another affair. She doesn't seem the faithful type,' Leonie said darkly.

'Nonsense, Leonie. You make her sound dreadful,' he retorted.

'I think she is,' Leonie said, taking her arm from him and walking away. 'She knew Tony was older, saw how much he loved her, got herself pregnant by him so that he married her even though he had the sense to know it would be foolish. She ought to make some effort, for the children's sake, anyway.' She was thinking of her own effort, thinking of how easily Clemmy had gone to Julian. Or had it been he going to her?

'You just don't understand,' he said petulantly.

'And I don't want to,' she said. 'Relationships are hard work. It's one thing if two adults can't make it work between them, but quite another when children are involved,' she said pointedly, leaving the room to go into the kitchen to sort out her business accounts and shopping lists for the morning. She was afraid he would start on again about the time he and Clemmy 'comforted' each other in bed, beg her to understand him and forgive him. She was trying so hard to make their marriage work, to give Eleanor emotional stability, she had no sympathy at all for people who comforted each other with other people's spouses.

★ ★ ★

181

Working with Caroline in the kitchen of a merchant bank the following day, Leonie said wearily, 'I feel that everything in my life is slowly coming unstuck.'

'I hope not you and Julian?' Caroline looked up from smoothing sugar over the surface of a *crème brûlée*.

'Nooo,' she said with a long sigh, 'but Philip's had enough of Anita, though I think he's a saint to have stayed with her so long. Clemmy and Tony are in trouble too. She's gone off with a young writer, and you know Mel's broken up with Jason.'

'Oh Leo, I am sorry,' Caroline said sympathetically. 'What a nightmare it all sounds. But as long as you and Julian are all right.'

Before Leonie could answer the door opened and James Myers, one of the directors, lurched in.

'How are you girls doing?' he said. He was a pleasant-looking, solid man, running to fat. He always came into the kitchen quite a few times in the mornings they cooked, to chat them up. Leonie did not much like him. She knew he had a drink problem and because of it his wife had left him.

'Fine,' she said, trying to appear too busy to become involved with him.

'Oooh, my favourite pudding,' he went up to Caroline and put his arm round her sturdy waist.

Leonie winced, but saw that Caroline was blushing, simpering delightedly. 'Good,' she said, 'I'll see that you get a double helping.'

'You're a darling,' he said, making her look even more delighted.

When he'd gone Leonie said, 'He is a bit much, coming in all the time like that. Do you mind him mauling you, Caro?'

Caroline blushed even deeper. 'He's not as bad as he seems. He's very nice really.'

Leonie looked at her in surprise. 'Caro, don't tell me you fancy him? I mean, not him of all people. You know he drinks – God knows how he's kept his job. His wife couldn't cope.'

'He's very lonely, under all that . . . that heartiness. His wife has even taken his children away, you know. They live with her in Ireland and he hardly ever sees them.'

'How do you know all this? Have you been out with him?'

Caroline looked defiantly embarrassed. 'Twice actually. I like him.'

She slipped the *crème brûlée* under the grill, watching it carefully.

'Don't get hurt, Caro.' Leonie felt a surge of protectiveness for her. Having not had any boyfriends, Caroline, she felt, was awfully naïve.

Caroline checked the *crème brûlée*, seeing the sugar darken and melt in little puddles over the cream. She pushed it under the grill for another few seconds. 'You thought you had the perfect man,' she said gently, 'and look how much hurt you've had. You know we all have faults, no one is perfect.'

'I know, but I didn't realise marriage to Julian would be so complex. If it hadn't been for his mother—'

'And his stepmother.'

Leonie had confided an awful lot to Caroline over the years. Caroline, unlike some of Leonie's other friends, did not gossip.

'I agree. But, Caro, don't you see, relationships are hard enough without taking on a man who's virtually an alcoholic?'

'Maybe I can cure him,' Caroline said, removing the *crème brûlée* and putting it on to the side to cool. 'He said his wife didn't understand him.'

'Where have I heard that before?' Leonie said darkly. 'Caro, do be careful. I'd hate to see you hurt.'

'I'm prepared to take a chance. You don't know how much I want to be like you, like Jessica, Sophie, and all the others, with a husband, home and family,' Caroline burst out suddenly, her face going quite pink. 'I know I'm fortunate in lots of ways, with my job and no money worries. I have a lovely flat of my own, but unless I make an effort to invite someone round, I'm alone most evenings. I know you and the others are kind, asking me to supper, but I want someone of my own. I think I could save him, make him happy.' Her poignant eagerness smote Leonie deeply, making the tears jump to her eyes. She'd never realised before quite how lonely Caroline was.

Why did women like Anita and Clemmy have all these men swarming over them while such good and loving people like Caroline had no one? Now Caroline had at last found her star, however precarious it was, and was pinning her hopes on it.

'I'm sure you will make him happy, Caro,' Leonie said, instead of warning her off him any further. 'He's very lucky to have found you.'

She hoped fervently that Caroline would not become part of yet
another couple falling apart.

A week later Tony rang. He spoke to Leonie, as Julian was not back
from work.

'Clemmy's come back,' he said wearily. 'We're going away together
to try to patch things up.'

'I suppose the boys are at school?'

'Yes, they'll be fine. We've got various friends on stand-by should
there be a drama. I just wanted to give you our number in case you
should need us.'

She wrote it down. 'I don't know what to say, Tony . . . I wish you
luck,' she said gently, wondering how many more patchings-up there
would be before Clemmy left him for good.

He sighed. 'I don't think she knows what she wants. When she
married me she was in a bad way, had been hurt dreadfully by some
young chap. Now that her confidence is back . . .' He trailed off,
leaving a painful silence. Before Leonie could think how to fill it, he
continued, 'I've always known that I was far too old for her, though
she swore she could handle it. But we have the boys to consider, we
can't hurt them.'

'No one is perfect for anyone. One must just hang on to the good
things, not try to change the things that can't be changed.'

'It's easier said than done, Leonie,' Tony said gently. 'Goodbye, lots
of love.' He put down the phone, leaving her feeling sad and helpless
for his suffering.

Julian came through the front door almost immediately and she
turned on him angrily. 'Clemmy's come back . . . for the moment.
They are going away together for a holiday. Really, that girl doesn't
know how lucky she is with someone as kind and understanding as
your father.'

Julian looked at her sharply. 'I'll ring him,' he said making for his
study.

Lost and unsettled, Leonie reminded herself firmly of the advice
she'd so glibly handed out to Tony, about hanging on to the good
things and not changing what could not be changed. She got on with
cooking the dinner, knowing guiltily that Caroline envied her.

Chapter Twenty

After some months of good health, Anita's cancer flared up again. There was another operation, she seemed to be recovering from it, then she suffered a relapse. Early one morning Janet called Julian and told him that he must come at once as the doctor thought his mother had not long to live.

Leonie had just come back from dropping Eleanor at school and she found Julian, ashen-faced, about to leave the house.

'Mother is . . . worse.' He was hardly able to form the words.

'I'll come with you,' she said, guiding him to the car and starting towards Kensington. He barely spoke on the journey, sitting so still as if he were afraid he would shatter into pieces.

Leonie wished she could offer some magic words of comfort which would unlock this rigid, terrified figure, but not knowing what to say, and afraid that whatever she did say would be misconstrued, she stayed silent.

When they arrived he said, 'Don't come up to her room, but wait for me, please, darling. Are you working today?'

'No, and Eleanor's going home with Mandy. Of course I'll wait.' She pressed his arm, laying her head a moment against his shoulder. Distractedly he stroked her hair, then went upstairs like a man going to his execution.

'Call me if you need me,' she called after him, but he did not turn back.

The day drifted on with no news. It was very hot. Leonie could hear the hum of distant traffic. A fly trapped in the shutters buzzed exhaustedly, making her feel tired in sympathy. She got up, walked over to the window, peeled back the shutter, kept closed on sunny

185

days to stop the sun fading the rich fabrics in the room. She looked down on to the street, quiet and still in the heat. She could almost feel the tiredness of the trees, their leaves heavy and limp. She wished she could lighten her feelings, feel that life was still going on elsewhere.

The very sombreness, the feeling of approaching death, frightened her – alone in this half-shuttered room, waiting as if for a predator coming to snatch her away, as indeed it would snatch them all away one day. Yet, Leonie knew, it was the only way they would be free of Anita, the only way she and Julian could get back together as they had once been.

She glanced at her watch: three o'clock. In half an hour Eleanor would come out of school. She stayed all day twice a week now, so as to get used to 'proper' school later on.

She wished that Eleanor were not going home with Mandy today, and that she could be outside the school, waiting for her. On the afternoons that she picked her up, she felt a warm contentment, eager to catch the first glimpse of that shining face, to kiss that pudgy cheek and feel her warm hand curl into hers. Listen to her chattering of the doings of her day.

It was a time Leonie loved, the moment she felt complete again with Eleanor's busy little body skipping down the road beside her.

A shaft of sunlight enclosing dancing specs of dust made her suddenly want to leave this dark and gloomy house and go outside, to be with people hurrying down the streets, pushing prams, leading dogs, going to shops, to friends, not sitting there, waiting for death to come and take Anita.

A taxi ticked by, stopping outside. Diana got out of it. She glanced fearfully up at the house as if she expected to see Anita's spirit fly out of a window and engulf her. Leonie sighed – another person to support in this moment of crisis. She'd need all her tact and understanding as Anita's death was something she herself tentatively welcomed.

She ran down to let Diana in, at least pleased to have something to do.

'Oh Leonie . . . how . . .?' Diana's voice petered out as if she couldn't bear to ask the question whose answer either way would devastate her.

'I don't know. Julian is with her. I haven't heard anything for some hours. But you look marvellous,' she smiled at her, thinking how pretty Diana looked, even though there were signs of strain on her face. 'France must suit you.'

Diana blushed, appeared to be on the verge of a confidence, then said nervously, 'I . . . I'd better go up.' She ground her hands together, her whole body stiff with tension.

It wasn't the proximity of death that terrified her, Leonie knew, but seeing her mother. Death would release them from her power. It was the only way she and Julian – all of them – would escape.

'Do you want some tea or something?' Leonie said, wondering how Diana would cope when Anita died.

'I'd better go up,' Diana said again as if the words were fuel to move her trembling legs.

'Ask Julian if he needs anything,' Leonie said, wanting him to remember that she still existed. She followed Diana upstairs, stopping off at the shuttered drawing room. She was sure he would not want anything. Anita alive or dying would keep hold of him. She wondered suddenly with a cold shudder if her death would release or destroy him.

A little later Janet came in.

'She's still with us,' she said quickly.

'Oh . . . and Julian . . . shall I . . .?'

'Julian told me to tell you to go home. There's nothing you can do here,' she said gently. 'He'll stay with her and he has Diana with him now. He thinks you should be at home with Eleanor.'

'OK, I'll go.' Although the last thing she wanted was to lurk round Anita's deathbed, Leonie felt hurt that Julian had asked her to go, and through Janet, that he had not even bothered to come down to tell her himself. She felt, as so often before, like an outsider.

There was the sound of the front door opening and Janet said, 'I expect that's Philip. I'll go and see.'

Leonie followed her downstairs. Philip was taking his key from the lock, about to close the door.

'There's been no change. She's still with us,' Janet told him in a reverent voice.

'I see. Good.' He looked into the hall and saw Leonie. 'Oh Leonie, hello. Have you been here all day?'

'Yes, I'm about to go home. Julian said I should.' She stood there awkwardly on the stairs.

Philip said to Janet, 'Shall I go up to her, or is it better to leave her?'

'I think it's better if just Julian and Diana are with her at present. There's a nurse too, and the doctor's coming back.'

'Diana's back, then?'

'Yes, she flew over today,' Janet said.

'Well, I'll go then. You can reach me at my flat, or on my mobile, if you should need me.' He looked relieved, Leonie thought. He retrieved his key and turned to go. Then he stopped and came back.

'Do you want a lift anywhere, Leonie? I've got the car here.'

'Oh yes, that would be kind. Then I can leave mine for Julian.' She came out on to the front step with him. The air was warm, the sun more golden with the dying day, touching the trees with light, making them glow. She felt a little spark of euphoria, as if she were free, had been let out of captivity.

'Please, Janet, tell Julian I'll be at home in a couple of hours or so. I've got to pick up Eleanor from a friend's first. I'll leave him the car.'

'I'll tell him.' Janet smiled a stiff, brave smile and closed the door on them.

'Was it hell?' Philip said as they drove down Kensington Church Street, past St Mary Abbots, where a wedding was spilling out through the arched entrance.

'I was alone all day, not wanted in the sickroom. Not that I minded, I wouldn't be much good in there . . .' Her voice petered out, not wanting to mention the hurt she felt at Julian shutting her out of his anxiety and grief.

'I hate sickness, death. But I had to show up. You never know with Anita if she is breathing her last, or if it's just a huge dramatic cry for attention,' he said wearily.

'She might well die this time. She seems to have developed an allergy to the treatments.'

'I know, poor thing. It is so dreadful for her. She's fought so hard, but she might pull through yet.'

'If she doesn't you'll be free.' She looked at him, at his hands, relaxed on the steering wheel.

'So will you.'

'I hope Julian will be free . . . free as he was in Florence.'

They passed the park and the imposing statue of Robert Napier on his horse and went down Queen's Gate. Philip slowed the car. 'Let's go and have some tea,' he said, 'have you time?'

She glanced at the clock on the dashboard. 'Yes . . . thanks, I'd like that.'

'Good. Do you want to go somewhere, or come to my flat? I've got a delicious fruit cake in a tin, sent from America, and I've been longing for an excuse to open it,' he smiled at her.

'That sounds great. I've hardly had anything to eat all day.'

His flat was close to Sloane Square in one of the large comfortable red-brick blocks that spoke of respectable luxury. He parked the car in the residents' parking place and they went inside and up in the lift to the top floor. She had never been to his flat before and when he opened the door she was confronted by the slim, elfin figure of a naked girl.

He laughed. 'I love this sculpture, all youth and hope.' He led her into the drawing room, a large room, sparsely furnished, but each piece expensive and well designed, the view the skyline of London. Everything was clean-cut, the *objets* made of glass, the furnishings pale blue and sand-coloured silks, various other sculptures standing around. There was a modern bookcase of suspended shelves, filled with books. The place, with its rooftop view, had a feeling of space, of light, of being part of the sky.

'Quite different to Anita's taste,' he said, following her eyes.

'Yes . . . it's wonderful. Uncluttered. I long for that, but then I'm a cluttered person, collect things as I go.'

'You have to be ruthless, selective. Now tea, or coffee? I have good vintages of both.'

They sat drinking a very delicate china tea in white, translucent bone china cups, and eating huge slabs of his sticky, American cake. They talked easily of this and that and Leonie thought how nice he was, how wasted on Anita.

She said at last, 'Do you think Anita will ever get better?'

'No. She didn't go to the doctor soon enough, for a start, and she's not responding well to the treatments. She might hang on another year or two . . . you never do know with cancer. It can lie low for a while, for quite a long while if you're lucky.'

'So what will you do when she's gone?'

He shrugged. 'I'll be fine. You may have noticed I've been away a lot these last few months. But I'd like to keep in touch with you . . . and Julian and Diana.' He added their names almost as an afterthought.

'I hope you will. I wonder what Diana will do.'

'I wonder what Julian will do,' he said, looking at her intently.

'What do you mean?' she said, afraid that he knew something she did not, that with his mother's death he would leave her.

He smiled. 'Don't look so anxious. I just meant I wonder how he will react to being without her. She's been such a strong force in his life. Everything he's done, he's done in the hopes of gaining her affection, though, poor chap, he has never realised Anita is unable to give love.'

'Not even to you?'

He laughed. 'Especially not me, though she was attracted to me, as I was once to her. But when she does go, it may be the saving of Julian, make him live his life for himself – for you and Eleanor.'

'I do hope so,' Leonie said with fervour. 'In Florence we were so happy together, but I didn't know about Anita. When we first fall in love, we think we can survive anything. We don't realise that it's not the big things that kill it, but the drip, drip of small things that erode us beyond repair.'

'Oh Leonie, what are you saying?'

'I just . . . I just don't know how much of our love for each other is left. Sometimes it's there and sometimes . . .' she paused, 'I feel it's gone. We're just together like a habit, hard to give up.'

He didn't say anything, leant back in his chair, and watched her gently, quietly as if his silence would be healing.

She said suddenly, 'He adores Eleanor – of course we both do. I often feel it is she that keeps us together. If we could have had more children, lots of them, he would have been so caught up in them, he might have stayed with us more. Not kept going to his mother . . . to Clemmy.'

'Is there a reason why you haven't more children?' His voice was very quiet.

'I don't know. My gynaecologist thinks I'm all right. He says that Julian should have a sperm test, but I haven't liked to suggest it. He said also that sometimes men and women are perfectly healthy but the woman's body rejects the man's sperm. I may be doing that. Julian would take it as a further rejection of him if that was found to be true.' She smiled bitterly. 'I keep putting off having the problem investigated properly. I'm so afraid of what the doctor might find, of how it would affect Julian . . . affect us. After all, we achieved Eleanor; next month I may be pregnant again.'

Philip said, 'But if you do reject his sperm, or he has a low count, it's hardly the fault of either of you. I mean, it's like saying you have a different blood group or short-sightedness.' He cut her another slice of cake, got up and put it on the table beside her.

'I know, but . . .' She shrugged, then made herself smile brightly. She did not want to bore him with these intimate details, and changed the subject.

'My great friend and partner, Caroline Smythe, is about to marry an alcoholic. She's been carrying about a load of love all her life, waiting to deposit it on someone. She adores him. I don't know if she's mad or a saint.'

'She may reform him.'

'But it means my job might finish. He wants to live in Wiltshire, and she's longing to be a housewife. But still,' she smiled bravely, 'the recession hasn't been too good for us. Directors often have sandwich lunches now.'

The telephone rang. Philip stiffened, then got up to answer it.

'Janet . . . yes.' He listened intently and Leonie saw his body slump, heard the effort he put into his voice.

'All right. Yes, I'll be round. Fine. See you in a while.'

Anita's dead, Leonie thought, feeling a lurch that the news of death brings with its terrible finality. She half rose. She'd have to go with him to be with Julian. How would he take it? How would she cope with his grief? Thoughts whirled into her brain. Should she ring Ruth, Mandy's mother, to ask if she would keep Eleanor overnight?

Then Philip put down the receiver and turned to her.

191

'Anita seems to have perked up,' he said levelly. 'She wants me to go round.'

'Oh . . .' Leonie, expecting Anita to be dead, didn't know what to say or how to react. She looked at Philip and caught his agonised eyes. We're still trapped, they seemed to be saying, still trapped.

Leonie didn't know how it happened, who made what move, but suddenly she was in his arms and they were clinging together like lost souls. Their lips were together, drawing on each other in a mutual feeling of desperation. She felt him lift her, carry her to the sofa and he was making love to her and she was responding with a sort of helpless franticness as if they were lovers saying goodbye for ever, trying to get as much of each other as they could before they were torn apart – as if, having brushed with death, they were snatching greedily at life.

At last they fell back, spent. She lay under him, her body beginning to ache from his weight.

'I must go,' she said at last.

He opened his eyes, leant up on his elbows and looked down at her. 'What have we done?' His voice was gentle.

She sighed, not wanting suddenly to leave this intimacy, the scent of him, the warmth of his skin against hers.

'Perhaps it was just a reaction to the news.' She didn't want him to blame himself.

'I think this has been waiting to happen.' He got slowly off her and began to get dressed. 'Don't let this ruin your marriage, Leonie. Let's keep it to ourselves as just . . .' he smiled, bent quickly and kissed her, 'just a lovely aberration.'

She felt sad, wishing he would take her in his arms again, but she knew he spoke the truth. Her marriage must last for Eleanor's sake. This act had nothing to do with it. It was just a release of tension. She did love Julian, she told herself firmly, and if only Anita would let him go free, they would be happy again. She was sure of that. Wasn't she?

She went to the bathroom, washed and dressed herself. When she looked in the mirror her face was shining, there was a bruised look about her lips like overripe fruits. Her whole body felt alive, vibrant with life.

She could not go to Julian now, with this glow of Philip's lovemaking on her, she thought wildly. He would notice at once, or would he? Would he still be only thinking of Anita? She came out of the bathroom and Philip was standing by the window, waiting for her.

'Ready?' he smiled.

'I don't think I'll come with you. I'll just go and fetch Eleanor.'

'As you want. Where is she? I'll drop you.'

'No, she's on my way home in Fulham. You get on to Anita.' She forced herself to appear relaxed, keeping her eyes firmly away from the sofa where minutes before they had been entwined in lovemaking. Though in the brief second she'd glanced that way she saw that the cushions were taut and plump again, leaving no clue to her and Philip's passion.

The truth was she wanted him again, wanted him to make love to her slowly, without the pressure of time, without the thought of the other people in their lives. She wanted to take away the pain in the back of his eyes. She wanted to love him.

'If you're sure? I'll drop you at Sloane Square. Then you have the choice of the tube or bus.' He picked up the tea things and took them into the kitchen, behaving now as if she were just a friend who had popped in for tea.

'No. I'll walk. It's such a lovely evening and I've been cooped in all day,' she said, forcing herself to match his mood.

In the lift they stood in opposite corners and he asked her about Eleanor, but she knew he was just using the words as protection against becoming close to her again. They parted on the steps. He slipped his hand under her elbow.

'Goodbye, Leonie.' His voice was gentle and she saw that his eyes held her with a kind of desperation.

'Philip . . .' She moved closer to him, not wanting to leave him. She saw a steely firmness come over his face. He gave her a tight smile.

'Goodbye,' he said, and walked away, leaving her without turning back.

Chapter Twenty-One

Leonie discovered she was pregnant on Caroline's wedding day. She had pretended not to notice the first symptoms, but standing in a queue at her local chemist that morning, her eyes had homed in on the shelf displaying the pregnancy testing kits and almost robotically she had put one in her basket. Once home she found it impossible not to try it.

A pink dot stared up at her from the card. It was positive.

She stayed in the bathroom, sitting on the edge of the bath, weak with shock. If only she hadn't done the test today, when she was looking forward to the wedding and seeing lots of her old friends. This knowledge had ruined her day, ruined her life, probably all their lives, she thought desperately, waves of panic gripping at her stomach.

Julian had made love to her quite a few times in the last month, quickly, with a sort of desperation, as if the act would help him forget his mother's ravaging illness.

But sitting there, hearing Eleanor singing to herself as she played next door in her bedroom, Leonie was certain that the child was Philip's. She felt half pleased and half terrified at the enormity of what she'd done, what they'd both done, and how nature had had the last laugh on them.

What made it worse was that she couldn't even tell Philip. Two weeks ago he had announced he had to go to South America to help start up a new bank there. Leonie had not seen him since that afternoon they'd made love, but she had heard through Julian and Diana that his firm needed someone of his experience, so he had been sent there for however long it took to have the bank up and running.

Anita was furious. 'If he's the only person with experience I don't think much of his firm,' she said one afternoon when they were visiting. 'Here am I dying and he deserts me.'

'He hasn't deserted you, Mummy, and he telephones you every day,' Diana said.

Leonie felt angry with him too for running away from them all. Half her anger, she knew, was caused by envy that he could escape this increasingly intolerable situation. Anita, she thought with a hint of guilt at her unkindness, was rather like a sinking ship, determined to pull everyone down into the sea with her. She was facing her death with fury, not fear.

'Leonie, are you all right?' Julian banged on the bathroom door. 'We should be having lunch soon if you've got to dress Eleanor.'

'I'm coming,' she started guiltily, thrusting the pregnancy test to the back of the cupboard. Her mind spun again with all the things she had to do before they left for the church. The thought of abortion whirled in with everything else. If she could get rid of the baby before anyone knew about it, it would solve everything. The thought hovered for a moment, then she dismissed it. She could never live with that. She cared for both men, she could not kill the child of either.

She dressed Eleanor in her white bridesmaid's dress, tying the yellow silk sash in a huge bow on the side of her plump tummy. Caroline and James were having a blessing, he being divorced, and Caroline wanted it as near 'the real thing', as she called it, as possible. She had chosen a conventional wedding dress, white with a long train and a flowing veil, and her numerous godchildren were to be pages and bridesmaids.

'I'd have liked to have included his children,' she told Leonie, 'only his ex-wife has made some excuse to keep them with her in Ireland. It's a great pity as I've never even met them yet.'

To her surprise, as recently he seemed to think only of his job and his mother, Julian noticed Leonie's preoccupied mood.

'She'll be fine,' he said, thinking she was worrying about Caroline marrying an alcoholic. 'She looks lovely and so radiant. It's just sad about your job going with her moving to the country, but I'm sure you could find someone else to team up with.'

'I don't think so,' Leonie said, knowing that *if* she was having another child – she had now half-kidded herself that perhaps the pregnancy test was faulty, and that it might be advisable to do another one – it would make working very difficult. Eleanor had a full life of activities after school, and coping with a baby as well would take up enormous amounts of Leonie's time and energy.

Besides, their business was dwindling anyway. The recession, coupled with Marks and Spencer's ready meals, which more people were using instead of getting Caroline and Leonie to cook their dinner parties and office lunches, would make it difficult to find enough work to pay for a good nanny.

At the reception, held at the Hyde Park Hotel, Leonie laughed and talked with old friends. But she felt sick as she drank the champagne, and all the time the knowledge of her pregnancy tortured her.

It was like a ghastly joke, she thought. Here we are at a wedding, with me pregnant with my mother-in-law's lover's child. There could not be a more dreadful scenario, especially as the mother-in-law was Anita.

'I'm going to change now. Come up with me?' Caroline said, and Leonie followed her upstairs.

The room was full of other girl friends, mostly from school. They lay on the bed or sprawled on the chairs and window seat, all giggling and chattering just as if they were still fourteen and in the dorm. There was a feeling of excitement and warmth. They had all performed their best, looked their best and could now be themselves, relax with abandon.

'Have another drink.' Sophie poured out some champagne from a bottle that stood by the window.

'I've hardly had any,' Caroline said, pulling off her veil and taking a glass. 'Ow, those pins hurt.' She rubbed her head where the small diamond tiara had been pinned in place.

'It looked marvellous – you looked marvellous,' Jessica said, picking up the tiara and inspecting it. 'Some diamonds! Is this yours?'

'Sort of. It was my grandmother's. The insurance was horrendous to take it out today, and I'm meant to lock it in the safe the minute I take it off, but I'll put it back in its bag. No one will know.'

'I'll do it,' Leonie said, feeling apart from this merry throng. She carefully extracted the tiara from the veil, wrapped it in tissue paper and put it in the brown paper bag Caroline gave her.

'Mummy will put it in that Harrods shopping bag she has, put her cardigan, tapestry and whatever on top and no one will ever know she's carrying it,' Caroline said, standing still while willing hands undid the long row of tiny buttons running down the back of her dress.

'So where are you going tonight?' Camilla asked, with a laugh in her voice and a wicked twinkle in her eye. She was the schoolfriend they all talked about with delighted shock, as she'd had numerous love affairs since losing her virginity at sixteen to a young man the other girls had longed for but didn't dare speak to.

Caroline blushed. 'Well . . . it's a secret really,' she said happily.

'Tell us. We won't spoil it,' Becky, who was on her second husband, begged her.

'I don't really know about tonight – some hotel in the country – but we're flying to the Seychelles tomorrow.'

'Great! Oh for another honeymoon . . . without being pregnant,' Jessica said. 'I felt so sick on mine.'

'Serves you right for jumping the gun, not waiting like a good Catholic girl should until she's married,' Sophie laughed.

'Surely we all jumped the gun, I just got caught,' Jessica retorted.

Caught, that's me, Leonie thought bitterly. She felt a sudden closeness to these old friends, laughing and fooling with the easy camaraderie they'd shared as children. She yearned now for those days to return when their only worries had been spots, fat thighs, boys and exams. How little they had known about life then.

She longed suddenly to tell them of her dilemma, longed for the strength, the warmth of their sympathy, their advice, even if it would be tempered with shocked delight. But before she could form the words, there was a knock on the door.

Thinking it was James, the girls screamed, 'Don't come in, she's starkers.'

'It doesn't matter now she's married.'

Jessica went to the door while Caroline struggled into her going away suit. It was her mother.

'Only me, darling. How nice that looks, such a lovely blue. Now where's the . . . you know . . .' she said pointedly at Caroline as if the room were thick with thieves waiting to snatch the tiara.

'Leonie's got it.'

'Thank you, dear.' Mrs Smythe took the brown paper bag from Leonie and stuffed it, as Caroline said she would, into her Harrods shopping bag. 'You looked so lovely, darling. Everything all right?' Her smile was too bright.

'Fine, thanks, Mummy.'

There was an emotional moment when it looked as if both Caroline and her mother would burst into tears. Camilla saved it by saying, 'Don't forget to throw me your bouquet. I could do with a husband.' The laughter broke the tension. Caroline finished dressing and then James, rather pink in the face, knocked loudly on the door, saying, 'Is my wife in there?' which made Caroline blush even more.

'Be happy.' Leonie kissed Caroline goodbye, hugging her tightly to her for a moment. She found she was nearly crying herself.

'I will,' Caroline said, flushed with happiness.

James looked rather drunk already. He gallantly took Caroline's arm and wove his way out of the hotel to the waiting car, trying to dodge the confetti.

After waving them away, the cosy group of girls dispersed back to their own lives, with screams of 'We simply *must* meet soon,' and hugs and kisses all round. Leonie felt suddenly depressed. So many wedding days start with such hope, she thought, praying that Caroline would not be disappointed with her own dream of marriage.

Zinnia came up to her. 'I'm so glad she's married at last. She's such a sweet girl,' she said, as if marriage were the final accolade.

'But to an alcoholic, Ma.'

Zinnia squeezed her arm. 'She'll make a go of it, see if she won't. You don't look well, darling. Is it this Anita business? It is horrid when an illness drags out like this.'

'I'm pregnant.' The words shot out before she could stop them.

'Oh my darling, I'm so pleased.' She hugged her. 'I was beginning to wonder if Eleanor were to be an only child – and our *only* grandchild, by the look of the others, Melanie having broken up with

199

Jason, and Harry with such anorexic girlfriends they're sure never to be able to bear children. When will it be born?'

Her joy almost made Leonie weep. Zinnia seeing this said anxiously: 'Everything's all right, isn't it, darling? Julian is pleased? It will take his mind off his mother.'

'He doesn't know.'

'Why ever not, Leonie?' Zinnia looked bewildered. George came up to them and she shooed him away, saying impatiently: 'Just a minute, dear. I'm having a quiet word with Leonie.'

Leonie knew now she had to make a quick decision. Either she told her mother straight away about Philip, or she said nothing and let everyone assume that the child was Julian's, which it could possibly be.

Since that afternoon they'd made love, she'd thought constantly of Philip. She longed to ring him, just to hear his voice, but she knew that if she did, she would go with him – if he asked her – abandon Julian and Anita, and Tony and Clemmy, let them all work out their lives together. Only Eleanor would she take with her. But of course she wouldn't whisk Eleanor off to South America, tear her away from her secure life.

But would Philip want her? One frenzied act of lovemaking, taken in a moment of extreme stress, did not mean undying love. Also Philip was, in reality, still looking for his dead wife. She did not think she could bear to share a man with another woman again. Mother or dead wife, these women had spun a web around these men, making it impossible for them ever to commit themselves deeply to another woman. Even after they had gone, their power remained behind like invisible chains, tight round their emotions.

'I only found out I was pregnant this morning, when I did one of those tests,' she said to her mother. 'I haven't had time to tell Julian. It's just come as rather a shock.' She forced a smile.

'But you wanted another baby, surely? If you don't mind my saying so, darling, you have left quite a big gap between this one and Eleanor.'

Leonie knew better than to tell her that that was unintentional.

'So it's just as well your job has folded and you can take things easy. You'll have quite a time juggling Eleanor and a new baby, you know. She's been used to being the only one for so long,' Zinnia went on.

'I know, Ma.' Leonie felt weary. Once everyone knew of her pregnancy they would smother her with advice.

Melanie, looking rather strained in a beige suit and pale pink hat, joined them. 'What are you two gossiping about?' she said.

'The wedding. Caroline looked wonderful, didn't she?' Leonie said quickly.

'It was all right as weddings go,' Melanie said. 'No doubt it will soon fade from the memory like all the others. Only if something goes wrong – the bride doesn't turn up, or someone denounces them – would one remember one wedding from another.'

'Now, darling, you remember Leonie and Julian's,' Zinnia said, taking her arm. 'That's such a pretty suit, expensive too. Is it new?'

Leonie knew she was saying this to take Melanie's mind off being alone again, and not having a wedding of her own to look forward to. She saw that Melanie realised this too.

'Very expensive, Ma, but as I seem to have been asked to so many weddings lately I thought I'd buy one marvellous suit and be done with it. The hat is expensive too,' Melanie spoke in a flat, rather hard voice that Leonie had noticed she used since Jason had left her. But at work she'd got her promotion and was winging her way up the ladder with a calm detachment Leonie found disturbing.

'I must be going now,' Melanie said, kissing Zinnia and Leonie goodbye. 'At least Caroline doesn't have any in-laws,' she said, smiling at Leonie. 'Yours still alive, Leo?'

'You know she is,' Leonie said in a low voice, seeing Julian with Eleanor skipping beside him, her wreath of flowers over one ear, coming towards them.

'I thought her death was imminent,' Melanie whispered, seeing them coming too. 'I must say, I did rather fancy her boyfriend. Is he still around?'

Her remark caught Leonie off guard and she blushed, struggled desperately for something to say. Melanie laughed. 'Don't tell me you fancy him too?'

'Whom do you fancy?' Julian said, reaching them.

'Oh, no one,' Leonie said quickly, 'just one of Melanie's jokes.' She bent down to straighten Eleanor's wreath, but Eleanor whipped it off and threw it like a boomerang into the crowd of guests dispersing into Knightsbridge.

Later that evening, after a scrap dinner, Leonie rehearsed silently to herself ways to tell Julian about the baby. She was feeling very tired and had a headache, but she knew she must tell him before he heard it from anyone else.

'I . . . I think I'm . . . *we* are having a baby.' She sat in the shadows of the room so he could not see her face.

'A baby? Are you sure?' He looked up from his newspaper.

'Yes, I did a pregnancy test this morning, it was positive.'

'Why didn't you tell me at once?'

'Oh, the wedding . . . and Eleanor was listening and you know how she goes on about things. She would have told everyone at the wedding, taken the spotlight off Caroline on her big day.' Now the lying starts, she thought guiltily, hating herself now for believing that it might be Philip's child, hating herself for cheating on Julian.

'That's wonderful, darling.' His face lightened as if it had been trussed up by great tension. 'When will it be born?'

'Oh, next April, May. I'm only just pregnant.'

'I'm so glad, darling,' he said as if he couldn't quite believe it. He folded the paper up with exaggerated care, looking at it intently all the time. He said slowly, 'You know, I was scared, silly really, but I was scared I couldn't have children, that Eleanor was just a fluke. Now I know that we must have got our timing wrong. There are only two or three days a month that you can conceive, did you know that?'

'Yes, I did.' She looked at him, thinking, why could we not have talked about this fear of not conceiving a child before, shared our worries together? Both of us have been torturing ourselves with anxiety about it on our own. She did not like to admit that there must be something seriously wrong between them if they couldn't voice their fears to each other.

Over the years she and Julian must have hit the days of ovulation many times. It was strange how he didn't seem to realise that, she thought. But maybe he didn't want to think about it.

'You must take care, darling.' He came over and sat beside her, putting his arm round her and dropping a kiss on her cheek. For a second tears welled up in her, she felt like clinging to him, confessing her guilt, but she knew it would destroy him and she must keep it to herself for the rest of her life.

He must have felt her trembling for he said gently, 'You're tired, it's been a hectic day. It's a good thing in the circumstances that your job has come to an end.'

His tenderness almost made her break her resolve. Instead she forced herself to say, 'Ma said that.'

'Did she?' He frowned. 'How come she knew before you told me?'

'She guessed,' she said quickly, 'mother's intuition.'

'I see. I must tell my mother, it might make her feel better,' he smiled. 'I think I'll go now. She doesn't go to bed for ages. Will you be all right? Shall I tuck you up first, bring you some hot chocolate in bed?' He looked young again, as if the news had loosened the age lines on his features.

'I'll be fine.' Now she felt hurt that he was going to Anita, not staying here with her. But perhaps, she thought, closing her eyes, it was better if he did go. If he were too kind and tender she would find it impossible not to break down, tell him the truth and ruin everything.

When he had gone she was so tired and racked with such conflicting emotions that she did break down and cry. She cried for their marriage, sucked dry by Anita and to some extent by Clemmy. Then she found she was crying for Philip and when she realised this, she clamped her mouth tight shut in case Eleanor should hear her.

She tried to conjure up his face. Did he look so different from Julian that everyone would know at once that the child was his? Philip's hair was very fair and straight, whereas Julian was strikingly dark with wavy hair. Eleanor looked quite like her now, but with Julian's wonderful eyes, though Leonie would never forget that at her moment of birth she had been the image of Anita. Maybe everyone would expect this baby to have those same distinctive eyes.

Panic hit her as she imagined the drama that a baby looking like Philip would cause. Anita would, with her last strength, massacre her, blame her entirely. After all, she had committed the worst sin: carrying Philip's child when Anita herself could not. Even though she was too old for child-bearing, it would be taken as a double insult as she had lost her womb through cancer. Her revenge would be terrible. She would turn Julian completely against her; she might even succeed in having Eleanor taken away from her as well.

This thought made Leonie spring up in terror. Anita had influential friends – could she so blacken her character, so want to hurt her, that she would find a way for Julian to have custody of Eleanor? She thought of Caroline telling her that James's ex-wife would not let him see his children. It was not so difficult to arrange, make conflicting appointments, say they were ill.

Anita must die, Leonie thought suddenly, her thoughts running out of control. If she died before the baby was born Leonie would be safe. Even if Julian guessed, with Anita dead, she doubted he would question the child's paternity. He had admitted that he was afraid he could not father children, with two babies in the nursery, he would feel the family was complete.

'I'll make it up to you, Julian,' she breathed aloud. 'Just let this child be yours, look like you, and I'll put up with anything.'

But for the rest of the evening and most of the night too, she tossed and turned, worrying what to do, wondering whether to confide in her parents, get them ready to help her fight for Eleanor. In the silent house, alone and overwrought, Leonie was aware of her thoughts spiralling into a bizarre nightmare, but she felt helpless to control them. She waited in trepidation for Julian to come back, the knowledge that Anita must die before the child's birth consuming her like a poison.

Chapter Twenty-Two

As the months of Leonie's pregnancy progressed, Julian seemed to become increasingly distanced from her. He spent a lot of time with his mother, and Leonie, feeling guilty because of her lapse with Philip, made little fuss. Melanie couldn't understand it.

'Doesn't he want this baby then?' she demanded, finding Leonie alone on yet another evening, when she came round to return the electric drill she'd borrowed. 'He wasn't here the other night, he's not here now, surely he should be with you, helping with Eleanor. Thank goodness I didn't fall for this marriage game. It's far more exhausting and boring than my job, and you don't get paid.'

'Anita is very ill,' Leonie said lamely, her advanced pregnancy taking much of her usual fire.

'She only lives down the road, and has all that help. Honestly, Leo, I'd make a stand. Shall I tell him that his place should be here with you and Eleanor? It may be easier coming from me.'

'Oh no, Mel. Leave it,' Leonie said alarmed. She wished she could confide in her sister, explain that she didn't want to antagonise Julian and Anita at all, fearing and dreading a far worse battle; explaining away a baby with Philip's blond straight hair.

Melanie looked rather put out at her refusal. 'I think it's extraordinary, a grown man besotted with his mother and cowering so pathetically under her thumb. You're going to have trouble with him when she does die, wait and see,' she said encouragingly, and packing in a few more warnings on how Leonie should cope with her husband, she kissed her and left, congratulating herself loudly on staying single.

But Leonie had far worse things to worry about. The arrival of the baby filled her with fear of a possible catastrophe ahead. It obsessed and worried her, disturbing her sleep, and because she could confide in no one, she allowed her irrational fears to fester and grow, denied a calming voice of reason.

'We won't leave you any longer,' her gynaecologist said as she struggled to her appointment with him. 'Come into hospital on Monday if nothing happens at the weekend.' Then, seeing her face, he said, 'There's nothing worrying you, is there? You do look very tired. Perhaps you should come in sooner for a rest. I assure you I have no concern about your or the baby's health.'

Leonie looked up at his kind, fatherly face and had a sudden urge to confide in him.

'I . . . I feel dreadful saying this, but I don't know if it is my husband's child.'

'I see.' He sat back in his chair and put the tips of his fingers together, looking intently at them, not her. 'Is there a chance that it might be his?'

'Yes, but we've had so much trouble conceiving. As you know, Eleanor took ages and then this one took nearly three years. And the first, the only time, I made love to someone else, I found myself pregnant.'

'Does your husband suspect that it might not be his?'

'No, I'm sure not. It was just an impulse sort of thing . . . with this . . . other person. I haven't seen him since. He's . . .' she blushed now, 'it sounds worse and worse, he's my mother-in-law's lover.'

The doctor lifted his eyebrows, smiled at her. 'I think, my dear, that you are suffering from an overdose of guilt. These things do happen, you'd be surprised at how often. But it seems there is every chance that the child is your husband's, so don't let your guilt tell you otherwise. The other man isn't a different race and hasn't any very distinguishing features that will appear, has he?'

'No, but he's got quite different colouring, and his eyes are not so,' she laughed awkwardly, 'beautiful.'

The doctor got up and patted her hand. 'I think you'll be fine, stop worrying,' he said. 'Perhaps the baby will look like you. Young Eleanor does. I'll see you Monday if not before.'

Leonie thanked him. She felt better, though, having worked herself

206

into such an extreme state of panic, not completely reassured. She made her way slowly round to Anita's house where she had left Eleanor.

Diana had still not gone back to her widower in Limoges. Leonie had tried to persuade her to go, even for a weekend, but every time she had agreed, and even once when she'd been packed and ready to go, Anita succeeded in changing her mind at the last minute.

'Mummy's not too well. I'll go next week,' she said, not looking at Leonie. Or, 'There aren't any flights at the time I want to go.' Leonie stopped pressing her, knowing that Anita had got to her with her emotional blackmail.

'I'm sorry I'm not dying any quicker. Would you like me to put a plastic bag over my head?' she said tartly, after Pascal, the widower, had telephoned Diana and asked her to come, and Diana, unable to leave the room to speak to him privately had stumbled in French that she couldn't this week after all.

Leonie, watching all this, had said, 'You're not going to die for ages. Surely Diana can pop over and see . . .' Anita's icy stare made her falter. Should she say 'boyfriend', 'friend'? '. . . Pascal and her other friends,' she finished lamely.

'I trust *you* will stay with your mother should she become ill,' Anita said.

Leonie did not answer, knowing her mother would be the last person to expect them all to be lurking round her, waiting for her to die.

Julian was taking Anita's illness very badly. He feared that if he left his mother for long, she would die. By just being there, telling her he was returning later in the day, he ensured that she stayed alive to see him.

'It can't be much fun for her, knowing you are waiting for her to die. I think it would be far kinder to get on with your life as if she were going to live for a long time. After all, the doctors say she could go on for ages,' Leonie had said the previous evening as he gulped his dinner, ready to go back to his mother, almost resenting each piece of meat he had to chew in case she would die in the time he took to eat it.

'I don't want to talk about it,' he said in the tight-lipped way he'd adopted since she'd got worse, afraid that by talking of death he would make it come at once and claim her.

'The baby will be born very soon, and Eleanor needs you,' Leonie tried another tack.

'I'm sorry, darling,' he made a real effort to look at her, 'but you must see how very difficult things are for me at the moment.'

How she longed for Philip to be there – Philip who understood everything.

He had made two visits back, but both times she had missed him. She heard from Diana that he'd spent two days at the house, then later another three. He never rang her. The first time she found out he'd been there, she felt hurt, cheated, but later she'd been relieved. How could she face him with this pregnancy? His reaction, unless she got him alone, might betray them. She wondered if he even knew she was pregnant, and tried to question Diana.

'I don't know,' she said. 'I mostly talked about his job, and his life over there.' Leonie saw her eyes still held a slight glow when she talked of him.

All this time, Leonie could not quite forget her prayer of the lonely dark hours that Anita would die before the child was born so she could never guess at its paternity. But as the months of her pregnancy passed, Anita rallied, got stronger each day, so that now, with the birth only days away she seemed almost back at her full strength.

Diana and Janet had offered to have Eleanor some afternoons to give Leonie a rest, and although she was concerned about the atmosphere in the house and worried that Anita's sharp tongue might be harmful for Eleanor, she recognised that Eleanor's cheerful presence was a welcome relief in the gloom of the house. She also saw more of Julian that way.

Today, while Anita was resting, she gratefully accepted the cup of tea Janet put before her and said to her and Diana, 'I'm to go into hospital to have the baby induced on Monday.'

'You must be pleased,' Janet said. 'You must be getting so tired.'

'Shall we look after Eleanor when you go in?' Diana said. Eleanor was lying on her stomach, head propped up in her hands watching television in Janet's sitting room.

'Thank you, but my mother said she'd have her,' Leonie said.

Zinnia loved being needed and had suggested herself that the minute Leonie felt a twinge of labour she'd be in the car and on the road.

'I've plenty of neighbours and friends to leave Eleanor with until you get here,' she said.

'But, darling, that's so unsettling for her. I mean, you rushing away like that, dumping her somewhere.'

'Ma, she's very sensible. Anyway, we've made a game of it, and she's looking forward to it.'

When they got home from Kensington, Leonie explained to Eleanor that she knew the day she was going into hospital and that Granny was coming the day before to look after her. Eleanor was disappointed.

'I thought we were going to Mandy's or Toby's in the middle of the night,' she said.

'We don't need to now.'

'It's not fair. Now it won't be fun,' she pouted. 'Silly baby, why can't it come in the night?'

'It still might.'

It didn't, and Julian drove Leonie into the hospital early in the morning after the weekend to have the baby induced.

'The minute it's born I want to come and see it,' Eleanor demanded.

'All right, darling, Granny will bring you.' Leonie kissed her goodbye.

Julian was not very talkative as they drove to the hospital and checked in. She felt that he'd rather be hovering round his mother than going through this birth with her.

They induced her and her labour started in earnest about ten o'clock. Julian rang Diana almost every hour to ask about his mother, until Leonie finally cracked and said sharply, 'Can't I give birth in peace without all this telephoning?'

'I'm concerned for Mother. She had a bad night.'

'But she's so much better and, after all, Diana knows where you are,' Leonie said, certain that Anita was just tweaking the cord, asserting her influence even while Julian was supposedly helping his wife through childbirth.

'Here we are,' the gynaecologist said after the last heave. There was a cry and instinctively Leonie looked towards the blue-red, bloody baby that he held up. It was a boy and he looked like Harry. She burst into tears.

'Oh darling, a boy. Isn't he great?' Julian said, looking animated. He kissed her with a return of his old love, and took the child from the nurse, holding him to him a minute before putting him carefully into her arms. 'One of each, perfect,' he said, smiling down on them.

'He looks like Harry,' she sniffed, the relief after her nagging anxiety making her weepy. She couldn't take her eyes off the tiny, wrinkled face.

'Does he? I can't see that he looks like anyone,' Julian said, peeling away the towel to see his face better.

'He's a great chap,' the doctor said, 'quite a big boy, too.'

'I'm going to fetch Mother so she can see him at once,' Julian said as a nurse took the baby away to wash and the doctor tidied up Leonie.

'But I'm quite tired and Eleanor's coming, couldn't she come tomorrow?' she said.

'I think she ought to see him,' he said gravely, and before she could protest further he kissed her and left.

Some time later, in her own nightdress and back in her hospital bed, the baby beside her, Leonie lay back exhausted. Suddenly the door opened and Julian, Anita and Diana came in.

'We won't stay long, you must be so tired,' Diana said. 'It's so exciting, a little boy.'

Leonie tried to smile. She looked at Anita so elegant, so beautifully dressed, despite her now too-thin figure, standing beside Julian. Leonie couldn't help admire her for her stand against this illness. Anita did not even look towards the cot where Diana was now bending over, her hand carefully pulling back the blanket from his face.

'He doesn't look at all like Eleanor,' Diana said.

'Doesn't he?' Leonie suddenly felt so agitated with her old fears she began to look round for means of escape.

'Leonie thinks he looks like her brother, but I can't see it,' Julian said. 'Look, Mother, isn't he great?' He was standing proudly by the cot now, Diana having moved away. Leonie felt sick, blood pounding in her ears. She couldn't bear it if Anita saw Philip's likeness in the baby's tiny face and said anything to ruin Julian's pride, ruin all their lives.

'He's sweet,' Diana said, smiling at Leonie. 'Have you thought of a name yet? You said you'd wait until you saw what it was.'

'Frederick,' Julian said at once.

'I like that,' Diana said. 'Eleanor and Frederick, very chic.'

Leonie, her whole body tense, waited with fear for Anita's verdict. She couldn't look as Anita threw a cursory glance towards the cot. Anita said: 'At least it's a boy,' then backed away and sat down on a chair.

'He's quite big,' Julian said eagerly, hoping his mother would praise something about the child.

'I suppose he would look different,' Diana continued cheerfully, 'being a boy. Eleanor has such a neat little head, but that would look a bit stupid on a boy, wouldn't it?' She beamed happily at Leonie, and Leonie forced herself to smile back, relieved that Anita took no interest in the child.

'I think we'll go now,' Anita said, getting up. 'I've had enough of hospitals to last me a lifetime.'

Diana opened her mouth as if to persuade her to stay, then obviously thought better of it, for she smiled sympathetically at Leonie and said, 'I'll try and pop back tomorrow, if I may? Do you need anything?'

'No thanks. My mother is bringing Eleanor in a little while.'

'Let's go,' Anita urged. 'I've some friends coming for bridge, remember.'

''Bye, darling. I'll come back when I've dropped Mother. Get some rest.' Julian kissed her, and so did Diana, but Anita just nodded at her and left the room.

When they'd gone Leonie lay back with a sigh, her worst fears over. She wondered if the guilt of her passionate coupling with Philip would keep inducing panic attacks over the baby's paternity, or if it was just Anita's presence that affected her so.

Soon her mother and Eleanor appeared.

Zinnia thought Frederick looked like Harry too. 'Makes me quite emotional,' she said, sighing. 'I wish he was like that now, so little and sweet, not breaking my heart with all his odd girlfriends and peculiar causes.'

Eleanor climbed into Leonie's bed, put her arms round him and tried to lift him. 'He's a bit red. I'll wash him,' she said.

'He's been washed. That's just how he is,' Leonie told her.

'How horrid to look like a tomato,' Eleanor said, wrinkling her nose. 'Will he look like that for ever?'

While Zinnia explained to her about new babies, Leonie lay back and closed her eyes. She had one arm round the baby, the other tight round Eleanor. She felt a great surge of relief. He was Julian's baby – surely he was – but how lucky he looked liked Harry.

Chapter Twenty-Three

From deep in her sleep Leonie heard the telephone ring. She struggled awake to answer it. It was Janet.

'I . . . I've got some very bad news,' the voice was flat with resignation. 'Mrs Maitland has died in her sleep.'

'What?' She couldn't believe it, but by now Julian had woken up. He snatched the receiver from her. 'Hello . . .'

Anita's dead, Leonie kept telling herself over and over again. It seemed impossible, after so much time and so many false alarms. Death had come just like that, catching her unawares in her sleep.

She looked at Julian. He was ashen, stunned. She took the receiver from his hand and put it back on the phone.

'You're free,' she wanted to say, 'free at last,' but she didn't. She took him in her arms and held him to her, the shock of the news making her feel cold and empty. At first he didn't respond. Then he gave a low moan like an animal in pain. She tightened her grip on him but he struggled free and got out of bed.

'I must go to her,' he said, bewildered as a small child.

'I'll come with you,' Leonie said, her mind alert now, going into overdrive, making plans. He needed her. She must put the children aside and stand by him through his initial grief until he saw the freedom his mother's death had given him and how they could be happy again.

'No.' His voice was firm, his expression decisive. 'No, you stay here.'

Again, Leonie felt the hurt. She was in one compartment of his life, Anita in another.

'I can leave the children with Jenny across the road. You need me

213

with you, darling. I know it's a terrible shock for you, even though we knew it would happen sooner or later,' she pressed on, wanting him to need her, wanting him to realise that now he would not be torn between them any more.

'No,' he said again, this time with more force, pulling on his clothes.

'Please let me come,' she said, wanting to support him, comfort him.

'Diana is there. I want you to stay here.' For a second his face softened, then she saw the taut look of grief come back, and she thought it better to do what he wanted for the moment. Now, at last, they had a lifetime of just each other and the children ahead of them.

Determinedly pushing away the hurt of his rejection, biting back any more pleas to let her come with him, she lay back in the bed, watching him dress. His face was set hard, his body drooped in despair. She felt suddenly that she could understand his momentary rejection of her. They both knew she had not cared for Anita. He was holding this against her now at the hour of her death.

When he'd gone Leonie wondered what would happen to the house, to Janet, to Diana. Then Eleanor bounced into her room. 'I looked at Freddie and he's asleep,' she said, curling into the bed beside Leonie with a collection of teddies, monkeys and Piggy.

'Eleanor,' she said hesitantly, then wondered if she should wait for Julian, for them to tell her about Anita together. But with sinking heart she knew he wouldn't be able to cope, would be no support at all.

'Darling, something very sad has happened,' she began, stroking Eleanor's firm little back.

'What?' Eleanor tried to make Piggy sit down.

'You know Granny . . . Granny Anita has been very ill . . . well, she's died. She's gone to Heaven,' she added as a sweetener, remembering how the nuns at her convent school rejoiced when one of their order died as she had surely gone to God.

'Do sit, Piggy,' Eleanor said, pushing Piggy down on his soft backside.

'Did you hear me, darling? Granny Anita has gone to Heaven.'

'That's all right then,' Eleanor said, looking at her with Julian's beautiful eyes.

'What do you mean?'

'I thought you said she was dead, but if she's only gone to Heaven then that's all right.' She retrieved a teddy bear from the floor.

Leonie sighed. 'But, darling, she is dead. You can only go to Heaven when you're dead.'

'Oh.' Eleanor regarded her for another moment, but she did not seem in the least perturbed. A wail came from two-month-old Freddie in his room, and she bundled herself off the bed calling, 'Coming, Freddie. Here I am.'

Leonie followed her quickly. Eleanor adored Freddie, but she was apt to treat him in the same ham-fisted way she treated her toys.

Perhaps it was just as well Eleanor had not taken in the fact of her grandmother's death. Leonie doubted she could cope with her and Julian both overcome with grief.

The day of Anita's funeral was heavy with gloom. Everyone talked in whispers, crept about the house fearful of wounding each other with intrusive noise. Julian behaved as if he were in a trance. He would not allow Leonie anywhere near him in his grief, but shut himself away for long hours in his study, or stayed in Anita's house in Kensington.

Diana seemed bemused, like a bird bred in captivity who had suddenly had the cage door opened and was afraid to fly away. Watching them, on the few times she saw them before the funeral, Leonie wondered with fear if their freedom without their mother would, instead of making them carefree with the loss of their burden, cause more damage than her imprisonment of them. Leonie had not foreseen this and, with Zinnia and George away with friends in Portugal, she felt very alone.

'Shall we come back for the funeral?' Zinnia said doubtfully when Leonie rang her. 'It does mean buying new plane tickets as ours are bucket shop and can't be changed, and we have only just arrived.'

'No, Ma, don't worry. I'll explain to Julian.'

'I suppose he's taking it awfully badly, though really it was a blessed relief for her I should think, and for you. I can't say I liked her much, far too selfish, but a horrid end for her, especially as she was so beautiful,' Zinnia rattled on in her muddled way.

'I can't really believe it. I keep expecting her to walk in and say something crushing,' Leonie broke in eventually, 'but I am worried about Julian, he's—'

'I know, darling,' Zinnia interrupted. 'She was a lethal sort of woman, but hang on, he'll get over it,' she added briskly as if Julian were only suffering from something ordinary like measles. 'Now I am sorry we can't come, but it's a shame to make Daddy break his holiday, he does work so hard. Organise some flowers from us, darling. I'll settle up with you when we get back. Lots of love to Julian, to you both.' She rang off, leaving Leonie feeling bereft.

Philip came back from South America for the service. Leonie longed to see him again, yet dreaded it. In her weaker moments, when she was alone at home with the children sleeping upstairs, she found herself daydreaming that once they saw each other again everything would miraculously slot into place.

He flew in late the night before the funeral and her first glimpse of him was in the church.

He greeted her solemnly, kissing her quickly, chastely on her cheek, then moving on to the other people. She felt her heart pounding and was afraid everyone in this silent church would hear, but he did not look at her again.

I must stop remembering that afternoon when we made love, she told herself firmly, stop turning it into something more serious than it really was. She'd dreamt that he would greet her with love, with the tenderness she craved and which Julian now withheld from her.

Philip had made no reference to her pregnancy, had sent her no messages over the last months. He was either disinterested or afraid to ask about it. It was safer to leave it that way, she knew, even though she longed for him to know.

Leonie hated funerals. They were so unlike anything in life, so alien to the person deceased. She would rather the body just disappeared and a service was held without it. Somehow then, she thought you could remember the person with less awe, less fear, smile, relax and recall the good times, feel that they were still there, but just out of sight. The starkness of the coffin holding the remains cut any feelings of reality and warm remembrances from her.

But this coffin holding Anita filled her with a sickening dread bordering on fear. She could not believe that her mother-in-law was really dead. She felt that she might suddenly rise out from under the huge spray of flowers, her beautiful eyes dark with malevolence, and start ruling their lives again. Looking surreptitiously at Julian and Diana, so white and stiff, she wondered if they didn't feel the same way too.

Gloomily they followed the coffin to the crematorium.

In the car Julian said tonelessly, 'Mother wants to be scattered in the gardens of Hopewell House, where she lived when she was a child.'

'But it belongs to the National Trust now,' Leonie said, suddenly seeing a ghastly picture of them creeping into the grounds with Anita's ashes under their coats, to scatter them secretly.

'She wants them there, so they'll be put there,' Julian said, shutting his mouth firmly, making an end to the matter.

Leonie knew that it was pointless saying anything. She wished Philip were in the car with them to make Julian see the impossibility of this plan, but after the service he had got into a car with some of their friends.

Trust Anita to leave behind such difficulties for everyone, Leonie thought. Even death would not eliminate her from their lives.

When the coffin slid behind the curtains to the fire, accompanied by rather tinny music, Julian collapsed. Dazed, afraid, she bent down to him, but Philip, standing on the other side, lifted him up quickly and walked him outside. Leonie went with them, holding on to Julian's other arm.

As she'd seen the coffin slide away, she had experienced another surge of fear, that even the fire would not consume Anita and she would come back, clawing her way through the flames. Leonie felt Anita's force on her back as she walked away down the aisle, and was too frightened to turn round.

'Take a few deep breaths, Julian,' Philip said. He walked him about outside. 'You'll be better in a minute.'

Leonie hovered behind them, feeling helpless. She didn't know how to help Julian. She hadn't been able to reach him since Anita's death and she'd kept going by telling herself that after the funeral there would be a magical cure. He would accept that his mother had gone and turn to his wife. But his collapse frightened her.

She was angry with Anita for leaving behind this broken victim for her to care for. She wanted the old Julian back, her husband, a father for her children, someone who would stand beside her as a strong partner to help her guide them through life.

Seeing the two men together, she could not help but compare them: Philip, taking charge, strong and decisive, stalwart as a sturdy tree; Julian, limp, ashen like a broken sapling after a storm. She had a sudden, almost physical longing for Philip. It was so strong she had to close her eyes and turn away in case he saw it.

The rest of the mourners came out of the church and crowded round Julian, Tony amongst them. He had played no part in the arrangements or the service. Clemmy had not attended. Diana took Julian's arm and with Leonie following behind they got back into the car to take them to the house. Philip did not travel with them. They slumped unspeaking, utterly drained by the event. Leonie held Julian's hand, which lay cold and still in her own.

When they arrived back at the house Leonie went over to Philip. 'What will happen to everything?' she said to him as an opening, wishing she could say so much more.

'She left no will,' he said. His eyes flashed a quick, warm look at her, but it faded almost at once. 'There are just instructions to scatter her ashes in the gardens of Hopewell House.'

'Trust her,' Leonie said furiously, 'to leave behind such a mess that she'll keep everyone occupied with her for ever, instead of being able to tidy everything up and get on with their own lives.'

'Hush,' Philip said softly, putting his hand on her arm and for one wild moment she thought he was going to kiss her. She looked up at him and in that moment she saw the naked pain in his eyes, a yearning, a love.

'Philip,' she breathed, almost faint with wanting him, wanting his strength, his support, his love.

The desire hung between them, potent as a drug.

'Philip?' Far away Leonie heard the voice. 'Philip?'

He turned slowly. 'Oh Diana, what is it?'

'I . . . well, how do you think we can get Mummy's ashes to Hopewell? Should we write to the family who lives there . . . or the National Trust?' She looked up at him helplessly. Leonie wondered if she had noticed their emotion, so strong she felt the whole world must know about it.

Philip became capable again. He took Diana's arm and said, 'I don't know. I think there are laws about these things. I mean, one can't just scatter ashes wherever one pleases.'

He looked across at Julian who was drinking a glass of brandy as if without it he would collapse. 'Watch his drinking,' he said gently to Leonie. His expression was impassive, his feelings locked away again. 'You must look after him, Leonie. He's going to need all your love and understanding for a while,' he added, giving her shoulder a little squeeze. She felt that he was reminding her of her duty as Julian's wife, and that anything they might feel for each other had to be held back.

'I . . .' She began to say that she couldn't cope with Julian, not without him by her side, but perhaps guessing her thoughts he said warmly, 'I know you can do it, Leonie. You have so much courage and strength. I admire that so much in you.' He smiled, kissed her swiftly on her cheek and walked away with Diana into the crowd of Anita's mourners.

She looked after him, watching him talking to the others, comforting Janet, moving round the room, confident and charming. Her whole being longed for him, longed to walk away from all this and escape with him. But she thought of the children, staying today with a friend, and knew she could not leave them. Rosemary and David came up with other friends to talk to her.

Then Philip reappeared, saying, 'I'm afraid I must be off. Goodbye.' He kissed Rosemary and the other two women and then turned to Leonie. David began to speak to him earnestly, monopolising him.

'So sad, and what a brave, courageous fight she put up. We'll miss you, Philip, miss the bridge fours. Going back to wherever, are you? Jolly good, keep in touch . . .' On and on he went.

Philip kissed Leonie and said very quietly, 'Everything will work out once he's over this, you'll see. Take great care.' His eyes lingered on her for a second before David's intrusive questions forced him to release her.

'Flying out tonight, are you, or would you like to come to the club for a spot of dinner?'

'Sorry no, I've a lot of things I must catch up on, I'm only back such a short time,' he said with a quick smile, and left them.

Leonie stood there in the chattering group feeling utterly alone. She wondered what Philip was catching up on. She couldn't help thinking that it was another woman.

The others started to go too, Tony giving Leonie and Diana supportive hugs, then slipping out discreetly. He had long since drawn a line under his relationship with Anita.

Leonie, seeing Diana looking more and more desolate as the room emptied, said impulsively, 'Come back home with us, Diana. Stay as long as you like. It will be more cheerful with the children around. You don't want to be alone just now—'

'She won't be alone. I'm staying here,' Julian broke in. His face was so white, his eyes enormous, burning with almost a manic desperation.

'But aren't you coming home, darling, with us?' Leonie said as gently as she could.

'Not at the moment. I want to stay here.'

'But you must come home. The children will want you,' Leonie said frantically. She'd been prepared to nurse him through his grief as Philip had decreed, but not if he stayed here as if the house were some sort of mausoleum. Surely, thankfully, it would have to be sold. None of them would be able to afford the upkeep of such a house, and Janet. Anyway, whose house was it? She felt sick at the thought of years of legal jargon and commotion ahead to decide who had inherited what.

'I'm staying here,' Julian said firmly, going back to the brandy bottle. 'You can move in too if you want to, with the children.'

'Oh no, Julian!' Leonie cried out in horror. 'We can't live here.' She imagined them having to sleep in Anita's bed, her things left lying about as though she would appear at any moment.

'*I* am staying here,' he said again and went out of the room. She heard him going upstairs. She felt alone and rejected.

'What shall I do?' she said to Diana who was lying exhausted on the sofa.

'I don't know. I don't know what any of us will do,' her voice was weary.

'You'll live your own life, now you're free,' Leonie said vigorously, annoyed now at the apathy of the two of them. 'You can go back to Pascal, make a life with him if you want to. Don't waste your life mourning your mother.' She just stopped herself saying, 'She wasn't worth it.'

'Please, Diana, I'll help you, but you must live,' she entreated, seeing her almost shrinking into the sofa.

'I'll see.'

'I'm going to ring Philip,' Leonie said suddenly, unable to bear Julian and Diana any more, yearning for his strength, his support.

She dialled his number but his phone went unanswered, ringing on and on. She held on for some time, then rang again and again. She rang finally about midnight from her bed, the children asleep beside her, but still there was no answer. She wondered whose bed he was in and wished so much it was hers.

Chapter Twenty-Four

Julian woke to the sharp, fresh light of another morning. At once he felt the sickening ache deep in him, the feeling of dread that he still hadn't done what his mother had asked of him and scattered her ashes at Hopewell House. But each day somehow passed before he had planned how to get them there. They sat at the top of the wardrobe, on a shelf to themselves in her bedroom. He had cleared out her neatly packaged jerseys to make room for them. He was sleeping next door in the room Philip had used as his dressing room.

Julian felt that by staying in her house he was close to her. He felt she wanted that, and found it difficult to accept that Leonie didn't understand this. He was torn between them still. Leonie had the children, but his mother had no one but him and Diana, and soon she would be gone, back to this man in France who telephoned her most days.

He didn't want to think ahead to what might happen to the house, to her things. Janet had suggested that any of her clothes Diana didn't want should be packed up and given to the Red Cross, but he couldn't bear to think of them hanging limply with other cast-offs to be pored over by strange, uncaring people, to be tried on by dirty, ugly women. So they stayed where they were on her silk-covered hangers, in her house, away from prying eyes and grubby fingers. He could not help feeling that she was still here, just waiting somewhere, watching what they did with her possessions.

Though they hadn't said a word about it to each other, he was sure Diana felt the same way. He tried to explain it to Leonie, but she said it was unhealthy. She was trying her best to make him leave the house, forget Anita, as if he ever could. It upset and angered him that she just didn't seem to understand so he stopped talking about it, stopped talking to her altogether unless he had to, as if protecting a gaping wound from an intrusive weapon.

Leonie wondered if she should insist that Julian come home if he wanted to see the children, hoping that once home he might stay there with them. He asked her to bring him the clothes and things he needed. She refused once, saying that at least he could come and fetch them himself, but he just shrugged and seemed not to care. So she kept bringing round what he asked, not daring to break his contact with them, hoping that if he kept seeing them all together as a family, he would pull himself together and come home to them on his own.

As he became more and more withdrawn, his beautiful eyes turned into huge pools of pain in his ashen face. He would acknowledge her and the children, hold them in his arms with a sort of dumb gratitude, but he barely had enough energy to play with them, or to tolerate Freddie's crying. He still went to work, but Leonie could not believe he was much good at it. What if they sacked him, how then would they live?

She tried to talk to him about this, but he barely listened to her. 'Just leave me,' he would say wearily, as if he could not bear to take on any more.

Janet continued her duties as housekeeper and Diana continued living there too, pale and listless, not knowing what to do with herself.

'Aren't you going back to Pascal? I hear he rings you most days – he must be missing you,' Leonie asked her, hoping that if she went to France, Julian would come back to her.

'Perhaps later, when Mummy's affairs are settled,' she said.

She wondered what Julian and Diana talked about together when she was not here. She only came to the house for just enough time to see him, hating it here with Anita's presence still lurking.

'Julian worries me,' Leonie said, keeping her eyes firmly on Diana as if pinning her down so she would listen. 'He hardly talks, unless it's about scattering your mother's ashes, and he's done nothing about that yet. I wish your father were here to talk some sense into him, but I don't like to worry him any further. Clemmy is enough for him.'

Diana jumped as if Leonie had uncovered something secret. 'We *must* find a way of scattering her ashes at Hopewell House,' she said.

'Diana, don't you see, it isn't a feasible thing to do? Why don't you find another place?' Leonie tried not to sound impatient.

Diana looked at her with horror and muttered, 'But we must do what Mummy wanted.'

Tony rang her from time to time, and when she hinted about her anxiety over Julian, he told her he knew it would be a rough ride, but to give it time. His remarks, and others like it from her family and friends, made Leonie feel guilty. She knew bereavement was a savage cross to bear, and one which had never really touched her.

'You are always a little mad in grief, though they say you suffer more if you didn't have a good relationship with the dead person. Your feelings are mixed with guilt and regret of not measuring up,' Zinnia said, when Leonie went to see her on her return from her holiday. 'He'll come to terms with it soon. We all have to,' she said briskly.

Leonie did not tell her mother about Anita's ashes, afraid that Zinnia, though meaning well, would do something drastic like send Father Bennet round to dispose of them in a religious way.

But she told Harry who said, 'She ought to have had a sky burial like they do in Tibet. There's hardly any earth there to bury people in so they take the bodies to a special mountain and feed them to the vultures.'

'Oh Harry, how disgusting.'

'No worse than being eaten by worms and earwigs,' he said. 'I'd let them scatter them in Hopewell. Put them in a coat pocket with a hole in it and as they walk the ashes will spill out. I wouldn't want them in my pocket, though.'

'Nor would I,' Leonie said with feeling, though she was also amused by Harry's practical suggestion.

Julian finally got round to writing to the Keatings, who lived at Hopewell, to ask if he could scatter Anita's ashes in the garden. He explained it was her last wish to go back to where she had been so happy as a child. He had a firm, but sympathetic letter back, refusing his request.

'The house is open to the public so we must go in one day and just do it,' he said to Leonie on one of her visits.

'But we can't,' she said. 'Look, darling, it's hardly your fault that they won't give you permission. You've done everything you can for your mother, but you just can't do this.'

'I shall do it,' he said, his face defiant.

Leonie was about to say Anita would understand when she knew that she wouldn't. She said tersely, 'I suppose we could go down at night time and scatter them in the hedge outside the property.'

Julian looked horrified. 'You just don't care, do you?' he said. 'You never liked her.'

'She never liked me. You are making too much of this, Julian. Why not just find a pretty church yard and put her there?'

'No!' he cried, his eyes dark with anger and pain. 'I won't . . . don't you see I can't? I must do what she says.'

'Julian,' she said gently, taking his hand. 'She can't hurt you any more. She's dead, finished. She cannot reach you now.'

He snatched his hand from hers. 'What nonsense you talk,' he said. 'What do you know about it?'

'You need help,' she said gravely. 'Serious medical help. Come with me to Dr Wharton. You know he'll help you.'

He ignored her. 'Where's Philip? He can help me with the ashes.'

'I don't know, South America still, isn't he?' Her heart lifted for a second, thinking Julian might tell her that he'd returned to London. Since the funeral she'd heard nothing from him. When she rang him there was just the empty sound of his telephone ringing on, unanswered. It made her immeasurably lonely. She wanted him, not just for himself but to help her with Julian. She wondered how much longer she could cope alone.

One morning Julian rang her at home. He sounded calm, almost normal. 'Can you leave the children with someone, darling, and come round here? We're going down to Hopewell.'

'But—'

'If you're not here in an hour, I'll assume you're not coming,' he said and put the phone down.

The last thing she wanted was to go off into the country with

226

Anita's ashes and try to sneak them into this garden, but Julian had made up his mind at last and if she didn't go he might hold it against her and they would never get back together again.

As she got the children ready, she thought that perhaps once Anita's ashes were gone, Julian would be better. It must be very sinister for him, having his mother's remains sitting about like some menacing idol right where they were living.

It was the end of August, and she had to ring quite a few friends before she found one at home who would take Eleanor, but she couldn't manage Freddie.

'Don't worry, I can take him,' Leonie told her friend, seeing by the clock that time was fast running out.

She arrived at Julian's ten minutes past the hour he had given her. Diana opened the door. 'We're just going. Oh good, you've brought Freddie,' she kissed him.

'I couldn't leave him, everyone's away on holiday.'

'He'll be no trouble.' She smiled nervously and Leonie noticed her eyes kept reluctantly straying to a dark brown shiny gift bag on the hall table. She knew at once what it contained. She turned away, fighting an overwhelming surge of hysterical giggles. Really, this whole episode looked set to be utterly bizarre.

Julian came downstairs. 'Hello,' he said. He did not kiss her. He picked up the bag.

'Are we all ready?'

'Is it just us? I thought Philip might be coming,' Leonie said, hoping to glean some information on his whereabouts.

'He's gone back to South America,' Diana said.

'I didn't know he was here. When did he go back?' Leonie said, feeling sick that he hadn't contacted her.

'He came back briefly for a meeting. Now come on,' Julian said, leading the way out of the house into the garage.

'I see.' Leonie felt terribly let down.

The brown bag, folded over at the top, was put in the car boot under Julian's coat. Leonie wondered what would happen if the ashes spilt, working their way into the fabric, clinging there for always. She resolutely pulled herself together. The situation was macabre enough, without such gothic embellishments.

227

They arrived at the long wall surrounding Hopewell and drove into the car park.

The day, which had started off dull and grey, had now turned stormy-looking, so Julian carrying a coat over his arm to hide Anita's ashes did not look out of place.

They paid their entrance fee and began to walk round the large garden. Most of it was in view of the house and through the windows Leonie could see people inside, looking out admiringly at the garden.

Leonie noticed how nervous Diana and Julian were, as if they were carrying a murdered corpse to bury. They walked down a box path to the orchard and walled garden.

'This would do,' Leonie said, looking round hurriedly. 'No one can see us here, and it's empty for the moment.'

'I'm not putting her in a vegetable garden,' Julian said shortly.

Leonie gave out a manic giggle which she fought to turn into a cough.

Despite the dull day there were quite a few other people wandering round the garden and every time they thought they'd found a place, someone would turn the corner or appear from behind a shrub.

'We must hurry up,' Leonie said, thinking she could hardly bear this macabre farce for much longer.

'We must find the right place,' Diana said in a small voice, glancing nervously at Julian.

A bus load of Japanese tourists poured round the corner, all jabbering and flashing their cameras at everything in sight. Leonie then did laugh, though in a frenzied way, imagining them being filmed scattering their ancestors' ashes on some flowerbed.

'We must just get on and do it,' Leonie said, biting back her hysteria. 'We are here, in her garden, it doesn't matter where we do it, but we must, quickly, before someone sees us. I mean after they wrote and told you you couldn't scatter them, people may be looking out for you,' she added firmly.

'She's right,' Diana said. 'Let's go back to the orchard.'

Nobody else was there just then. Julian opened the bag and after a moment's hesitation poured the black ashes out on to the ground. They lay there like black pepper on the grass. Then, in an almost biblical manner there came a wind that whipped up the grasses and bent the trees. It picked up some specks of the ashes and blew them towards the four of them. Instinctively Leonie jumped back, but saw too late that one had become embedded in Freddie's white shawl.

She gave a cry of horror, whipped the shawl off him and threw it to the ground, waking Freddie and making him cry. She was shaking and afraid. She could see it as the shawl lay on the ground, a dark flaw on the white wool like an accusation, as if Anita knew of her coupling with Philip and was renouncing her.

Chapter Twenty-Five

'I've met a new man,' Melanie said to Leonie as the two tramped over the Downs. Eleanor and the dogs ran on ahead; Zinnia had stayed at home with Freddie. 'But don't tell Ma. He's not at all what she'd think of as "suitable".'

'I'm so glad, Mel.' Leonie shot a smile at her. 'I thought you seemed happier, but why won't she like him? He's not married or anything, is he?'

'No. But he comes from quite a different background to us. I can't face Ma being kind to him, as if he has somehow suffered for not being sent away to some public school to be beaten and bullied. I can tell you he's far more balanced and together than many public school men I know.'

'I think she's better now about people,' Leonie said. 'She's even got quite fond of some of Harry's weird girlfriends.'

'I don't want to tell her yet, it's too new and special.' Melanie glowed and Leonie felt a little pang of envy, remembering how special it had once been with Julian.

'You know how ignorant the parents are about people different to themselves, being surrounded in their narrow little world by clones of themselves,' she went on. 'Anyway I can't face any more of her talk about my body clock ticking on. Steve and I are great together, but I don't want to ruin everything with marriage and babies.'

Leonie didn't, as she used to, pick up her argument. She had always wanted marriage and a family, thought it would be the most important thing in her life. Now she was beginning to see Melanie's point of view. If only she had realised that that deep and passionate love she and Julian had experienced in Florence was a one-off, magical experience, unfettered as it was by responsibilities. Love was all-consuming, a selfish indulgence that didn't always cater for other people. Once Anita and, to a lesser extent, Leonie's parents and Tony and Clemmy had appeared it had stretched their love out of shape. Only the children held it together.

'So how is Julian?' Melanie asked, as if she guessed her thoughts.

'I told you, still living in Anita's house, hardly speaking, well to me anyway. I think it's because he knew I disliked his mother. But you can't change and like someone just because they're dead.'

'She's much easier to like dead than alive, I'd have thought,' Melanie laughed. 'But what I really meant was, how do you feel about him? Will you stay with him, let him go on in this selfish way?'

'I have the children to think of,' she said, looking ahead at Eleanor who was throwing a stick for Mitzi, shouting, 'Fetch it, fetch it for me, Mitzi.'

'It can't be good for them seeing their father like that. I know marriage is for better or worse, so it's bad luck on you to get the worse. Why don't you shock him into sense, say you'll leave him unless he comes back to your house?'

'I must do something,' Leonie said vaguely, not wanting to tell Melanie of the letter from Philip that she carried in her bag. It had arrived a week ago. The address was his firm in New York. She knew the words off by heart.

'My dear Leonie, I am going to stay out here for a while as I cannot trust myself to see you. You have too much on your plate right now to make any decisions, but if you should ever need me, I will come to you. My love always, Philip.'

She did not know what she would do about it. She kept it close to her like a talisman, taking it out and reading it when she felt particularly lonely or sad. She longed for him, but she knew that to destroy Eleanor and Freddie's life was too high a price. They depended on her for so much. Eleanor, old enough now to sense the rocky ground they lived on, would often seize her with her large beautiful eyes – Julian's eyes, Anita's eyes – and say accusingly: 'Why doesn't Daddy live in our house any more? Why does he live in a dead person's house? Doesn't he love us?'

'Of course he does, he's just there because . . . because he's lots of papers to see to. When people die they leave a lot of important papers to deal with,' she struggled valiantly, inwardly cursing Julian for causing his daughter distress.

'Why can't he bring the papers here, with us?'

'There are too many . . . and there are other things to do.' She could not meet her eyes, and would end up hugging her, holding her close so she should not see the lies in her face.

Freddie was too small to know anything, but he wriggled with delighted pleasure like a plump puppy each time she came into his room. His unconditional love and need of her touched her heart and she knew once more she must fight for her marriage for their sake.

She did not know if she still loved Julian, or indeed if she did love Philip or was just attracted by his strength and his obvious charm and sexual attraction. Actually to leave Julian and go to live with Philip was too big a risk to take. If she'd been alone, it would have been different.

'You must do something, Leo,' Melanie said firmly, digging her gloved hands into her pockets as if to emphasise her point. 'He's an awfully weak person, isn't he? I know it was his mother's fault to a certain extent, but he could have been stronger right at the beginning and gone to live with you in Florence.'

'I know . . . but I sort of see how he couldn't get away. She was dreadfully possessive and knew just how to make her children feel guilty. He wasn't too bad, in fact he stood up to her many times until she got cancer. It was that that really finished him.'

'Well, now she's dead you must give him a choice: come back to you, or you'll leave him. If you don't do anything it will only get worse, letting him wallow in this.'

'I will do something,' she said wearily, knowing Melanie spoke the truth.

They turned back and as they reached the last field before the house, they saw Harry calling and waving.

'What on earth does he want?' Melanie said, craning her head as if to hear better. 'What . . . Leonie what?'

'Freddie!' Leonie said, breaking into a run.

'What's happening?' Eleanor said, clasping a struggling Mitzi in her arms.

233

Leonie reached Harry. 'What's happened? Is Freddie all right?'

''Course. It's Julian . . . he's had a fit.' He dropped his voice as Eleanor and Mitzi came closer. 'Mum said not to tell her.'

Leonie felt cold and sick. 'What's happened?' she said.

Zinnia appeared. 'Oh darling, there you are, and Eleanor. Sweetie, you're filthy, put Mitzi down.'

'Ma, what has happened?' Leonie said fearfully.

Zinnia took Mitzi from Eleanor's arms and dropped her on the ground where she ran thankfully away. 'Run in, darling, and wash. Take everything off at the door, please,' she said to Eleanor. 'I don't want all that mud inside.'

When she'd gone, Zinnia said, 'Diana rang. Apparently Julian's had a sort of breakdown.' She said the word as if it was something shameful. 'He's all right, he's in hospital, well a private nursing home.'

'How . . . what?' Leonie felt pain, fear and anger that he should cause them more upset. 'A breakdown? What do you mean?'

'I expect he's just flipped,' Melanie said. 'I'll come back with you.'

'Daddy will take you. Leave the children here.' Zinnia was calm in a crisis. 'Don't worry, they'll be fine with me. Country air will do them good.'

'But . . . a breakdown . . .'

'My darling, he must just snap out of it. He's taking this death thing far too much to heart. It's staying in that dreadful, overdone house that's brought it on,' Zinnia said unhelpfully.

They set off to London, Eleanor happy with the prospect of being left behind to bath Mitzi. George drove, every so often making cheerful bracing remarks. Leonie slumped beside him, feeling she couldn't cope with any more. Melanie sat in the back of the car going over some balance sheets. They arrived at the house in Kensington. Diana let them in.

'Whatever happened?' Leonie said, her fear made worse by Diana's terrified face.

Diana waited until they were all inside, then she said, 'He just screamed and screamed, said . . . Mummy was looking at him. H-he tried to jump out of the window.'

'Oh God, what did you do?'

'Janet held him, and I rushed to ring our doctor, who luckily only lives round the corner. He came at once. He gave Julian an injection and he's now in a nursing home.'

'I must go to him immediately.' Leonie could almost feel Anita in this house, malevolent and gloating. She shuddered, resolving that Anita would not claim him, take him away from her. 'Come on, Daddy, we must go. What is the address, Diana?'

'Well . . . the doctor says—' Diana started.

'Stuff the doctor,' Leonie said. 'He's my husband and I'm going to him at once.' She felt suddenly strong, determined to go and get Julian away from these doctors and bring him home to Putney. 'Come on, Dad,' she said, taking George's arm. 'Please drive me there.'

'Do you mind if I don't come?' Melanie said, glancing surreptitiously at her watch. 'I said I'd meet someone later, and if I come all the way to the nursing home I might not get back in time.' She gave Leonie a meaningful look signifying that she had to meet her new lover.

'No, we'll be fine. Thanks for coming so far.' Leonie kissed her distractedly and pulled George, protesting mildly, to the car. They drove to the nursing home, which was in Richmond, in silence. Leonie, having never seen anyone with a breakdown, had lurid pictures of Julian secured in a strait-jacket, foaming at the mouth.

The nursing home was set in a pleasant garden up a drive. They parked the car and went into the large hall.

'I don't like the feel of this place. I hope they don't think *we're* mad,' Leonie said, shivering slightly, her determination to rescue Julian waning now that they were here.

'I'm sure they won't,' George said rather too loudly. 'Now, let's find someone who is in charge.' He tried to look purposeful as they looked round the empty hall. 'There's reception.' He pointed to a sign that led down a corridor. 'Let's go there.'

A rather vague woman that Leonie thought seemed like a patient herself showed them to a desk where two nurses sat. One listened calmly to Leonie's rather frantic request to see Julian.

She smiled kindly as if Leonie were about to go berserk herself, referred to some notes, then said quietly, a smile still clamped to her lips, 'Come back tomorrow, dear, when the doctor's here.'

'I want to see him now,' Leonie said, feeling that she might well erupt into insanity in the face of this overcalm woman.

'Your husband is fine. He's been sedated, he must not be disturbed tonight.' She smiled at George as if she hoped he would understand. 'It is imperative that he stays quiet. He won't know you tonight anyway. Please go home and come back tomorrow.'

'Better see him in the morning, darling,' George said quickly, taking her arm. 'I'm sure he's in safe hands. Come on.'

'I want to see him,' Leonie said, but weakly now. Sedated? Would he not know her? Had he truly gone completely mad?

She let her father drive her home. Just as they walked in, Tony rang her. She burst into tears.

'My dear, you've had such a rough time. I'm coming down on the early plane. I'll sort it all out, don't you worry.' His pleasant voice soothed her and then he spoke to her father and as she slumped back on the sofa, listening to the hum of their voices, she thought, that bloody woman, she has succeeded in her death in ruining our lives.

The next morning, after a wretched night, Leonie drove herself back to the nursing home, assuring her father that she was fine, and that she would rather go alone. She pretended not to see his relief as she left him. She suppressed her longing to have his comforting figure beside her, but she was determined this time to see Julian, and she knew that if George was with her, he would agree with the doctor, if he said she couldn't see him, and take her home again.

She walked into the nursing home purposefully as if she had a right to be there, but not, she hoped, slightly hysterically, as a patient. She half expected someone in a white coat to come and round her up with soothing noises and possibly a syringe.

She walked down the empty passage bright with cream paint and restful pictures, towards room 44, which she hoped, from having caught a glimpse of the numbers on the doctor's notes last night, referred to Julian's room.

It was mid-morning and although she could hear the soft sounds of people moving and talking, there was no one in the passage. She got to the desk where the nurses had been last night. It was deserted, but the door to one of the rooms was slightly ajar, and Leonie could see two nurses tending to an elderly man. She went past the desk to room number 44, opened the door and went in.

The curtains of the room were drawn and, to her relief, Julian lay on the bed, his eyes closed. She crept over to him, sat down and gingerly took his hand. He started, opened his eyes and looked at her uncomprehendingly.

'It's all right,' she whispered, taut with fear, having never been anywhere near a mentally ill person before, 'it's only me. How are you?'

He stared and stared at her as if he couldn't remember her, but he left his hand lying in hers.

'You're going to get better and come home to us. We'll go to Florence like we said we would,' she said gently, terrified at this change in him.

He smiled then, a faint smile as if a memory stirred in his befuddled mind.

The door opened and a nurse marched in.

'Mrs Hunter,' she said evenly, 'you must not disturb your husband. You should have seen me first. Come with me now, please.'

'I want to stay with him,' Leonie said, still holding his hand.

'First you must see the doctor. I insist you leave him at once. He is in safe hands, but he must have complete quiet for a few days.' Her voice was hard under its whispering tones.

'I . . . want . . .' Leonie faltered. She felt alien here, unsafe, and wished with all her heart that she could take Julian away from this quiet and sinister place. Surely he'd get better somewhere else more normal?

She bent over and kissed him, fighting back the tears that blocked her throat, hating leaving him here. She thought how lost he looked. 'I'll come back,' she promised, wishing she could tell him that she would rescue him at the first opportunity, but knowing she couldn't in front of this nurse. 'Don't worry about anything, I'll come back, I won't leave you.'

For a second his hand tightened on hers and there was understanding in his eyes.

'I love you,' she heard herself saying. 'I'll come back very soon.'

She kissed him again and slipped her hand from his, all the time feeling the sinister presence of the nurse hovering behind her as she left the room. She fought with her tears as she did not want them to think she was weak and could not fight for him.

'You can do a great deal of harm disturbing these patients,' the nurse said angrily when they were outside and Julian's door was shut again.

'But he's all alone, and being ill, haunted I'm sure he thinks by his mother's ghost, he should have someone he knows with him,' Leonie said defiantly. 'I am his wife and he needs me.' She glared at the mottled face of the nurse as if daring her to dispute it.

'He is under medication and must not be disturbed,' the nurse said, and then as another nurse appeared added, 'His doctor will see you now. Please go with Nurse Simpson, and please, Mrs Hunter, check with us before you visit your husband again.'

Leonie was shown into a large, sunny room to see a Dr Hale, who, Leonie thought after a few moments with him, was disturbed himself. He insisted that she went away and left Julian in his care.

'He feels overpowered by women,' he said. 'Women are bad for his self-esteem at the moment. You must give him a chance to heal.'

'But I am his wife,' she said firmly, looking with dislike into this doctor's pale, pink face with tufts of ginger hair on his head. 'I must stay near him in case he needs me.'

'He will not need you,' Dr Hale said. 'I insist you give him a chance to recover. He is very seriously ill, and I am sure you want him to make a full recovery.' He gave her a sharp look.

'I know my husband better than you do,' Leonie said firmly. 'He needs to be with people he knows. I will come every day to see him.'

'You will see him *when* I think fit,' the doctor replied.

Leonie decided to go home, ring Dr Wharton and insist that he cope with it.

She was relieved that Tony telephoned her just minutes after she got home.

'I can't leave Julian with that dreadful man,' she said desperately, after she'd told him about her visit.

Tony calmed her. 'I've already made enquiries and he is meant to be a good doctor. I know it's hard for you, but if he seems to think the best treatment is to keep Julian sedated for the next few days you will have to accept it. You don't want Eleanor upset by this any more than you can help. I'd take the children away for a while, if I were you, until he's better,' he said. 'I'll see you this afternoon and we'll talk some more.'

Leonie was thankful for Tony's imminent presence, and let herself be persuaded by his words.

'This place must be sold at once,' Tony said later that day as he sat with Leonie and Diana in the upstairs drawing room of the Kensington house. 'I will buy you a flat, Diana. It's bad for you to stay on here.' Janet had given in her notice after Julian's breakdown, saying she couldn't take any more.

'I might go to Limoges,' Diana said. She too looked terrible, shattered by Julian's breakdown.

'That's a good idea,' Tony said, 'then come and stay with us, don't come back here. The memories are not good.' He shuddered. 'I'm horrified at what went on, the ashes and everything. Trust your mother not to leave you in peace,' he said to Diana.

'And you, dear Leonie,' Tony said when they'd gone back to Putney and were alone. 'You've had the worst of it, but the doctor's hopeful, you know, that Julian'll make a full recovery. It will take time, though.'

'As long as I don't go near him,' she said bitterly. 'I don't think psychiatrists like marriage, do you? Every married person I know who has been to one has had their marriage wrecked. But I don't know what I feel. The Julian I loved has been gone a long time.'

Tony put his arm round her and said sadly, 'I know, my dear, and I'll understand if you feel you can't take any more.'

Thinking suddenly of Clemmy, Leonie said, 'It's all such a mess. But how are you and Clemmy?'

He smiled, but she saw his eyes were sad. 'She'll stay with me for the moment,' he said, 'but I fear there will be other young men. It wouldn't matter if I didn't love her so much, but I have to accept that I am so much older than she is, and I will surely be gone long before her, or,' he shuddered, 'become ill and be a burden on her.'

Leonie hugged him, knowing there was no answer to his situation.

'We're both stuck,' she said. 'I just feel so drained, I can't make any decisions at the moment.'

'Don't until you've been right away for a break. Look, let me treat you to one, take the children. Where would you like to go?'

'Oh Tony, I couldn't . . .' but even as she protested she had a sudden urge to return to Florence, to see the pictures, the statues she and Julian had loved, to walk the streets where they had been so happy together. She wanted to feel that once everything had been magic between them. 'I would love to go to Florence,' she said, kissing him. 'Oh Tony, thank you.'

Leaving Freddie, who would not appreciate Florence, with her mother, Leonie reserved a room in a nice little hotel she and Julian had discovered, and went to Italy with Eleanor.

'We'll see some pictures first, then we'll have an ice cream,' Leonie said to encourage her.

'Can it be chocolate and nuts?'

'If you want. Now these pictures are very special. Some were painted over four hundred years ago and their colours are the most beautiful you'll ever see.'

'I might have pis . . . how is it . . . pistish?'

'Pistachio.'

'Pistachio *and* chocolate.'

'Let's just look at a few pictures first,' Leonie said, feeling the same rush of excitement she had when she'd first come here years ago. She looked happily round the walls, greeting each picture with joy. She tried to infect Eleanor with her pleasure, and Eleanor did her best, pointing out, 'such a darling baby,' and 'why are those ladies all bare?'

She came at last to Botticelli's *Magnificat Madonna*. It had been in front of this picture that she had first met Julian. She stared at it for a long time – at the gentle face of the Madonna, who seemed to be touched with sadness as she looked down at her child, as if she knew the pain and sacrifice that lay ahead. Here was the perfect, all-loving mother who gave up everything for the love of her son.

'Why are you crying?' Eleanor tugged at her hand.

'Oh, am I? How silly of me,' Leonie said, wiping her tears away and looking down into Eleanor's large concerned eyes – Julian's eyes, she thought, remembering how it had been his eyes that had first attracted her to him, here on this very spot.

If only she had known then what heartbreak that meeting would bring, that a mother could destroy as savagely as she could love.

'Can I have an ice cream now? We've seen lots of pictures,' Eleanor said hopefully.

Leonie smiled down with love at her eager little face. She had the children; something good had come out of that fateful meeting.

A boy and a girl, arms round each other, moved in front of her to look at the picture. They were very young and they held each other with a kind of desperate intimacy as if they sensed the fragility of love. Leonie turned away, sick with longing, wishing loving were easier.

'We must buy Daddy a postcard, and Freddie and Granny and Grandpa and Aunt Diana and Mandy and Grandpa Tony and . . .' Eleanor chimed in, lightening Leonie's thoughts. There was a string of people in her life, she thought, most of them in it because of the meeting in front of this picture. It was strange to stand here again and look back on her marriage, a marriage that might now be over.

'I am simply *dying* for an ice cream,' Eleanor tugged at her hand.

'Come on then.' She walked away from the Madonna, getting comfort from the warm little hand in her own and Eleanor's now exuberant chatter.

The next day they went to Mass at the church of the SS Annunziata, one of Leonie's favourites, with its extravagant Volterrano ceiling.

Leonie tried to pray that Julian's health would return and they would be happy again, that Anita's ghost would leave them in peace. She prayed too for Philip. But she felt hollow inside, empty, her prayers just a meaningless jumble that would solve nothing. Suddenly she remembered her grandmother, Zinnia's mother, whose husband had come back so wounded from the war that he spent the rest of his life in pain.

'It's no good fussing,' she would say briskly. 'Offer it up to the

Holy Souls. There are lots of people worse off.'

Perhaps, Leonie thought desperately, I too will have to nurse a wounded husband for the rest of my life. In her grandmother's day, she knew, people didn't give up on relationships so quickly as they did today. Now with the emphasis on happiness, youth, beauty and everything perfect, relationships were often tossed aside as soon as any flaws appeared. But were people any happier? She thought of newspaper stories of well-known 'beautiful' people, who drank and drugged their way through series of relationships, leaving helpless children in their wake. Were they any happier than her grandmother, who had devoted her life to the man she loved when he had come back a shadow of his former self? But he had come back, unlike so many others. For that, her grandmother would often remark, she was eternally grateful.

After Mass, when everyone had left, Leonie wandered round the church with Eleanor, hoping that the beauty and the peace would somehow seep into her and soothe her. Eleanor ran off every so often to play hopscotch on the diamond pattern marble floor, or to explore some dark recess.

Passing a side chapel, Leonie heard the soft sound of crying and saw in the darkness a young woman sitting in the pew, her head in her hands. As she looked more closely she saw that she was sobbing into a baby's garment. The pain, the utter poignancy of the tiny white sleeve that overlapped her hand shook Leonie to the core. The despair of this woman crying for a baby that she had lost made the tears rush into her own eyes. Swiftly she moved away so as not to intrude upon this grief, offering a silent prayer that she would be comforted. How small suddenly her troubles seemed, compared to this girl's grief. How grateful she felt for her healthy children.

She saw Eleanor then ᴜy a statue of the Virgin Mary, pushing yet another candle into the crowded higgledy-piggledy arrangement she'd just made in the iron rack in front of the statue.

'Eleanor,' she rushed over, 'darling, you have to pay for the candles.'

'I did, I had two pence in my pocket,' Eleanor said happily, picking up another candle and trying to cram it in. 'I'm putting them up for

Daddy so he can get better and stop resting and come home to us again.'

Leonie, hastily pushing a handful of lire into the tin beside them, did not attempt to hide her tears.

Chapter Twenty-Six

'Damn, stupid glass keeps moving,' James said as the red wine he was pouring himself spilt on to the cloth.

'Let me do it.' Caroline got up from her place at the table, took the bottle from his hand and poured a little into his glass. 'Now take it next door with Julian,' she said pleasantly, 'while we clear the table.'

'I'll take the bottle too.' He made a grab for it, but she was too quick for him. 'That's enough for tonight, darling,' she said firmly, putting the cork in and putting it in the cupboard.

Leonie watched her with compassion. They were here for the weekend in this beautiful old vicarage that Caroline was in the process of restoring. James had been all right during the day, but now he seemed to have sunk pretty fast into drunkenness. She looked quickly at Julian to see how he was taking it. He was not allowed to drink alcohol at the moment because of the pills he was on. He smiled back at her, slightly raising an eyebrow.

James's two children, Peter and Annabel, did not look at him, but stared fixedly at their plates. Caroline said cheerfully to them, 'Take your plates to the kitchen, please, and put them in the dishwasher. Then you can watch television for half an hour or play a game. How about Racing Demon?'

'Let's . . . will you play with us? It's more fun with more of us. Will you play, Dad?' Annabel asked, her small face shining eagerly.

'What, my darling? Play? Play what?' James got up and swayed a little before setting off out of the room. He looked rather like a clockwork toy that once wound up had no choice but to lurch forward until it ran down, Leonie thought with amused pity.

'We'll let the men off,' Caroline said, 'but we'll play, won't we, Leonie?'

'Yes, of course,' Leonie said. 'I'll just check on the children first. Freddie's a bit grumpy with his tooth coming through.'

'I'll do that, darling,' Julian said and quickly left the room.

'Thank you,' she smiled after him. Julian and she were struggling along like two sleepwalkers in their marriage, Leonie doggedly playing the part of wife and mother as if nothing had changed, though of course they had. Julian was a different person since his breakdown.

He had been home from the nursing home for two months now and was back at work. Christie's had been very understanding and kept his job open for him. To people who didn't know him well he was much the same – a little quieter, more thoughtful perhaps – but Leonie, with the image of Anita still strong in her mind, felt she was living with a clone. They were like two actors playing a part, going through the motions of a relationship without any warmth, any feelings of reality.

They talked about the children, his work, Diana's courtship with her widower, and his father and Clemmy, but Anita was never mentioned, though Leonie felt her presence, like a massive tumour between them.

Philip had telephoned her once to ask if he could do anything to help. For a few seconds she had been stunned to hear his voice.

He had said, 'Can you hear me, Leonie?'

'Yes . . . I'm sorry . . . Julian is better. He's home now and he should make a full recovery. Anita's house has been sold.' The words poured out of her as if she felt they would somehow keep him with her.

'Good. But how are you?' His voice was warm, alive.

She longed to say, 'Struggling to keep the family together, wanting Julian to make a spontaneous gesture to show he really cares and wants us to stay together. But how I wish you were here, to help me, to love me.' Instead she said, 'I'm fine.'

'And the children?'

She wanted to say, 'Come and see your son, he is such a happy child,' but she said instead, 'They are fine too,' and she went on to tell him about them and listened to his laughter, hating the social game they were playing, but suspecting that they were both too afraid of the devils and the destruction that would be unleashed if they said what they really wanted to say to each other.

'I'm sorry it all ended how it did,' he said. She wondered for a moment if he meant their brief affair and was about to say it needn't have ended, was there not some way they could all be together? Could he not come back and work here so at least she could see him? But even as she thought this, she knew it would be impossible without hurting the children.

He said, 'It was terrible for you to have to go through Julian's breakdown as well as everything else, but with any luck it will purge him of his relationship with his mother, and you can start again with a clean slate. I'm sure you'll both be happy together again. You've so much to build on.'

She agreed mechanically, wishing she could see him, see in his eyes what he felt for her – feel the vigorous passion of his body. But after a few more polite, restrained words he rang off. There seemed to be so much they couldn't say.

'Take care of yourself, Leonie.' His words echoed through her for the rest of the day, curling into her mind for her to bring out and yearn over when she wished for his strength.

'Ready, steady, go!' Peter yelled, jumping up, throwing the ace of hearts on to the table and quickly covering it with a two. Annabel threw out the ace of diamonds and the three of hearts, Caroline and Leonie followed more slowly behind them. For a few minutes all was frantic with the slapping of cards on the table as they raced to finish their pack.

'Out!' yelled Peter.

'Oh, I only had two more to go,' Annabel wailed. 'Let's have another.'

'Two more games, then bed,' Caroline said.

Leonie sank back in her chair when the children had gone up. 'Goodness, it's exhausting. I haven't played that for ages. I must teach Eleanor. Do you think she is old enough?'

'Almost, if you went slowly.' Caroline smiled, put on the lamp beside her and picked up a pair of Peter's jeans to mend.

Leonie watched her across the softly lit room. The night sky, sprinkled with stars, was visible through the open curtains. Woman with sewing, woman at domestic tasks, she thought, seeing various old masters in her mind, portraits of women depicted in their role of carers for the family. People like Melanie would scoff at them, insist that there were more important roles for women than being door-mats to their family, dismissing the raising of children as a less important task than being a high-flyer in a top career. But Caroline, despite her obviously drunken husband, had blossomed. She had become, Leonie thought now with surprise, almost beautiful.

'So the children live with you now. How do you like it?' she asked over their companionable silence.

'It's perfect.' Caroline looked up from her sewing and smiled. 'They've only been here a couple of months but I almost feel they are mine. I know I shouldn't – I'm only their stepmother after all, but we do get on so well.'

'Why did his ex-wife change her mind, let them come?'

Caroline blushed. 'Well, it was her boyfriend. He . . .' she swal-lowed, 'he tried to abuse them.'

'You mean sexually?' Leonie said, horrified.

Caroline nodded. 'Thankfully Peter told James about it before much happened. He rang us one evening, hysterical. James went over at once and fetched them both here – told Penny, their mother, he'd have her boyfriend in court if she didn't let them come.'

'How dreadful! But surely she'd get rid of the boyfriend to keep the children?'

'You would have thought so, but apparently he convinced her the children were lying. Anyway, she let them go.' She smiled. 'They seem very happy here. We're going to buy Annabel a pony for her birthday next month, and Peter wants a dog for Christmas, so . . .' she smiled over at Nelson who was snoozing noisily by the window, 'we might breed from him before he's past it.'

'So it all worked out?' Leonie said fondly, though she could not help thinking of James's drinking.

As if she guessed what she was thinking, Caroline said, 'I have always wanted a family of my own, now I have one. We might have a baby together when life is more settled. I don't believe in looking too deeply into the flaws of one's life or I think they swallow up the good bits, don't you?'

'I suppose so.' Leonie thought a drunken husband was a pretty big flaw, but then so was a man overpowered by his mother who now, since his breakdown, seemed unable to relate to them.

The door opened and Julian came in.

'James is upstairs,' he said. 'I've put him to bed. He . . .' he laughed awkwardly, 'I don't think he would have managed on his own.'

'Oh thank you, Julian,' Caroline said warmly. 'I'll go up to him, make sure he's all right.' She put down her sewing and left the room as calmly as if James were another child she had to check on.

Julian sat down on the sofa beside Leonie and picked up the paper, skimming through it. 'Poor chap, he's got an enormous problem with that drink,' he said. 'It's a terrible shame when he's got such a super wife, house, and his children back.'

He didn't look at her as he said this, keeping his eyes on the paper, but Leonie thought he meant his remark to refer to them, that his mind was clearing and he was making a statement. They had everything, everything that mattered, a home, children. It was so easy to let them go if you looked only at the flaws, as Caroline had said.

'Yes, it is, but she's happy. She thinks only of the good bits,' Leonie said. 'In her mind, they outweigh the bad things.'

'She's right,' he said, putting the paper down and for the first time since Anita's death he looked at her steadily. 'We have more good things than bad, don't we?' His beautiful eyes, soft now like Eleanor's, perhaps a little apprehensive, homed in on hers, holding her.

'Yes, we have,' she said, feeling his hand curl into hers. She knew suddenly that they would keep on together, using the good times to help them through the bad. That a good relationship, as Philip had once said, was built of bricks, made slowly and sometimes painfully, one by one. Or, she thought, like making a patchwork quilt, stitching this experience to that one, patching over the flaws, carefully creating a varied, rich and lasting marriage.